Praise for Aurora Rey

"Rey's frothy contemporary romance [*Built to Last*] brings two women together to restore an ancient farmhouse in Ithaca, N.Y. Tension mounts as Olivia's colleagues and her snobbish family collide with Joss's down-home demeanor. But the women totally click in bed, as well as when they're poring over paint chips, and readers will enjoy finding out whether love conquers all."—*Publishers Weekly*

"*Built to Last* by Aurora Rey is a contemporary lesbian romance novel and a very sweet summer read...I love, love, love the way Ms Rey writes bedroom scenes, and I'm not talking about how she describes the furniture. This is a wonderful light romance with a slow burn that paid off for this reader. The combination of construction tools, paint, drywall, and two really attractive women who are hot for each other was a heady mix for me."—*The Lesbian Review*

"*Winter's Harbor* by Aurora Rey is a charming story. It is a sweet, gentle romance with just enough angst to keep you turning the pages. This is a sweet romance that keeps you captivated to the end. It is a light but fun read. Perfect for a weekend of escapism."—*The Lesbian Review*

By the Author

Winter's Harbor

Built to Last

Crescent City Confidential

CRESCENT CITY CONFIDENTIAL

by

Aurora Rey

2017

CRESCENT CITY CONFIDENTIAL
© 2017 By Aurora Rey. All Rights Reserved.

ISBN 13: 978-1-62639-764-4

This Trade Paperback Original Is Published By
Bold Strokes Books, Inc.
P.O. Box 249
Valley Falls, NY 12185

First Edition: February 2017

Credits
Editor: Ashley Bartlett
Production Design: Stacia Seaman
Cover Design by Jeanine Henning

Acknowledgments

When I joined the Bold Strokes family two years ago, I felt proud to be part of such a talented and respected group of writers, editors, and individuals committed to LGBT publishing. I never expected that so many of those people would become dear friends, family even. I remain grateful for their inspiration, motivation, exceedingly high standards, and sense of humor. I'm especially indebted to Radclyffe and Sandy for running such an amazing company and Ruth for providing insight and mentorship. And perhaps most importantly, Ashley, for being the best punk-ass editor a recovering good girl could ask for. You humor me, keep me in line, and make me a better writer. Every damn day.

Writing a book set in Louisiana was both an indulgence and a challenge. There is no place on earth where I feel both completely at home and utterly foreign. I haven't called it home in many years, but it remains a part of me. I'm profoundly grateful to the women—aunts, neighbors, teachers, cousins, nuns—who taught me how to be me, even when I had no idea who that was.

Finally, my deepest thanks to Andie. You are smart and patient and funny and a force, all rolled into one. Our little life out in the country feeds my soul. I'm so very glad that you love me.

For all the Southern women who taught me about food,
family, strength, resilience, and love.

CHAPTER ONE

*C*layton stood in the shadows, panting. A mixture of adrenaline and triumph made his pulse race. He looked down at his gloves, sticky and discolored with blood. This was his first.

The woman had seen his face, had seen him at work. He couldn't risk letting her live. The decision to kill her was split-second. The blade, in his hand to cut a canvas, slid across her throat so easily. Like slicing a pear. Other than the brief gurgle of blood in her windpipe, she hadn't even made a sound.

He surveyed the body beneath him. He'd had to do it. His very survival depended on it. He knew now, though, that it wouldn't be his last.

He stayed longer than he should have, looking at her face, her body. Something in her unseeing stare enthralled him. The unnatural angle of her limbs invited his caress.

He removed one of the gloves and touched her, timidly at first, as though she might wake. He was careful to use the back of his hand so as to not leave fingerprints. Clayton didn't know the science behind it, but he would have sworn her skin already felt cooler, waxy almost.

He traced his knuckles over her face, her hair. Feeling bolder, and more aroused, he moved his hand down to her breast. He squeezed it through her clothing, pinching her nipple.

Clayton lost track of how long he crouched there, but he'd given himself quite a hard-on. He needed to get away, before anyone found him and before his desire made him do something stupid.

He gathered the painting that had been the reason he came here in the first place. The thrill he'd felt when he'd first seen it, held it, was *gone. In its place was a feeling far more powerful. He tried to ignore the sudden hollowness that filled his chest. He'd worry about that later. Right now, he needed to get out cleanly and before anyone stumbled across him.*

Clayton rolled up the painting, sliding it into the cardboard tube he'd brought with him and into his bag. He indulged in one final look at his victim, imagining what it would be like to slide his bare fingers over her lifeless flesh. He adjusted himself, trying to ease the pressure of his erection straining against his trousers. Once he was clear of the building and safely back in his apartment, he'd be able to jerk off, all the while imagining his cock sliding into her.

Sam leaned back in the plush club chair and smiled. She wondered, sometimes, whether it was healthy to take such delight in murder, especially when the violence was laced with perversion. She imagined some would wonder whether such depravity could spring from an entirely healthy mind.

She shrugged and the concern passed. A little late to worry about that now. She popped the last bite of bagel into her mouth, finished her coffee.

She checked her watch. Boarding should be starting in just a few minutes. She lingered in the first-class lounge, in part to skim the few chapters she'd written thus far and in part to avoid the awkwardness she always felt sitting in her nice, wide leather seat while dozens of people streamed by to the coach section. Maybe it had something to do with her upbringing—traditional, Cuban, Catholic—but as much as she appreciated the luxury of flying first class, she hated the smugness that seemed inherent in it.

Shaking her head, she turned her attention back to the computer screen. It was good to remember one's roots, especially in her line of work. It made her characters more interesting, both in background and motivations. Clayton Gentille would be no different.

She was happy with what she'd sketched out so far in terms of character and plot. She'd had the idea for the story long before she'd chosen New Orleans as the setting. Now that things had taken a more sinister turn, she knew that choosing the Big Easy, complete with its dark history and tradition of black magic, would be the ultimate backdrop for her darkest mystery to date.

Once Sam was in New Orleans—living in it, absorbing it—the rest of the story would start to flow. She'd research the city's art scene, its history and culture, but she'd also find a way to work in some of its more sordid underbelly. She planned to enjoy its culinary delights, and maybe a little of its famous hospitality as well. After all, what good was moving to a new city every six months if it didn't include all the local charm?

Sam glanced at her watch again, then up at the monitor on the wall. Time to go.

CHAPTER TWO

Since her car and most of her things wouldn't be delivered for a couple of days, Sam took a cab to the house she'd be renting—a fully furnished Greek revival in the Garden District. She'd expected to stop by the rental agency to pick up her keys, but was assured someone would happily meet her at the house. By the time she pulled up, a woman stood at the front gate waiting for her.

The property agent looked exactly how Sam would imagine a woman born to sell. She owned her surroundings and drew attention in a way that was compelling without being obnoxious. Her blond hair fell halfway down her back, perfectly straight; her emerald green dress was perfectly tailored, short enough to draw attention, but not so short you'd question her professionalism. Sam appreciated the way her long silver necklace drew attention to the hint of cleavage that, again, was more hint than promise.

"You must be Samara Torres. I'm Kelly. I am so pleased to meet you."

"Please, call me Sam. I can assure you, the pleasure is all mine. Thank you for meeting me here."

"We try to take care of all of our clients as best we can."

Kelly's coy smile made Sam nod in appreciation. "It's good to know I'm in such capable hands."

Kelly walked down the gravel path and up the steps of the front porch. She slid a key into the lock, pushed the door open, then stepped back so Sam could enter first.

The ceilings were the first thing Sam noticed. Twelve if not fifteen feet, they created a sense of airiness throughout the house. What was it about high ceilings in old houses? They seemed practical in a way that newer buildings couldn't mimic. Sam would need to find a way to work that into the story. She realized that Kelly was speaking again and pulled herself back to the conversation.

"It's a charming property, has all the character of a historic home but all of the modern conveniences built in. Central heat and air—you'll probably need both while you're here—and a gas fireplace. There's a sound system throughout the house, with control panels in the kitchen, living room, and master bedroom. And, of course, high speed internet and premium cable with DVR are included."

They walked through the spacious foyer to the living room. The decor was a bit over-the-top for Sam's tastes, but the space itself was gorgeous. "It's perfect."

"There's an office on the first floor and a formal dining room that seats twelve should you want to entertain while you're here." Kelly gestured toward the rooms to her left. "The real star, though, is the kitchen. Fully remodeled only a couple of years ago with professional-grade appliances."

Sam wasn't about to tell her she only cooked in states of emergency. Even then, it rarely went beyond boiling water for pasta. Or eggs. Sam knew her way around eggs. "Mmm-hmm."

"Three bedrooms upstairs with two full baths. There's also a powder room next to the office. Any questions?"

"No, I think you've covered it."

"Excellent. It looks like the rent is set up on a direct pay, so unless there's a maintenance issue, we'll stay out of your hair."

"Great. Thank you."

Kelly tipped her head slightly to the side and smiled. "Of course, if there is anything at all you need, you shouldn't hesitate to ask."

Sam got the clear message Kelly wasn't talking about her services as a rental agent. Unless, perhaps, those services included showing off some of the more interesting things that could be done in beautiful rooms with tall ceilings. Sam returned the smile. "That is a very generous offer. I may have to take you up on it."

"I hope you do." Kelly walked up to Sam, a little closer than necessary, and handed her a card. "The number on the back is my personal cell."

Sam accepted the card. "I'll be sure to keep it handy."

"Good. I have an appointment across town, so I'll leave you to settle in. Welcome to NOLA."

Sam walked Kelly to the door, then watched her walk—sashay really—to her car. The view of the back was almost as nice as the one from the front. She closed the door reluctantly.

Sam wandered the house. Perhaps it was a bit more space than she needed, but she liked to be comfortable. She was admiring the six-burner gas stove when her phone rang. Seeing who was on the other end made Sam smile. "Hello, darling."

Prita didn't bother returning the endearment. "I take it you've arrived?"

"I have and I think you may have outdone yourself this time." Prita, who dabbled in real estate as a hobby, had taken on hunting up Sam's digs each time she ventured to a new city.

"Really? I love when that happens. Do tell."

"The place is gorgeous—old New Orleans charm, but with all the creature comfort upgrades. The kitchen might even inspire me to cook."

"Okay, let's not get carried away."

Sam chuckled. "I mean it. It really is perfect. And the rental agent who met me to give me the keys was nice, too."

"And by nice, do you mean pretty?" Prita and Sam had been friends since college. After one date and some painfully awkward kissing, they decided to be best friends instead of girlfriends. She knew Sam better than anyone.

"She was nice and pretty. I think I might develop a thing for Southern hospitality."

"I'm sure you'll find all sorts of ways to take advantage of it, but let's not forget why you're there."

Sam shook her head. The problem with having a best friend who is also your agent is that they're always trying to keep you on task. "I seek inspiration in all forms."

Prita laughed. "Don't I know it. So, that form of inspiration aside, where are you going to start?"

"First order of business will be to find sustenance."

"Right, because it's probably been three hours since you've last eaten."

"Four and a half, and that was only coffee and a bagel."

"Mmm-hmm. Then what?"

"Probably just driving around, trying to get a feel for things. I'll head over to Tulane in the morning. My appointment with Professor Chastain isn't until next week, but I can wander around campus, check out the art buildings and the library."

"And the coeds."

"Hey, now. I gave that up once I hit thirty. It started feeling creepy."

Prita snickered. "Fair enough. Maybe you'll stumble across a sexy librarian."

"You laugh, but maybe I will."

"I laugh precisely because you will."

"I can't decide if I should take that as a compliment or an insult."

"Merely an observation. Don't forget you have to get page proofs for *The Ninth Informant* done by next week."

Sam scowled even though Prita couldn't see it. While she understood the importance of page proofs, and certainly wouldn't let a book go to print without that final knowledge everything was just so, proofs were a pain in the ass. "Yes, boss."

"Eat something delicious for me and call soon."

"Will do."

❖

Based on her Google search, there was a restaurant and oyster bar only about four blocks from her new place. Hopefully, it was good. Even in a place like New Orleans, she liked the idea of having a regular place. Since she didn't cook, it was the closest thing she got to homey.

She threw on a jacket and headed out, making sure her Moleskine was tucked in her pocket. Despite the fact that it was January, the temperature hovered in the low fifties. It was nice, if a little unnatural. Sam may have lived in more than a dozen cities over the last ten years, but Philly remained her frame of reference.

She walked the short distance to St. Charles Avenue and turned right. When a streetcar rattled by, carrying more people heading home from work than tourists, she couldn't help but smile. As promised, Superior Seafood and Oyster Bar sat on the corner of St. Charles and Loyola. The red neon sign, along with the building's curved lines and chrome accents, gave it an art deco feel.

The inside was spacious, but with booths and partial walls that made it cozy. Dark wood and warm lighting reinforced the ambience. A girl—tall, but probably still in her teens—stood at the hostess station.

Sam smiled. "Hi."

"Good afternoon and welcome to Superior Seafood. Can I get you a table or would you prefer the bar?"

"Can I get oysters at the bar?"

The girl grinned. "You certainly can. You can also sit at the oyster bar in the back. Take your pick."

Sam walked into the bar area. Mirror-backed shelves stretched to the ceiling and boasted an impressive inventory of liquors and cordials. Heavy stools and brass trim created a vibe that was old school without being stuffy. She was in heaven.

The main bar lined the entire side wall, while the oyster bar was about a third of the size and situated in the back near the kitchen. Several groups sat and stood, chatting with each other and the bartender. There were two men, one older and one younger, behind the bar. The oyster bar, on the other hand, was staffed by a woman.

Sam headed in her direction.

Only one other couple sat on the dozen or so stools, so Sam took a seat at the other end. The woman behind the bar, who'd been facing away from her, turned and smiled. "Good afternoon."

Sam felt a quick surge of desire. Not uncommon, but the intensity of it caught her off guard. "Hi."

"What can I get for you today?"

"Ah, I think I'm in the market for some oysters."

The woman flashed a smile that made her even more stunning. "Well, you came to the right place. A dozen?"

Sam nodded. "That would be great."

"Would you like a drink as well? Or a drink menu?"

Sam set her elbows on the bar, crossed her arms, and leaned forward. "What would you recommend?"

"A Bloody Mary if it's brunch time, but in the afternoon, a French 75."

Sam wasn't familiar. "What's that?"

"Gin, champagne, and lemon juice."

Sam couldn't think of a better pairing. "Sold."

"Coming right up."

The woman gestured to a passing waiter and Sam took the

opportunity to study her. She was petite; Sam would guess five-two at most. Her hair was sandy blond and cut pixie short. She had a heart-shaped face and high cheekbones, which only added to the overall pixie look. As did the whimsical, handmade earrings. Sam noticed the name Tess embroidered on the white chef coat she wore under a long black apron.

With the drink order in, Tess got to work on the oysters. Sam had the perfect seat to watch her work. After scooping some crushed ice onto a metal platter, she picked up her knife—a stubby little thing with a black handle that looked to be plastic. The blade was rounded and not more than five or so inches in length. Sam thought about the chefs who traveled with their own knives, sets worth thousands of dollars tucked into special cases and treated with reverence and respect. This was not one of those knives.

But to watch Tess wield it, you'd think it was an object of beauty and precision. With practiced movements and an easy rhythm, she slid the blade into the seam of the shell, right at the thickest part. After wedging it in, she made a practiced flick of her wrist, prying the two halves apart. She discarded the top shell, sliding the blade around the full circumference of the meat and flipping it over so it was smooth and plump and succulent. Before setting the shell into the ice, she lifted it toward her face. It looked like she was studying it, but Sam realized she was smelling each one for freshness.

Despite her diminutive size, she worked quickly and efficiently. In what had to be less than two minutes, she'd made a ring around the outside of the platter. Small metal cups of horseradish and cocktail sauce went in the middle, along with slices of lemon.

"Enjoy." She set the platter in front of Sam and started the process again.

As she ate, Sam realized that every ticket that came out of the small printer on the back counter was for an order. As Tess filled each tray, she slid them through an opening into the kitchen. Moments later, a waiter or waitress would emerge, carrying the tray to one of the tables in the dining room. Sam was mesmerized. "So how many of these would you say you do in a night?"

Tess thought for a moment, offered a slight shrug. "Probably about two thousand?"

It seemed like a huge number to Sam, but eaten by the dozen, she could see how they added up quickly. Partly out of curiosity and partly to keep her talking, Sam asked, "How long have you been doing it?"

"I learned as a kid, did it with my dad at all our family parties. When I started here, it was as a bartender. I filled in doing oysters one night when they were short staffed. Turns out I was faster than the regular guy. And having a female shucker is a bit of a novelty. The tourists really liked it."

Sam imagined plenty of people would come in as much for her as they did for the oysters. "So you got reassigned."

Another shrug. This time it was accompanied by a smile. "I make more in tips here than I did at the bar."

That didn't surprise Sam in the least. She'd known Tess all of five minutes and she was enchanted. She wondered what she could do to spend more time with her, short of eating two dozen oysters every day. Sam loved oysters as much as the next person, but she had her limits. "Are you here every day?"

"More days than not."

"And always here, at the oyster bar."

"Pretty much."

Sam plucked the last of her oysters from the shell, popped it into her mouth. She wished she'd eaten them more slowly, and not just because they were delicious. She had no desire to leave. "I'm Sam, by the way."

Tess smiled, but her brow arched slightly. "And I'm Tess."

"It's a pleasure to meet you, Tess."

"Can I get you another round? Or something else?"

Bingo. "I can order other food here?"

"Of course." Tess reached under the counter, then handed Sam a menu. "Let me know what you'd like and I'll put it in for you."

Sam scanned the menu and Tess started to work on another order of oysters. The oysters had been surprisingly filling, so she decided to go with a couple of appetizers. She caught Tess's eye. "I'll have the crawfish cornbread and an order of fried green tomatoes."

"You got it."

This was perfect. Since she was now waiting for food, Sam could sit there and watch Tess work. It was easy to do. Tess's hands were small, but efficient. And even though she wore the bulky apron and mesh gloves, there was something innately feminine in her movement.

"So, are you visiting from out of town?"

Sam was so busy watching that the question took her by surprise. "Sort of. I'm here for a few months for work."

Tess glanced up and smiled without breaking her pace. "And what kind of work is that?"

Sam thought of the fictitious answers she sometimes gave to that question—professions she'd researched for one book or another. It wasn't like she relished being dishonest, but it was often easier and helped keep her shell of anonymity. But whether it was the promise of getting to know her better or something else, Sam didn't want to do that with Tess. "I'm a writer."

"That sounds like fun. What kind?"

Sam couldn't tell if she was curious, or if chatting up customers was part of her job. Given her comment about tips, Sam feared it might be the latter. But still. "A little of this, a little of that."

Tess gave her a quizzical look. "Anything I would know?"

Sam chuckled. Even if people didn't read Sid Packett's books, most people had heard of him. Deciding to keep herself completely detached from her pen name meant she couldn't use it to impress women. That was okay. She had plenty of other tactics.

"Nothing that glamorous, I'm afraid. I'm here to research a couple of art historians." That wasn't an untrue statement. Her next novel centered on an art history professor turned counterfeiter, a man who made millions using his expertise to fool black market collectors. A man who then became a serial killer.

"I don't know about art historians, but the local art scene is great."

Sam was about to ask her to elaborate when her food arrived. A couple sat down at the other end of the bar and Tess moved down to talk to them. Sam turned her attention to her food. She'd picked the dishes at random, but they both turned out to be delicious. It would be easy to eat here every day. She might gain twenty pounds in the process, but it might be worth it.

Tess didn't come back until Sam was nearly done eating. "Did you save room for dessert?"

"I really wish I had. I guess that means I'll have to come back."

Tess smiled. "The bread pudding is worth it, I promise."

Sam took the black billfold Tess handed her and slid in her credit card. She scribbled in a tip for the waitstaff, but was sure to stuff a ten into the snifter glass that served as a tip jar. "Then I promise I'll be back, for the bread pudding and the company."

"We'll look forward to it."

Sam reluctantly slid off the stool and put on her jacket. It shouldn't irritate her that Tess said "we" instead of "I," but it did. It was probably just habit. Either way, she planned to be back very soon. And while the bread pudding probably was spectacular, it would not be the reason why.

CHAPTER THREE

It was just before eleven when Tess peeled off her apron and chef coat. She dumped them in the restaurant laundry and opened her locker. She grabbed her coat and gloves, slung her bag over her shoulder, and headed out the back exit. Her bike was locked to an old gas meter at the back of the building. She lined up the combination, then climbed on.

The ride from the restaurant to Canal Street was just under three miles and took her about twenty minutes. Despite the cold dampness in the air, she enjoyed it. The city was far from asleep and her route down Magazine Street offered an eclectic mix of sights, smells, and sounds. People walked dogs in their pajamas while others stood outside bars, smoking and laughing. Next to a taco truck, a man who looked to be in his eighties stood on the curb playing a trumpet. Just by passing through, Tess felt like a part of it. Considering she worked more nights than she went out, it was nice.

At the ferry station, a dozen or so people waited to board the boat that had docked only minutes before. She lined up behind them, walking her bike and flashing her pass as she embarked. She parked her bike and headed inside to warm up for a few minutes.

It didn't take long for the boat to cast off and begin chugging across the muddy water. Not ten minutes later, they docked on the opposite side of the river. Tess collected her bike and started the brief final leg of her commute.

As she rode, she thought about the crepe myrtles that would soon be in bloom. It seemed wrong to wish for spring when summer followed so close on its tails, but she couldn't resist. She longed for the vibrant colors and sweet fragrance of a whole city in bloom.

She pulled into her driveway and hopped off the bike, walking it through the narrow space between her car and the side of the porch. After locking it to the post of the old chain link fence, she headed up the side steps and let herself into the house.

At the sound of the door opening and closing, Marlowe came running—one of many habits that made him seem more like a dog than a cat. Before Tess could set down her keys and take off her coat, he rubbed up against her ankles, then set his two front paws on her knee.

"Did you miss me?" He meowed in reply. Tess scooped him up and nuzzled his nose. He purred. She set him down to pull off her coat and kick off her shoes. "I can never tell if you missed me or if you're just hungry."

Another meow. She opened a can of food and dumped it into a clean bowl. She'd given him canned food once when he was sick and had never been able to break the habit. She couldn't begrudge him, though. She wouldn't want to live on dry kibble either.

She walked from the kitchen to her bedroom, peeling off clothes as she went. She paused long enough to drop everything in the laundry basket, then continued to the bathroom. In the shower, she washed her hair, then lathered her entire body with orange blossom shower gel. High-end bath products were one of her favorite indulgences.

Clean and clad in a pair of fleece pants and a sweatshirt, she returned to the kitchen for something to eat. After surveying the contents of the fridge, she fixed a bowl of cereal. She took her combination dinner and late-night snack to the living room at the front of the house. She found an old black-and-white movie on television and curled up on the couch. Marlowe hopped up to join her.

She'd not seen this movie before, but the hero was the brooding, mysterious type. Absolutely the last kind of person she'd want to get involved with. Still, she could appreciate the appeal. Without warning, the image of Sam popped into her mind. She didn't know why, except perhaps the fact that Sam exuded all those things—tall, dark, handsome. Tess rarely found herself attracted to customers, so Sam was definitely a standout on that front. She'd probably never see her again. Tess was okay with that. It didn't mean she couldn't enjoy the way Sam smiled at her, or the generous tip she'd left in Tess's jar.

After finishing her cereal, she set the bowl of leftover milk on the coffee table for Marlowe. He lapped it up, then returned to curl up against her and purr his appreciation. It didn't take long for Tess's lids to grow heavy. She clicked off the TV and looked at the ball of orange fur asleep next to her.

"You'd think you were the one who put in a ten-hour day." The cat opened one eye, then stretched. "I know, you're too pretty to work."

She stood and he stretched again. Tess shook her head, but chuckled. Marlowe slinked down from the couch as though he'd been waiting for her all along, then followed her to the bedroom.

❖

Tess didn't love the evening shift, but there was something to be said for never setting an alarm. She had never been a late sleeper, but she did enjoy waking up naturally and after the sun was up. She glanced over at the clock and saw it was just after seven. Since she wasn't meeting Carly until nine, she had plenty of time to be leisurely.

She climbed out of bed and smiled at Marlowe, who didn't even stir. After making coffee and putting on a load of laundry, she showered and dressed. She contemplated a bowl of cereal, but decided to indulge in a pastry at the market instead. She drank a couple of cups of coffee at the kitchen table before pouring what remained into a travel mug.

The sun was out and it was chilly without being cold, so Tess unlocked her bike instead of her car. The farmer's market was only a fifteen-minute ride from her house. She arrived, happy to see a good-sized crowd. After parking her bike and grabbing her coffee, she headed to meet Carly at the honey stand. She'd not quite made it when she spotted Carly walking toward her. Tess waved to catch her attention. Carly grinned and returned the greeting.

They exchanged a brief hug and Carly said, "Good morning, lady. How goes it?"

"It goes, it goes. How about you?"

"Can't complain."

Tess smiled. "Hungry?"

"Always."

Officially, Tess and Carly started every trip to the market at the honey stand. While the honey was awesome, it didn't merit a weekly purchase. In truth, they met there because a local bakery had a booth directly across the aisle. They wandered over to peruse the selections.

Baguettes and boules and loaves of jalapeño cheddar bread sat artfully arranged in large baskets. Low, tray-like baskets lined the table, overflowing with muffins and scones, donuts and croissants. As far as Tess was concerned, the only downside was having to pick one thing. Carly got her usual chocolate chip muffin while Tess hemmed and hawed. In the end, she settled on an apple fritter.

Breakfast in hand, they meandered through the market. The pickings were a little slim in the winter, but a few of the local farms kept greenhouses going year-round. Tess picked up a big bunch of collard greens and a pint of cherry tomatoes.

"Are you working tonight?" Carly asked.

"Yes, but not the closing shift."

"Nice. When's the next gig?"

"I've got one Sunday in the Quarter, then Thursday at Old Point."

"Maybe Becca and I will get a sitter next Thursday and come out. We haven't been out in ages."

"I would love that. And the nice thing about Thursday is you only have to get through Friday to get to the weekend."

"Truth."

"Are you still going to let me watch Dustin on Valentine's Day?"

"If you're sure you don't have to work and you're sure you won't have something better to do."

Tess smiled. "I can't think of a better date."

Carly shook her head. "It's not that I don't believe you. I just worry a little. I don't want you to be lonely."

They'd had this conversation at least a dozen times already. "I'm not lonely. I love my life, exactly the way it is. If someone comes along that fits nicely in it, great. If not, that's okay, too."

"Don't you miss sex?"

Tess rolled her eyes. "I have sex."

"Theresa Marie Arceneaux, you have occasional third-date sex. And by occasional, I mean like twice a year. That doesn't count."

Tess huffed and shook her head, but Carly's words stung a little, mostly because they were a fairly accurate description of her sex life over the last couple of years.

"The thirties are a woman's sexual prime. You don't want to miss out on yours."

"Okay, one, I don't believe that's true. Two, what do you expect me to do? Hop into bed with the next lesbian who tries to pick me up?" Without warning, Sam's face popped into her mind. She hadn't even tried to pick Tess up. She'd been flirtatious—not to mention gorgeous—but that was beside the point. Tess willed the image away.

"Maybe not the next one, but maybe every fifth or sixth. I know you're not wanting for willing participants."

Tess frowned. "That's not fair. I work at a restaurant and sing in bars. A lot of people slip me their number."

"That's what I'm saying."

"Quantity does not equal quality."

"I'm the first to agree with you. I just think you could be a little less picky without chucking your standards out the window. I don't think it's healthy when the lesbian couple with an infant is having more sex than you are."

"Well, shit, when you put it that way."

Carly nodded smugly. "Exactly."

They finished the loop of the market. Carly picked up a bouquet of flowers for her wife and Tess indulged in some beeswax hand balm. Carly, who'd parked close by, walked her to the bike rack. Tess tucked her purchases into the basket on the front of her bike. "It's lovely to see you, even when you make me feel bad about my sex life."

"You know I'm not trying to make you feel bad."

Tess smiled. Giving each other a hard time was part of being best friends. "I know. The only reason I feel bad is because you're right."

"Don't feel bad then, do something about it."

"Yes, ma'am."

Carly gave her a squeeze and headed to her car. Tess rode home and warmed up a slab of leftover lasagna for lunch before getting ready for work. She ate at her kitchen table, flipping through a magazine without much interest.

For the second time that day, she thought about Sam. Tess didn't have a type necessarily, but if she did, Sam would be it. Tall without being gangly, dressed in dark pants and an oxford that blurred the line between masculine and feminine. She had bronzed skin and short dark hair; Tess wasn't certain of her ethnicity, but guessed it was Hispanic. And her mouth—perfect teeth and a smile that exuded confidence.

Maybe Carly was right. She needed to get out more. Or perhaps more accurately, find someone to keep her in more.

CHAPTER FOUR

Sam woke to bright sunlight streaming through the window. She wanted to do some exploring and research in person before writing too much, but her most productive writing time was first thing in the morning. She decided to work on a few of the scenes already in her head, then venture out.

She put a pot of coffee on to brew, then headed to the office to set up a work station. She plugged in her computer, turned it on. Next to it went her thesaurus, writing journal, and her grandfather's fountain pen. The same might not be true of her wardrobe, but when it came to work, she packed light.

After returning to the kitchen for a cup of coffee, Sam sat down and got to work. She'd already sketched out a few chapters that would be fleshed out with detail later. Even though it irritated her editor no end, Sam had never written stories in order. She wasn't about to start now.

An hour later, Sam scowled at the screen. The pot of coffee was long gone and something felt off. She shook her head. It wouldn't be the first time a plot had gone sideways, but she usually figured out pretty quickly how to get it back on track. Feeling stuck did not sit well.

She skimmed over the previous two chapters. Clayton, her art historian turned counterfeiter, had just committed his first murder. Calculated, clean. He'd needed to silence someone he feared might be on to him. The sexual overtones had been a departure for her and she couldn't decide if the strategy was effective or a case of jumping the shark.

Maybe that was the problem. Maybe he shouldn't be a villain. Or he shouldn't be such an obvious one.

Sam turned away from the computer to the leather-bound journal where she kept notes and ideas. She flipped back to her initial character sketch of Clayton Gentille. *Old-money Southern. PhD from Clemson. Chip on his shoulder. Misogynist. Manhood questioned in past. Killing is about power as much as money/secret. Sees himself as a gentleman defending his honor/prerogative to do whatever he wants?*

Sam sighed, drummed her fingers on the desk. Clay was yet another variation on her bad guy archetype. Narcissistic and bold, undone eventually by ego-driven decisions and a belief they were too smart to be caught. She used it because it worked, but it didn't seem to be working now.

What if Clay had been an aspiring artist? Whose parents told him he'd never be good enough? If Clay started counterfeiting not for money, but for validation of his talent, it would make him a much more sympathetic character. Not Sam's usual type, but it might be interesting.

She reread the murder scene again. She'd have to scrap it altogether. Clay would be sloppy, driven by panic and then horrified with his actions, at least at first. She hated having to chuck entire chapters, but better to do it now than after the whole first draft was done. A lot of his internal monologue would have to change, too, and the scene where she'd alluded to some of his back story.

Should she keep the necrophilia? She wasn't concerned by the taboo nature of it so much as she didn't want to create a character with too many contradictions. Could a guy who murdered women and then found himself sexually aroused by them still be a sympathetic character? Sam sighed. She did like a challenge.

Instead of being irritated by the turn of events, Sam rubbed her hands together. After contemplating her options, she created a completely new project. Better to copy and paste in the good stuff instead of risk leaving something in that would contradict the new direction. She cracked her knuckles and started typing.

When Sam stopped long enough to glance at the clock in the bottom corner of her screen, she realized nearly five hours had passed. She leaned back in her chair, her smile of satisfaction morphing to a wince of pain. In not moving for so long, she'd given herself quite a crimp in her shoulders. She stretched her neck and pulled back her elbows, trying to work out some of the tightness. Before getting up, she did a quick check of her word count. If that didn't earn her a nice late lunch, she didn't know what did.

Part of the allure of New Orleans was the food. Theoretically, that meant exploring dozens of the city's restaurants. She still planned to do that, but for the moment, she found herself drawn back to the alluring woman shucking oysters.

The oysters had been exceptional. And the rest of the menu didn't look shabby either. Plus, it was walking distance, which meant she'd get a little fresh air and exercise. If she happened to be able to chat up the beautiful Tess again, well that would be icing on the cake. Or on the bread pudding. Or whatever one put on bread pudding. She intended to find out.

She grabbed her coat and headed out to take the same walk she had the day before. The sunshine and bright blue sky pulled her out of the dark head space her writing created. The promise of a delicious lunch helped, too, as did the thought of pleasant company.

By the time Sam arrived at the restaurant, her mood was ridiculously bright. The moment she walked in, her eyes went to the oyster bar in the back. Seeing Tess standing exactly where she'd been the day before made Sam smile. At the hostess's greeting, Sam turned her attention.

"Hi. Can I just grab a seat at the oyster bar?"

The woman, older than the girl who'd been working the day before, smiled. "Of course."

The woman gestured toward the back of the restaurant and Sam made her way to the same stool she'd claimed the day before. Unlike the day before, no one else sat at the marble counter. Tess had her head down, though, working on a platter of oysters. Sam took a seat and waited for her to look up. When she did, Sam thought she saw a flash of recognition. "Hi again."

"Hi."

Sam flashed her most winning smile. "The food and the company were so good yesterday, I couldn't resist coming back."

Humor danced in Tess's green eyes. "Is that so?"

Sam lifted three fingers. "Scout's honor."

"Well, I love a repeat customer. Can I start you with some oysters?"

"I think you can."

"And would you like a French 75 again, Sam?"

Sam didn't know if it was Tess remembering her name or hearing her say it, but she felt a flicker of pleasure. "I think I might. That's not bad form, is it? Having a cocktail at two in the afternoon?"

Tess laughed and it sent a shudder of warmth through her. "You do know where you are, right?"

"Of course. What was I thinking?"

Tess signaled to the bartender, then started working on Sam's oysters. They were just as delicious as the ones the day before. She followed them up with a bowl of gumbo. Unfortunately, with no one else to serve, Tess disappeared into the kitchen. The gumbo was tasty enough to keep her from being entirely disappointed. That's what Sam was trying to convince herself of when Tess pushed back through the swinging door with a smile.

"Did you save room for dessert this time?" Tess's tone, and the twinkle in her eyes, were totally flirtatious.

Even if she hadn't wanted dessert, Sam would have said yes to have a few more minutes with Tess. "I did."

"Would you like to see the menu?"

"I have it on pretty good authority that the bread pudding is the way to go."

"Coming right up."

Tess disappeared again and Sam made a mental note to keep her talking when she came back. She didn't have to wait very long. Tess returned with a huge square of bread pudding in a large, shallow bowl. It sat in a pool of creamy liquid that seemed too light to be caramel. "What's the sauce?"

Tess looked up at the ceiling, as though recalling the recipe. "Whiskey, along with butter, brown sugar, and cream."

It sounded even better than it looked. Sam scooped up a bite. It was a heart attack on a spoon and entirely worth it. "Whiskey sauce. That beats icing any day of the week."

Tess gave her a quizzical look. "I'm sorry?"

"I had a very productive morning and I told myself coming here for lunch, and dessert, would be icing on the cake. This beats icing any day of the week."

"Ah. I agree." Tess nodded. "Cake and icing have nothing on bread pudding."

"Of course, the company is a reward in itself."

Tess raised a brow, but it seemed more amused than judgmental.

"I'd love to have dinner with you sometime."

Tess smirked. "I appreciate the invitation, but I have to decline."

Sam cringed slightly. Maybe she'd read the signals wrong. "Are you straight? I'm sorry if I misread you."

Tess shook her head, but continued to smile. "No, you didn't misread."

Well, that was a relief. She'd hate to think she was losing her sense. "Girlfriend, then? Wife?"

Tess looked at her more earnestly now. "No. You seem very nice, but you're not my type."

Not her type? That could mean a thousand different things. Now she had to know. "Okay, I can't resist asking. What about me isn't your type?"

Tess shrugged slightly. "I don't date people who are just passing through."

Oh. Well, that wasn't so bad. Not like having something against Cubans or butches or charming writer types. Sam offered a flirtatious smile. "I'm going to be here at least six months. That has to count for something."

"That makes you an extended tourist, not a local." Tess folded her arms, but her demeanor remained playful.

Sam weighed her options. She could let it go, call up Kelly the rental agent, who seemed more than happy to go out with an extended tourist. Something about Tess had captured her attention, though. Sam felt compelled to get to know her. Besides, Tess didn't seem put off by their back and forth; if anything, she seemed to be enjoying it as much as Sam. And it's not like Sam was only interested in sex. "Would you have lunch with me, then? Friendly local showing an out-of-towner some of NOLA's hidden gems?"

Tess narrowed her eyes. That she was even contemplating it was a good sign. Sam had never been one to hound a woman to go out with her—for many reasons. Tess held her own, though, and sometimes, the pursuit proved more satisfying than an easy tryst. "You had to play the hospitality card, didn't you?"

Sam shrugged and did her best to look innocent. "You just seem so nice, and here I am, living in New Orleans without a friend to my name."

Tess laughed, a rich and sexy sound that Sam wanted to hear more of. "You're laying it on pretty thick here. Aren't writers supposed to have nuance?"

Sam laughed in return. Tess was even funnier than she'd thought. And she remembered that Sam was a writer. That definitely had to count for something. "Touché. I have to say, though, that romance isn't my genre."

"Well, in that case, I guess I'll cut you a break."

"And have lunch with me?"

Tess rolled her eyes. "And have lunch with you."

"Excellent. You pick the day and the place, then tell me where to pick you up."

"Wednesday at noon. There's a place called Willy's off Magazine Street. I'll meet you."

Sam enjoyed the way Tess walked the line between playing along and keeping her in check. "Sounds perfect. I'll be there."

Date, or pseudo-date, secured, Sam left the restaurant and meandered down St. Charles Avenue to explore the neighborhood and take some photos. She captured oak trees and palm trees, mansions and churches. Even at a leisurely pace, the walk felt good given the number of calories she'd just consumed. She eventually looped back toward home and had almost made it when her phone rang. She almost let it go to voice mail, but guilt kicked in. "Hi, Mama."

"Hi, honey. Did I catch you at a bad time?"

Sam climbed the porch steps, but sat in one of the white rocking chairs instead of going inside. "Not at all. I was just getting home."

"And where is that this week? Are you still in Texas?"

"No, I'm in New Orleans. I just started a new project."

"Did you tell me that's where you were going? I don't remember you saying so."

"I thought I had, but maybe not. I've only been here about a week."

"Your father and I honeymooned in New Orleans. Lovely city. You have a cousin there, you know."

As was often the case when she spoke with her mother, Sam had to work to keep up. "I don't think I knew that. Where did you and Dad stay?"

Her mother sighed. "It was this tiny little hotel a few blocks from Jackson Square, owned by a friend of your grandfather. I wonder if it's still there."

Sam enjoyed the moment of sentimentality. Her mother didn't have them often, or at least not with her. "If you give me the name or the address, I'll look for it. Send you a photo."

"I'll ask your father. I can't remember exactly, but I'm sure he will. Have you called up Elisa yet? How is she?"

Sam cringed. She had a vague recollection of her cousin Elisa, including the fact that she was a lawyer who lived in New Orleans. Sam hadn't seen her since Elisa's quinceañera, though, which was over ten years ago. What Sam remembered was a girl a few years younger than her, prettier and more feminine. In Sam's memory, Elisa had been aloof and uninterested in a tomboy older cousin, but maybe she'd just been shy. "I haven't seen her. I don't think I have her contact information even."

"That's nonsense. I'll get her number from your Aunt Maria. You have to see her while you're in town. What would she think if she knew you were living right there and didn't even call her?"

Sam wanted to say that she wouldn't think anything if she didn't know Sam was in New Orleans to begin with. She knew better than to go down that path with her mother, though. "You send me her number and I'll call her."

"I'll get it when I talk to Maria tonight."

Hoping the matter was settled, Sam tried to change the subject. "How are you? How's Dad?"

"Oh, we're good. Your father is clucking about retirement, but he does that every year around this time."

Sam's father had been a middle school music teacher all of Sam's life. She had no idea how he kept the patience and stamina to do it. "The problem with teaching is that you keep getting older and they stay the same age."

"So he says. He'll be glad for summer, but come August he'll be itching to go back."

"Not ready to have him around all the time?"

"We've already established he's going to have to get a part time job when he does retire. He'll go stir crazy without something to do."

"Not to mention driving you crazy in the process."

"Our staying happy and growing old together is contingent on him not being bored and underfoot all day."

Sam laughed. She shared her father's need to stay busy. "I'm sure you'll help him find something to do with himself when the time comes."

"I most certainly will. Tell me what you're working on now."

Sam gave her a brief overview, knowing her mother asked out of motherly duty more than genuine interest. She got the updates on her siblings, nieces, and nephews, then let herself get talked into a weekend in Philly for Easter. When she finally ended the call, Sam remained on the porch for a moment. It had actually been a nice conversation. She made a promise to herself to call within the week. She'd stay in touch and both she and her mother would feel better for it.

Sam went inside and straight to her office. She considered letting herself off the hook for the afternoon with the excuse that her concentration was broken. She opened her notebook, though, and read through her notes. Then she scrolled through the photos she'd taken over the course of the day. It was just enough to put her back in her groove and she got a solid two hours of writing in before her phone snapped her out of it.

As promised, her mother was sending her Elisa's phone number. That text was immediately followed by another. *Maria says she's a lesbian now!*

Sam sighed. Maybe this wouldn't be so bad, although her mother's use of the word "now" and an exclamation point gave her pause. She decided texting was an acceptable, if not downright preferential, way of communicating with someone her age. She crafted a greeting she thought blended enthusiastic with casual. Elisa's reply was both instant and friendly. Before she knew it, Sam had plans to meet her for dinner the following week.

CHAPTER FIVE

Tess had hoped agreeing to have lunch with Sam would settle things, make her think about Sam less rather than more. The opposite turned out to be true. Fortunately, she had the day off from work and a day of food, friends, and music to keep her occupied. The band got together every other week to practice, but they tried to make a day of it every couple of months, and today was one of those days.

Tess pulled into Jenny and Cedric's driveway alongside Zack's pickup. She grabbed the potato salad and brownies she'd brought and headed toward the house. When she was about ten feet away, the door opened, although there didn't seem to be anyone on the other side. She paused and, sure enough, a little face peeked around from behind it.

"Hi, Abby."

Big brown eyes blinked at her. "Hi, Miss Tess."

"May I come in?"

"That's why I opened the door, silly." Abby giggled, then ran down the narrow hallway that led to the kitchen.

Tess stepped inside, nudging the door closed with her foot. She followed Abby to the kitchen. Jenny stood at the stove stirring something while Zack and Cedric stood nearby, arguing about football. "Lazing around as usual, huh, fellas?"

Cedric turned and gestured at her with his beer. "I'll have you know I was up at six this morning to tend the smoker."

"Yeah. And I just helped him put on the chicken," Zack said.

"All right, all right. I guess you've earned your idleness." Tess set down her things and turned to Jenny. "Hey, girl."

"Hey, yourself."

Tess walked over to the stove and peered into the pot. "God, I love your dirty rice. Almost as much as I love you."

Jenny set down the spoon and gave Tess a hug. "It's good to know you've got your priorities straight. How you been?"

"Good, good. Work's not too busy. It's nice to have a little lull between New Year's and Mardi Gras. You?"

"Same. I'm trying to stockpile inventory for February, too, although the kids have had different ideas." Jenny did paintings on reclaimed slate roof tiles and had gone from selling them herself in Jackson Square to having contracts with half a dozen shops around the city.

Tess glanced over to where Abby and Maya were telling Zack a story, complete with spirited hand gestures and faces. "Why should Mama work when she could be playing instead?"

"Exactly."

"Hello, hello." The voice came from the direction of the front door.

"Come on in, Mo. We're in the kitchen."

A moment later, Maureen appeared. "Good afternoon. I see the gang's all here."

"And now that the beer has arrived, we can get this party started."

The guys pulled the chicken and sausage from the smoker while Tess and Mo helped Jenny set up a buffet along the counter. In addition to Tess's potato salad and Jenny's dirty rice, there was garlic bread, baked beans, and Mo's broccoli salad. As always, they had enough to feed a crowd twice their size.

Jenny set up the kids at their play table in the living room and the adults squeezed around the kitchen table. They ate and drank, told stories and laughed, then ate some more. Tess relished the laid-back time with the group almost as much as performing with them. As much as she liked to sing, she didn't think she could be in a band if she didn't enjoy their company when not playing.

She'd lucked out six years ago when she answered an ad for a band looking for a new lead vocalist. In addition to being a good fit musically, Sweet Evangeline had come to feel like her second home. After Carly and Becca, she considered her bandmates her closest friends. And with none of her immediate family left in New Orleans, it was the closest thing to family time she got on a regular basis.

Around three, Mo said, "I suppose we should probably rehearse."

There was some token protest, but no one really minded. They played together because they loved it. Even though a few of their gigs had gone from paying in food and drinks to actual money, the take-home pay for each show, divided five ways, barely covered a trip to the grocery store or a nice supper out.

They set up in Jenny and Cedric's living room. Unimpressed, Abby and her sister Maya went to their room to play store. Jenny took her seat at the drums, Zack at the keyboard. Mo propped her bass against her shoulder and played a few chords while Cedric picked up his guitar, plucking out notes with Zack to make sure he was in tune. Tess plugged in her mic and fiddled with the amps to have the right mix for the small space.

Once everyone was in position, they ran through a couple of their regular songs to warm up. Cedric had a couple of ideas for tweaking one of their newer songs, so they worked through that a few times, stopping here and there to adjust. Even though she didn't play an instrument, Tess liked the noodling around. It added a creative and collaborative element that she didn't get when doing standards at one of the hotel bars in the Quarter. After the fourth go, everyone agreed the updated version was a keeper.

Zack had been working on a new song. The only formally trained musician in the group, he often took the lead on new melodies and arrangements. He played what he had so far, then Cedric joined in with a series of chords.

"I'm thinking maybe a little more staccato," Zack said.

Cedric played the chords again, but with more force. "How's that?"

"Perfect." He then tapped out a beat with his fingers, which Jenny translated to drums and Mo embellished.

Meanwhile, Tess read through the lyrics Zack had sketched out. She liked the gist, but words were definitely not Zack's strong suit. She scribbled notes in the margins and picked out a different set of lines to use as the refrain. When the rest of the band was ready for her, she did a quick a cappella version.

Zack smiled at her. "I love when you change my lyrics. You make them say what I wanted them to say in the first place."

Tess offered a playful shrug. "I do what I can."

They put it all together, stopping and starting to make adjustments and offer feedback. Zack recorded them each time, playing back pieces that needed work. They closed out with some of the covers they threw into most of their gigs. The energy and comfort of such familiar songs made it feel more like a jam session than a rehearsal.

By the time they wrapped up, the sun had set. Tess couldn't think of a better use for her day off. After the instruments and equipment were packed away, Tess lingered to help Jenny and Cedric clean up the kitchen. She kissed the girls, who were attempting to negotiate a bath reprieve, and wished everyone a good night.

On the drive home, she found herself humming the new song. It didn't happen very often that new pieces came together enough in a single afternoon to be ready for public performance. This one was special, though, and she felt pretty certain their fans would agree.

For about the tenth time that day, Tess's mind turned to Sam. Gorgeous, flirtatious, persuasive Sam. Tess told herself she'd agreed to have lunch with Sam because it was the hospitable thing to do, which was true. Yes, she found Sam attractive, but that didn't need to factor into the equation. Sam was only passing through, so nothing was going to happen between them. Tess would make that clear and Sam would move on to flirting with someone else, a woman who would prove more susceptible to Sam's charms.

Of course, if all that was true, Sam shouldn't be popping into her thoughts uninvited. Tess brushed it off. It didn't matter. She'd enjoy the flirtation and then send Sam on her way. It might not be what Carly had in mind when she encouraged Tess to be more open, but it was exactly the kind of diversion Tess went for—a pleasant ripple that had no chance of making waves. She'd find a way to take Carly's advice and be more open, she'd just do it with somebody else.

CHAPTER SIX

Sam decided to take the day off from Tess's restaurant. It was a matter of principle, really. She'd gotten the date, or at least the pseudo-date. She wanted to make sure she didn't come across as overly eager. Besides, she had work to do.

She gathered up her journal and made sure her phone had a full charge for taking pictures. The Tulane campus was only a couple of miles from her house, but since she wanted to drive around a couple of the adjacent neighborhoods, Sam decided to take her car.

It was hard to tell where Loyola ended and Tulane began. Sam drove around until she found a place to park, then went exploring on foot. Like so many universities, old buildings covered with ivy bumped up against modern structures of concrete and glass. Oak trees sprawled, their roots rising from the ground with a circumference as wide as the branches dripping with Spanish moss. Sam was glad she arrived when she did and could do her scouting mission before the students returned from winter break.

Sam had arranged a meeting with Dr. Chastain before arriving in New Orleans. As the chair of the Art History Department, he had expertise both in the art periods she was interested in researching as well as the process of dating and verifying the legitimacy of paintings of the time. She also wanted to pick his brain about the culture of academic departments, but hadn't mentioned that in her initial inquiry to him. She didn't want to scare him off.

The directions he provided to the building were meticulously precise. She found the Woldenberg Art Center without having to check the campus map she'd pulled up on her phone just in case. After snapping a few photos of its columned exterior, she made her way up to the third floor.

The building felt eerily quiet despite the handful of open doors and illuminated offices. It reminded her of a museum after closing. She'd never thought about how different a university felt when no students were around. Wanting to be sure she captured the detail, she took a couple of photos and jotted a few notes in her journal.

The lights in Dr. Chastain's office were on, but the door was closed, so Sam knocked lightly on frosted glass. She heard movement, then saw the silhouette of a person on the other side. The man who opened it looked just like the photo on his bio page on the university website: tousled gray hair, small round-framed glasses, tweed blazer. Not that Sam had a plenitude of experience with art historians, but he looked exactly like she'd expect an art historian to look. Except this one had an earring, and he looked startled.

"Good morning, Dr. Chastain. I'm Samara Torres. We spoke on the phone."

"Oh, yes, yes. Of course. I was expecting you, but I got to working and it completely slipped my mind."

Sam chuckled. "I know the feeling. If it's not a good time, I'm happy to come back."

"Not at all. Please come in."

He stepped back from the door and Sam entered the office. The space was narrow, but long, with a tall window looking out on one of the countless live oaks sprinkled throughout campus. Paintings or bookshelves covered just about all of the available wall space. It was all neat and tidy, though, including the surface of the old wooden desk.

"Thank you again for taking the time to meet with me."

"It's my pleasure. Have a seat."

"Thank you." Sam sat in one of the chairs opposite the desk.

"You're working on a project, right? But it's not an academic one."

Sam nodded. "That's right. I'm doing some background research for a potential film project." It wasn't a lie. Several of her books had been turned into movies.

"How fascinating. Art history doesn't make it into film very often, I'm afraid. Well, aside from all those heist movies."

Sam couldn't tell from his tone whether his feelings on the matter were wistful or rejective. She decided to keep her planned storyline to herself. "I was hoping you might share your career path, maybe a peek into a day in the life. Then I have a few specific questions about your work."

An hour and a half later, Sam's knowledge of art history had increased tenfold. Dr. Chastain, or Herbert, as he preferred being called, walked her through choosing it as a major in college, the decision and process of pursuing a doctorate. Although he'd never had genuine aspirations as an artist, he'd dabbled enough to consider it. Since that was her plan for Clayton, it felt good to have the overlap of interest confirmed.

She debated asking him some of her more risqué questions, wanting to neither offend nor cause an early end to their interview. At this point, she figured she didn't have anything to lose. And Herbert had proved himself quite chatty. "Could I ask you about counterfeiting?"

Herbert leaned forward like a neighborhood gossip about to get a juicy story. "What about it?"

Okay, so clearly he didn't think it taboo. "Is it pervasive? I don't mean recreating paintings, or at least not just that. The science, the chemistry, of faking a painting's age. The kind of thing that fools even the experts. Is there a lot of that?"

Herbert considered for a long moment and Sam wondered if maybe she'd read his cues wrong. "At the museum level, the academic level, I don't think so."

Sam decided to press her luck. "I can't help but feel like there's a 'but' coming."

Herbert smiled. "But I think private collections are a different matter entirely."

Sam was growing fonder of Herbert every minute. "How so?"

"On one hand, pieces get handed down in families. Interesting stories become more important than documentation."

"That makes sense."

"There's also the matter of black market collectors."

Sam knew about this and planned to use it in her plot. Most of her knowledge of the subject, however, had come from the kind of heist movies he'd mentioned earlier. Having the idea corroborated by an art expert added a whole new dimension. "There's a lot of that?"

Herbert shook his head. "Sadly, yes. There are thousands of paintings and sculptures and artifacts that have been stolen or poached, then hidden away or sold on the black market. If these items ever turn up publicly, they must be returned to the rightful owner or heir."

"So they never turn up."

"Exactly. Because the buying and selling takes place behind closed doors, legitimate authentication is much harder to come by."

Sam loved where this conversation was going. "And because people keep their illicit collections private, there could be duplicates and copies floating around that would never be detected."

"Correct." Herbert's face took on a wistful expression. "I think, too, wanting something to be real can lead to clouded judgment."

Sam chuckled. That was true about many things in life, not solely art. "Do you believe there are professionals like yourself who are involved in this world, either full-time or on the side?"

Herbert sniffed, his disdain obvious. "Probably. People who couldn't cut it in the profession."

"Or maybe who found themselves looking for some extra income."

"Or that. Disgraceful, but I'm sure it happens."

"Do you think it's possible that people in your field might be some of the perpetrators?"

"What do you mean?"

She was pushing it at this point, but Sam couldn't contain herself. "Authenticating pieces they know to be counterfeit for profit. Or, if they've got artistic skill, creating counterfeits themselves."

Herbert's expression darkened and Sam realized she'd gone too far. "I don't mean to imply that you, or any of your colleagues, would engage is such nefarious activity. I'm only curious. It seems like every profession has a handful of unscrupulous bad apples."

He sighed. "I don't like to think of it, but I suppose you're right."

"I hope I haven't offended you."

Herbert waved a hand. "No, no. I just hate thinking about things like that."

"I'm sorry I brought it up. I'm sorry, too, that I've taken far more of your time than our initial arrangement."

"It's fine. I'm sure I rambled far more than you needed."

He still seemed disconcerted and Sam felt bad for souring his mood. "Let's end on a high note. Tell me about the most exciting piece of art you've ever worked on."

Herbert's face brightened and he launched into a story about a

Renaissance painter Sam had never heard of. She smiled and nodded, filing away terms and the way he talked about technique and style. She also congratulated herself on wrapping up the interview in a way that would hopefully leave Herbert with fond memories of their time together.

Sam shook Herbert's hand and thanked him profusely for his time. She paused outside the building to make a few final notes, then took a stroll around campus. After taking several dozen pictures, she climbed back in her car to drive around the neighborhoods. The homes were beautiful, if less grand than those right on St. Charles. The streets were narrow and riddled with a combination of potholes and slipshod asphalt patches. Within about twenty minutes, Sam's teeth were on edge and she was surprised she hadn't popped a tire. Realizing she'd given herself both a stiff neck and a headache, she decided to call it quits.

When she got home, the last thing Sam wanted to do was sit at her computer. She needed to organize her notes, though, and those page proofs weren't going to take care of themselves. Both tasks were in the category of least fun and least glamorous aspects of being a writer. Sam considered them some of the most important, though. Even if she didn't write the kind of literary fiction her parents would approve of, or write under her own name, she took pride in her work. Doing it well mattered.

After a couple of hours, her eyes felt blurry and her brain had gone fuzzy. Rather than give into the desire to take a nap, she switched over to her work in progress. She kept herself awake with a grisly murder and Clayton's sale of a counterfeit Manet to a New Orleans businessman with ties to the mob. At five, she shut down for the day and got ready to meet Elisa.

She arrived at the restaurant a few minutes early and was contemplating ordering a drink when she heard her name. Sam turned to find a stunningly beautiful and curvy woman looking at her. "Elisa?"

"A little more grown up since the last time you saw me. You look fabulous!" Elisa punctuated the statement with an enthusiastic hug.

"You, too. It's good to see you." Sam tried to reconcile the image of a gangly teenager with the woman smiling at her.

"I was so excited when you texted. Let's grab a table and catch up. I want to know everything."

They ordered a bottle of wine and a few small plates to share.

Sam learned that Elisa followed her first girlfriend from college to New Orleans, a relationship that lasted through her second year of law school. "Of course I had to pick the one state whose laws are entirely different from everywhere else," she said. "I'd kind of fallen for the city, though, so it wasn't all bad. Now I can't imagine living anywhere else."

Sam talked a little about her work. Although her parents and siblings knew about her pseudonym, she'd not shared the specifics with her extended family. Elisa seemed great, but Sam wasn't ready to share confidences, at least not yet. Elisa asked about where she was staying, which turned out to be only a couple of miles from Elisa's place.

Sam had forgotten how nice it could be to spend time with family. As much as she loved hers, they didn't have enough in common to make conversation easy. She didn't know if it was because Elisa was gay or approaching thirty and happily single, but Sam felt like she'd found a kindred spirit. She even let Elisa talk her into joining her for a yoga class on Saturday morning.

When they finally left, it was almost ten. "I'm sorry I kept you out so late."

Elisa waved a hand. "I can go into work a little late. As long as I get in my billable hours, my boss is a happy camper."

They hugged their good-byes and Sam made her way home. She flopped on the couch and put on a women's college basketball game. During halftime, she sent her mom a thank-you text for nudging her to reconnect with Elisa, then chuckled at the told-you-so reply.

CHAPTER SEVEN

On Wednesday morning, Sam woke at her usual seven, but she had a hell of a time concentrating. The image of Tess would not leave her mind. Sam tried to shake it free, but found herself hopping around the manuscript, unable to write more than a paragraph or two of a particular scene before feeling stuck.

At ten, she gave up and went for a run. She told herself it was in anticipation of having a big lunch. In truth, she needed to burn off some of the nervous energy that had been plaguing her the last couple of days. Despite her chosen genre, and the heart-pounding it sought to inspire, Sam did not enjoy the feeling of restless anticipation.

Three miles and a hot shower later, the unease had subsided. She sat back at her computer, figuring she could at least deal with a few emails before heading out. She took care of the couple that needed attention in her private account, then switched over to the one listed on her website and in her books.

Her assistant Peg monitored that account, responding to routine requests and fan mail and deleting the junk. They'd developed a system of flagging things that needed Sam's specific attention, using a color code system for different types and level of urgency. Pleased that nothing required immediate action, she switched over to her final, generic account. She used it mostly for online shopping and casual acquaintances.

She skimmed the long list, deleting offers from Banana Republic and Amazon. It was then she realized she had no fewer than a dozen messages from Francesca. Sam cringed.

When she'd announced her plans to leave Dallas, Francesca hadn't taken it well. Even though Sam had made it clear from the beginning she was only there for a few months, Francesca seemed convinced that Sam would change her mind and stick around. Instead of enjoying their final week together, Francesca went off the rails. Angry texts and tearful voice mails became more frequent and, eventually, Sam decided to block her number. Since arriving in New Orleans, Sam had put it out of her mind.

The first few emails overlapped with the phone calls and texts. For every one that called Sam names, another apologized and asked if they could talk. The last few seem resigned to the idea that they weren't going to get back together—not that they'd ever really been together in the first place. The most recent, sent only a few days prior, announced that Sam would regret turning her back on Francesca.

Sam stared at the list of messages for a minute. She'd never had a relationship end on such a sour note before. That was just it. She'd never intended it to be a relationship in the first place. Sam carefully avoided relationships and avoided getting involved with the kind of women who were looking for them. When they met, Francesca had been adamant that she never wanted to be tied down. She'd been adamant, at least, until she decided she wanted to do the tying.

Sam shook off the unease that had settled over her. Feeling guilty wouldn't help matters, nor would attempting to apologize. Again. She deleted the messages and closed her computer. She didn't want to keep Tess waiting.

Sam walked into the restaurant half an hour later and was enveloped by warm air and savory aromas. She had no idea what was cooking, but she wanted some of it. Even if everything with Tess turned out to be a total bust, Sam felt pretty sure learning about this place would make it worthwhile.

She scanned the small dining room and saw Tess sitting at a table, reading a book. She rested her cheek on her fist and had a look of relaxed concentration. That look, combined with the jeans and fleece jacket she wore, gave Sam a vivid image of Tess curled up on the couch with her, sipping wine and enjoying a cozy winter afternoon. Sam shook off the mental picture. That wasn't how her fantasies about women worked.

She approached the table. Tess glanced up and made eye contact. Her smile was warm. "Hi."

Sam swallowed the lump that had suddenly formed in her throat. "Hi. I hope you haven't been waiting long."

Tess closed the book. "Not very. I was running errands this morning and happened to finish early. I decided to come here instead of killing time somewhere."

"I think if I'd done that, I'd have ordered half the menu already. It smells amazing."

"Right? It reminds me of Sundays at my Mawmaw's house. She'd have half a dozen things going at once and we'd walk in after church and the whole house would smell like this." Tess glanced away. She didn't know why she'd shared such a personal detail. The whole point of this lunch was to be nice and to introduce Sam to parts of the city she wouldn't find in any guidebook. She looked back at Sam, who was smiling that charming smile at her again. She was going to have to watch herself.

"There's something about Sunday dinners for sure."

Tess nodded. "Must be. Have a seat and I'll tell you what's good."

Sam shrugged out of her jacket and sat in the chair opposite Tess. "Sounds great. I'm starving."

Tess handed her a menu—a single oversize page laminated in plastic. "Most people go for the meat and three."

Sam raised a brow.

"Like a blue plate special. One entree and three sides. You can mix and match whatever you want. I also recommend the po'boy. The seafood ones are good, but the barbecue beef and roast pork are to die for."

Tess watched as Sam's eyes scanned the menu. If the meals she had at Superior were any indication, Sam had one hell of an appetite. Tess wondered if she worked out like a crazy person or had one of those ridiculous metabolisms. Not that she was judging. She liked to eat as much as the next person. Probably more than the next person.

She considered the selections herself and settled on the roast pork po'boy. Much like the restaurant's aromas reminded her of Mawmaw, the sandwich made her reminisce about eating the leftovers of Sunday dinner. She set the menu down just as Andre made his way over to their table.

"Hey, Miss Tess. How y'all doing today?"

"Pretty good, Dre. Pretty good. You?"

"It goes. Can I get y'all some drinks or y'all ready to order?"

"It's my friend here's first time. She might need a minute yet."

Sam glanced up. "I'm good, I think."

Tess gestured to her. "After you, then."

Sam took one last look at the menu. "I'll have the pork roast with macaroni and cheese, sweet potatoes, and dirty rice."

Tess snickered before she could stop herself.

"What?"

"Nothing."

"Do those things not go together?"

"They go fine. It's just funny. Do you not eat vegetables?"

Sam shrugged sheepishly. "It's not that I don't."

"I'm sorry. I didn't mean to tease you."

"Is there a vegetable you'd suggest?"

"The collard greens here rock."

Sam winced.

Tess looked at Andre, who seemed amused rather than irritated by their back and forth. "You get exactly what you ordered. I'll get collards and you can try them."

Sam didn't look convinced.

"Just try them. One bite." She turned to Andre. "I'll have the pork po'boy with a side of collards."

Andre nodded. "Drinks?"

"Sweet tea," Tess said.

"Same," Sam added.

"Y'all got it." Andre turned to head back to the kitchen.

"Oh, Dre? Can I get fried okra, too?" He offered a small salute by way of answer. Tess smiled at him. "Thanks."

He disappeared into the kitchen and Tess turned her attention back to Sam. Her eyes were scanning the room like she was searching for something, or someone. "Looking for something?"

Sam brought her eyes back to Tess. "No. Sorry. Just taking everything in. Absorbing details."

"Absorbing details?"

"I'm a writer, remember. I live and breathe details."

Tess put her elbows on the table and leaned forward. "Right. A writer. What do you write, again? Something to do with art?"

"Sometimes."

Tess looked at her blandly. "Is that all I'm going to get?"

Dre brought over their sweet teas and Sam seemed to use that as a chance to think before responding. It made Tess wonder if the answer was going to be truthful. "I write places."

What? Tess couldn't tell if Sam meant to be vague or was referring to something she'd never heard of. "Places?"

"I go to different cities and I live in them for a few months. I try to capture their physical characteristics, but also the feel of them. The culture, the history. That kind of thing."

"So like a travel writer?"

Sam smiled and Tess sensed a coyness in it. "Not to be weird, but it's confidential."

"Seriously?"

"Not like CIA confidential. What I write doesn't ultimately have my name on it, so I like to keep a certain distance."

Tess still wasn't sure what Sam meant, but she wasn't going to be nosy about it. She shrugged. "If you say so."

"Besides, we're here to talk about you."

Tess raised a brow. "We are?"

"You, your city. You're my conduit to the real New Orleans."

"Right. So what do you want to know?"

"Have you always lived here?"

"From the day I was born."

"Interesting. And your family?"

"My brother moved to Houston after he finished school. We evacuated there for Katrina. After the storm and all the damage and the uncertainty that came with it, my parents decided to move there, too."

"But not you. Why did you stay?"

Tess thought back to the chaos and anxiety in the weeks—months even—after Katrina blew through. The arguments with her parents. The not knowing if she'd make it on her own. "I love it here. Even at its worst, I couldn't imagine living anywhere else."

"That's a pretty powerful attachment."

Tess smiled. "I think New Orleans can have that effect on people. It feeds the soul."

"What a great phrase." Sam was torn between wanting to learn more about Tess's New Orleans and wanting to learn more about Tess herself. Perhaps she could find a way to do both. Before she could try, their food arrived. The same guy that had taken their order set down Tess's sandwich and sides before putting down one of the largest plates of food Sam had ever seen in front of her. Even with her robust appetite, Sam thought it unlikely she'd be able to finish.

"Can I get y'all anything else?"

"Hot sauce for me, please," Tess said. "Sam?"

"Just a bigger stomach, maybe."

Her answer made both Tess and Dre laugh. Dre looked at Tess. "You a Crystal girl, yeah?"

"You know it."

Dre grabbed a bottle with a blue and white label from a shelf that looked to have five or six kinds of hot sauce on it. He set it down on their table. "Y'all holler if you need anything else."

Tess flashed him a smile. "Will do. Thanks."

Sam watched him move to a table of businessmen who had just walked in. She then returned her attention to the food, and the woman, in front of her. "You didn't tell me the meat and three was enough to feed three."

"I think you'll find that's the rule instead of the exception around here. Aside from your really fancy places, that is."

"Good to know." She unwrapped her knife and fork from the napkin it came in. "The hard part is going to be to stop eating before I burst."

"Well, don't forget you have to try the collards. You can try my okra, too, if you want." Tess nudged the small bowl of greens toward her.

Sam poked her fork in. It looked like there was ham in them, or maybe bacon. That was promising. Sam didn't know what she expected, but it definitely wasn't for them to be delicious. But they were. Salty and smoky, garlicky with only a hint of bitterness. And tender. She thought they'd be stringy and tough. "Okay, that's really good."

Tess grinned. "I told you."

Sam lifted her hands. "I promise to defer to your recommendation on all future food adventures."

Tess raised a brow, but didn't protest the assertion that there might be future adventures.

Sam gestured to her plate. "Do you want anything of mine? This really is more than I could possibly eat."

"I can't pass up macaroni and cheese." Tess reached over to snag a bite. "You should try the okra, too. I admit the slime factor can be a turnoff, but you don't get any of that when it's fried."

"Like I said, I trust you."

"With or without hot sauce?"

"Oh, definitely with."

Tess opened the bottle and dashed it generously over the top. "Help yourself."

Sam took one of the pieces and popped it into her mouth. "Yeah, that's good, too."

Tess picked up her sandwich and took a bite. "You're welcome to try this, but it's the same pork that's on your plate."

"I'm good, thanks." Sam picked up her fork again and tried the things on her plate. She wasn't disappointed. While it lacked the flash of some of the meals she'd had thus far in New Orleans, the flavors were complex and interesting. Not simple, necessarily, but she got the sense this was exactly how these dishes had been prepared for years and years. Although nothing like the food her mother or grandmother prepared, it managed to make her feel a little homesick.

Not wanting to dwell on those feelings, or waste her time with Tess, she shook off the sentiment. "So, what would you be doing with your day if you weren't having lunch with me?"

"Buying groceries and cleaning the house, probably. Nothing exotic."

"Does that mean I can tempt you into spending the rest of the afternoon with me?"

"A tempting offer, but I'm afraid I have plans."

"Please tell me 'plans' is not code for vacuuming."

"Not at all."

"Oh, good. Otherwise, I'd start to worry I'd lost all my charms."

"Yeah, I've got to wash my hair."

Tess kept her face straight and Sam realized she'd walked right into being teased. "I supposed I asked for that."

"Only a little. I do have some things to do, though, and I have to be at work by five. I'm not trying to get rid of you."

"Does that mean I might be able to talk you into doing it again sometime?"

Tess folded her arms and stared at the ceiling. When she looked back at Sam, however, she was smiling. "I guess maybe."

"I'll take it."

Dre returned a while later with the check. They both reached for it, but Sam grabbed it first. "I insist, especially since agreeing to go out with me was against your better judgment."

"It's not you," Tess insisted. "You're actually quite charming."

"Have dinner with me and I'll show you how charming I can be."

"Maybe."

"Maybe? You're killing me, here."

Tess shrugged, but her eyes had a certain sparkle. Sam found it impossible to tell if Tess was trying to let her down easy or making her work for it. Not knowing made Sam all the more interested.

"How about Café du Monde and a walk around Jackson Square? I've yet to get beignets since I arrived." When Tess made a face, Sam figured maybe she was trying to let her down easy.

"I don't have anything against Café du Monde, but if you're after the local experience, that's not it."

Sam perked up. "Okay. Tell me what is. I'll happily be your pupil in all things New Orleans."

"There's a place in City Park. Morning Call. I've got the brunch shift on Sunday. How about you meet me there in the afternoon? Around four."

"Sold."

CHAPTER EIGHT

Sam walked into the restaurant. She'd told herself to stay away for at least a day, but she couldn't seem to contain herself. Rather than satisfying her curiosity, having lunch with Tess had only made Sam want to get to know her more. Now here she was, not twenty-four hours later, sniffing around like an eager puppy.

As it always did, Sam's gaze immediately went to the oyster bar along the back wall. Only Tess wasn't there. A huge black guy stood behind it in her place. He was wearing the same white chef coat and black apron—probably about ten sizes larger—serving oysters and laughing with a handful of customers.

"May I help you?"

Sam glanced down at the hostess and realized that she'd been scowling. She hoped that was the only reason the girl had such a worried look on her face. Sam offered her a smile. "Yes, sorry. I was lost in thought for a moment. I'm just going to sit at the bar."

The hostess offered a hesitant smile. "Great. If you end up wanting a table, just let me know."

"I will. Thanks."

Sam looked over at the oyster bar again. The guy seemed nice enough, but since she was more interested in Tess's company than a dozen raw oysters, she opted to sit at the regular bar. She claimed a stool and tried to shake off her disappointment.

"Good afternoon. What can I get you?"

Sam studied the bartender, whose name tag said Gary. Skinny, with glasses and a handlebar mustache, he reminded her of the bartender at

Prita's favorite restaurant in Brooklyn. "Hi. I'll have a beer. Do you have any IPAs on tap?"

The bartender smiled. "Parish Brewing has a new one out, and I have one from Pennsylvania as well."

"I'll go local. Thanks."

"You got it." He picked up a pint glass and started pulling the beer. "Menu?"

"Please." He set the beer down and handed her the menu. Sam perused it. "I'll have the blackened redfish po'boy."

"Excellent choice." He turned to put in her order. Then, after checking in on the other people sitting at the bar, he returned to where Sam was sitting.

"I was surprised Tess isn't working today." She hoped she didn't sound too obvious.

"She's always off on Thursdays. It's her regular gig at the Old Point."

"Gig?"

"Yeah, she sings one or two nights a week over there."

Sam's curiosity was piqued. She wanted to press for more information, but tried to keep her tone casual. "The Old Point. I don't think I know that place."

"It's over in Algiers, across the river. Mostly a townie bar, but great vibe. A little out of the way for tourists, you know?"

Sam's mind turned over the new information. "Yeah. Sounds cool." A waitress appeared with Sam's food. After thanking her, Sam popped a fry into her mouth and returned her attention to Gary. She didn't want to seem too eager to track down Tess, so she asked him about other local spots he'd recommend.

After finishing her lunch, Sam didn't linger. Not that she had anything against hipster Gary, but he wasn't really the company she was after. She walked back to her house, then spent a minute researching the place Tess would be.

It turned out the Old Point Bar was, in fact, in the Algiers neighborhood on the opposite side of the river. The few photos she found online reinforced Gary's assessment. Not quite a dive, it definitely seemed to cater to locals more than tourists. Even without the promise of seeing Tess, Sam would have been tempted to check it out.

Sam didn't mind doing things alone, but since she'd been meaning to make plans with Elisa, she texted her with an invitation. Unfortunately, she was out of town for work. Undeterred, Sam looked at the clock and calculated she had a good four hours to kill. As she often did to keep herself motivated, she set a word target to hit before she could play. Given that she was the only one enforcing it, it always surprised her how well it worked.

She hit the mark a little after six. That gave her plenty of time to have some leftover takeout and put just enough thought into what she wanted to wear. She decided to change, wanting to look good, but not like she was trying. Satisfied with the result—dark jeans and a light sweater with a pair of brown boots—she pulled up directions on her phone and headed out.

The drive over the Crescent City Connection bridge was quick. Although she couldn't make out much in the dark, Sam got the sense of an old neighborhood. The houses were built very close together, and she couldn't be sure, but she thought most of them might be shotgun style. She'd have to come over during the day and poke around.

Although the bar sat on a street that paralleled the river, Sam realized it offered no view of the water or city skyline on the opposite bank. She'd yet to grow accustomed to the massive earthen levees meant to hold the river back from the city. The aesthetics left much to be desired, but she found the science of it fascinating.

Not seeing a parking lot, Sam took a spot on the street about a block and a half away. She passed a food truck serving barbecue. Based on the length of the line, she figured it must be pretty good barbecue. Despite the chill, a dozen or so people sat at old wooden picnic tables along the side of the building, eating, smoking, drinking beer, and talking. She nodded at the few who made eye contact.

Inside, the bar took up the right wall and a small stage filled the back of the room. She claimed a stool at the end of the bar farthest from the stage. As much as she wanted the best view possible, she didn't want to catch Tess off guard. Or seem like a stalker.

She ordered a beer from the middle-aged woman behind the bar, then positioned her back to the wall so she could observe. A few small tables sat near the door where she came in. Sam pegged the people sitting at them as regulars. Mostly older, they drank Budweiser and

Coors Light and seemed interested primarily in enjoying each other's company. The crowd around the bar and standing in the open space in front of the stage skewed a bit younger, more hip. Sam didn't recognize the labels on their beer bottles, but their clothes and mannerisms felt familiar. Much like Gary, they made Sam think of that bar in Brooklyn.

Sam resisted pulling out her notebook to jot things down. Instead, she tried to commit the details to memory. In addition to the people around her, she wanted to capture the aura of the bar itself. Neon beer signs shared wall space with license plates, vintage Mardi Gras decorations, and a pair of framed photos of dogs wearing Hawaiian shirts and sunglasses. Dark wood and brick made the space feel intimate, but not claustrophobic. Everything felt worn in, like an ancient but beloved sofa.

The stage lights came on and Sam redirected her attention. When Tess walked onstage, Sam realized she'd not seen her in anything besides her restaurant uniform. Well, except for their lunch date. Tess's outfit then was nondescript — jeans and T-shirt with a fleece hoodie. Now, she wore a long, dark green cardigan over what looked like a short floral sundress and boots. Cowboy boots.

Sam didn't know what she was expecting, but country pixie was not it. She realized she had no idea what kind of music Tess sang, either. Would it be twangy and wistful? Upbeat pop? Sam sipped her beer and waited.

While the band got into position, Tess took the microphone. It was one of those vintage chrome jobs that made Sam think of speakeasies. "Thank y'all for coming out tonight. For anyone who doesn't know us, we're Sweet Evangeline. We do a mix of old and new, and when the mood strikes, the occasional request. We're here more Thursdays than not and we hope you like what you hear."

The audience clapped. Welcoming cheers were accompanied by a couple of whistles. Sam watched Tess glance back, see that everyone was ready. The drummer nodded, then called out the count to get them started. "One, two. One, two, three, four."

Drums and an upright bass, keyboard and guitar, began in perfect unison. Sam had never heard the song before, but it managed to feel familiar. Not quite blues and not quite jazz, the tune was both catchy and unique. And then Tess started to sing.

Any and every expectation Sam had evaporated. From the first verse, Tess's voice captivated her. Sultry, but somehow playful at the same time. Silky, but not so smooth it felt predictable. Lower than she'd expected, too. Had she not known better, Sam would have pegged it as coming from someone at least twice Tess's age, and for that matter, size. Sam was mesmerized.

Only when the crowd erupted in cheers did Sam realize the song had ended. She clapped, still trying to reconcile the woman onstage with the one who'd shucked her oysters and harangued her about vegetables. Before she could do that, the music started again and Tess launched into the sexiest version of "Dream a Little Dream of Me" Sam had ever heard.

When the set ended, Sam considered seeking Tess out. Under normal circumstances, she'd offer compliments, offer to buy Tess a drink. For a reason she couldn't quite identify, Sam hesitated. She felt suddenly like she'd inserted herself into something intimate, private. That didn't make sense, given that she was at a public show in a crowded bar. Still, she couldn't shake the feeling that she'd entered Tess's space—without an invitation and without Tess's knowledge.

Sam set cash on the counter to cover the cost of her second beer and slipped out the same way she'd come in. As far as she knew, Tess hadn't seen or recognized her. Unless Tess brought it up the next time she saw her, Sam decided to keep it to herself. She'd just need to find a way to get Tess to talk about her music and, hopefully, issue an actual invitation. Because she definitely needed to hear her again.

Tess finished the set with "Midnight Stroll." Not only was it the first legitimate song she'd ever written, it was the kind of song that made her happy to be alive, and even happier to live where she did. When they got to the refrain, Tess could sense that some of the crowd sang along. That might be her favorite part of playing in the same bar again and again. She drank in their energy, channeling it back into the song.

When they ended, Tess saw Carly and Becca standing near the bar, waving at her like a couple of fan girls. She had the best friends.

She walked over to them. "Gin and tonic, extra lime," Becca said as she handed Tess a glass.

"You're a goddess. Thank you." Tess sipped the drink. "I'm so glad y'all came."

"Becca's little cousin is watching Dustin for us. It's a school night, though, so we'll have to sneak out before you finish."

"It's all good. I know it's a work night for y'all, too, so I'm impressed you ventured out this late."

"Well, we've been lamenting how old we feel," Carly said.

Tess shook her head. "Not old. You have an infant. That changes everything."

Becca smiled. "Even so, we don't want to get completely out of practice being cool."

"Fair enough. Feel free to practice with me anytime."

Jenny joined them and spent a few minutes catching up with Carly and Becca. They weren't close outside of Tess, but had spent enough time together to be casual friends. They talked mostly about each other's kids and Jenny offered a few baby items that hadn't already been handed down to someone else.

When Mo interrupted a few minutes later to ask if they were ready, Tess hugged Carly and Becca good-bye, and she and Jenny took their places back on the stage. Tess bantered with the audience between songs, talking about everything from the drink specials of the night to the start of Mardi Gras season.

When they ended an hour later, Tess took a small bow with her band mates, then stepped off the stage and out of the spotlight. The crowd's attention returned to conversation and to procuring another drink from the bar. Tess spent a few minutes helping pack up the speakers and wires, instruments, and other gear.

Jenny appeared with five beers. After distributing them to the group, she lifted hers. "To another great gig."

The other four bottles were raised in unison. "To Sweet Evangeline."

After a quick debrief of things that worked, and a couple that didn't, conversation turned to life. A few years ago, that would have been topics like making rent or buying new instruments, hookups and breakups. Now Zack was getting potty training advice from Cedric, and Mo asked Jenny about realtors in Metairie. Tess didn't mind. Even though she'd yet to jump on the start-a-family wagon, she liked the vibe of the older, more settled band.

Conversations began to wind down a little after midnight. They packed the instruments and gear into everyone's vehicles and Tess accepted Zack's offer of a ride to her house, which took all of three minutes. Tess wished him a good night and headed in.

After a shower and a bowl of cereal, she climbed into bed with Marlowe. Yet again, Tess found her thoughts wandering to Sam. Lunch had been pleasant enough. Sam was flirtatious without being pushy, which Tess appreciated. She also seemed genuinely interested in learning about New Orleans, and about Tess.

Even though Tess considered herself friendly, she didn't make friends all that easily. And Sam was definitely unlike any of the friends she had. Just because Sam might be interested in dating and Tess wasn't, it didn't mean they couldn't meet somewhere in the middle and enjoy each other's company. Feeling like she'd settled the matter, Tess drifted off to sleep. Maybe she dreamed about Sam, but that didn't have to mean anything either.

CHAPTER NINE

When Sam pulled City Park up in her phone, she realized just how huge it was—sports fields, walking paths, a sculpture garden, even a small amusement park. She tweaked her search to pull up the coffee shop Tess mentioned in the hopes of getting a more precise idea of where to park.

Seeing as it was a sunny Sunday afternoon with temperatures in the fifties, she expected it to be busy. But as she drove the winding streets into the heart of the park, Sam was surprised by just how many people there were. Kids climbed playground equipment and ran around in circles while moms, and a few dads, looked on. There were joggers and bikers and people sitting on benches reading. Although New Orleans was a far cry from the urban landscape of Manhattan, Sam couldn't help but think of Central Park.

Unlike Central Park, however, City Park offered plenty of parking. She pulled into an open spot and cut the engine. She could see Morning Call from where she sat, behind a large pavilion and some trees.

Tess stood in front of the café, wearing jeans and tall boots, a dark red sweater, and sunglasses. Usually, Sam found herself attracted to polished women—those who took a great deal of care with their looks and who liked being noticed. Tess seemed like the exact opposite. She was gorgeous, but Sam got the feeling she didn't spend a lot of time thinking about it. She doubted Tess dressed for the pleasure of others, or for attention. It was refreshing, and in some ways even sexier.

"This park is amazing," Sam said.

Tess smiled. "And just far enough out of the Quarter that it doesn't get too many tourists. I'm glad you like it."

"I like it even more knowing there's a beignet shop on the premises."

Tess shook her head, but continued to smile. "You're an eater, aren't you?"

Sam couldn't argue with the assertion. "One of my favorite pastimes."

"Well, you're in a good place for it. Would you like to meander first or go right for the goods?"

A pair of kids darted by, each with a small paper bag. Sam caught a whiff of hot grease and yeast and sugar. Despite thinking they should start with the walk, her stomach got the best of her. "We should definitely start with beignets."

They walked into the café. Most of the tables were occupied, so they snagged a pair of vacant stools at the long marble bar. A petite woman who appeared to be in her late sixties approached them. She wore a white jacket with a black bow tie and a white paper hat. She set down two small glasses of water and smiled at them. "Good afternoon. Y'all know what y'all want?"

"I think so," Tess said, glancing at Sam. Sam nodded. "Two orders of beignets and two café au laits, please."

"Comin' right up."

Sam took a moment to absorb her surroundings. Sets of French doors lined one wall, offering views of oak trees and people strolling by. A few of their fellow customers snapped photos of themselves and their food, but most seemed like locals. Although bustling, the vibe was far more relaxed than she remembered at Café du Monde, where stopping in felt more like something to check off the bucket list than a chance to relax and share a cup of coffee with friends. "Thank you for bringing me here."

Tess smiled. "It's not really hidden, but I suppose it's a place you have to seek out."

"Absolutely. I had an appointment at NOMA last week and didn't take the time to explore. I had no idea all this was tucked behind it."

The waitress returned with their order. "Y'all enjoy."

"Thank you," Tess and Sam said in unison.

The coffees were frothy and perfect, the beignets puffy and a deep golden brown. They were also bare. Sam frowned. Tess picked up a small silver can and handed it to her. "You get to sugar your own."

"Whew. I was worried there for a second." Sam took the can, shook a generous amount of powdered sugar onto her donuts, then handed the can back to Tess.

Tess took the can and put decidedly less sugar on her order. "You're hilarious."

Sam shrugged. "I take my sweets very seriously."

"Obviously."

Sam took a bite and moaned. She loved all donuts, but there was something about getting them fresh out of the oil that elevated the whole experience. The woman playing the accordion right outside may have helped, too. "I'm coming here every day."

Tess laughed. "A dangerous, but delicious, proposition."

"If I have a heart attack and die before I leave town, it will be a good way to go."

"I guess I can think of worse ways. I should have told you not to wear black. Sorry."

Sam glanced down at the front of her sweater, which was now dusted with powdered sugar. "I think I should have known better."

"A damp paper towel from the bathroom should take care of it."

"Since I've already made a mess of myself, would you judge me if I got another order?"

Tess chuckled. "I won't judge if you share."

"Deal."

After they polished off the second round, Sam pulled out money to cover the bill and excused herself to the restroom. Tess's paper towel suggestion did the trick, mostly. Not that she would have been terribly embarrassed anyway, but again, spending time with Tess had a much more laid-back energy than she was used to. Sam hoped it wasn't the fact that they'd landed squarely in the friend zone.

When Sam emerged, Tess stood. "I'm going to make a quick stop, too. I'll meet you outside."

Tess rejoined her a few minutes later. "Anything particular you want to see?"

"Anything. Everything. I put myself in your hands."

They left the café and took a path that skirted a small pond. Ducks paddled lazily in the water while sparrows, robins, and a few birds Sam didn't recognize hopped around, pecking at the ground. Some of the live oaks were so old that their branches dipped all the way to the ground, creating benches and crevices where even the most novice tree climber could have a field day. Spanish moss hung so perfectly, Sam had to remind herself it hadn't been placed there for effect.

"Do you mind if I take some photos?" Sam asked.

"Of course not. Take your time."

They made their way around one of the playgrounds and passed Storyland, which Tess described as an amusement park for little kids. Sam snapped photos of the trees and open spaces, of people in the distance. She wasn't sure how she could use this in the book, but she wanted to. She imagined the park at night. The shadows and hiding places that felt so charming in the daylight hours would be much more sinister in the dark.

When they got to the sculpture garden, Sam couldn't help but smile. Traditional figures stood opposite modern, abstract pieces of twisted metal and glass. There was a huge cutout of a cartoon blue dog and something that resembled an insect. They approached a bronze that reminded Sam of a mythical goddess and Sam stopped. "Will you let me take your picture?"

Tess took off her sunglasses and raised a brow. "Really?"

"Yes, really. When I remember this day, I want to remember you, too."

Tess rolled her eyes, but laughed. "If you insist. Where do you want me?"

Sam knew better than to articulate what she was thinking, which was some variation of "in my arms" or "in my bed." She pointed to the goddess. "How about next to her?"

Tess hesitated for a moment, then made her way over to the statue. She perched her sunglasses on the top of her head and glanced up. She turned back to Sam, pushing her chest and chin out slightly and letting her arms trail behind in a perfect mime of the statue's pose. Sam swallowed the lump that had risen inexplicably in her throat and snapped several photos. "Ravishing."

Tess walked back to where Sam stood. "Does this mean I get to take one of you, too?"

"But of course."

She seemed to think for a moment, then led Sam over to a rotund nude holding a baby. "Let me use your phone and then you can send them all to me."

Sam handed it to her and went over to the statue. Although she didn't have a baby to hold, Sam did her best to imitate the posture and stoic expression. "How's that?"

"Priceless."

They wandered a bit more before Tess began leading them back in the direction of their cars. Sam didn't want to press her luck, but she was in no hurry to end their time together. "I had a great time this afternoon. I appreciate you continuing to show me places the locals go."

"It's my pleasure. It's nice to have people show interest in the city beyond the obvious."

"Can I buy you dinner to say thank you?"

"I don't know, that's bordering on date territory."

"But—" Sam was trying to formulate a good comeback when Tess interrupted her.

"But, more importantly, I'm still stuffed with beignets. I can't possibly think about food for a few more hours."

Sam could think of a thousand ways to spend time with Tess that didn't involve food, but she knew that wasn't really the point. Normally, she would take the hint and move on. Something about Tess, though, kept her coming back for more. Maybe it was the thrill of the chase. Sam couldn't remember the last time she'd been so taken with a woman—and had to work for it.

"Fair enough. The walk has been really nice, though. Maybe we could get together again to burn off some calories." Again, Sam had to refrain from fully speaking her mind about possible activities.

"That sounds nice. I ride my bike a lot, but I'm usually more focused on getting from one place to the next than I am on simply enjoying the ride."

"You name the place, and I'll be there."

"Actually, there's a new path in my neighborhood that goes right along the river. I've only used it once or twice, but it's a great view of the city."

"I'm in." Sam resisted the urge to walk Tess to her car. She had a feeling that, too, might border on date territory. Since it didn't look like she was going to stop pursuing Tess anytime soon, she'd need to channel her inner tortoise rather than hare.

After saying their good-byes, Tess climbed into her car and sat for a moment. Despite her initial hesitation, she liked spending time with Sam. She hadn't dated much in the last few months and Sam reminded her of how much fun it could be to get to know someone new. It didn't hurt that Sam was nice to look at and a total flirt.

Sam seemed like she could hold her own and it was tempting to enjoy the ride. But something about Sam set off warning bells. Not that Tess feared Sam wouldn't take no for an answer, but more that Tess wasn't sure she could trust herself to say no in the first place. Assuming she wanted to say no.

Tess sighed. She had some pretty clear ground rules about getting involved and Sam broke just about all of them. The last thing she wanted to do was lead Sam on and then put on the brakes without warning. Tess hated women like that. She sure as hell wasn't going to let herself become one. And she had her rules for a reason. Didn't she?

Although she'd been looking to deflect Sam's invitation, Tess's comment about being stuffed had been true. So after getting home and putting on a load of laundry, she plopped herself on the bench of her ancient upright piano and started noodling. Her piano skills were barely better than her abilities on the guitar, but she picked out a few chords and hummed along.

Over the next half hour, she pieced together a refrain, extolling the virtues of resisting temptation. The tune was catchy, but the words fell flat. Tess chewed the cap of her pen and looked at Marlowe, who'd perched himself on top of the piano to sit in the sun and groom himself. He stopped licking his paw and stared at her.

"What?"

He set the paw down and tilted his head to one side, giving her his judgy face. She didn't know how she knew it was judgy, but she knew. She sighed and scribbled a line through the words. In their place, she laid out an argument for giving into temptation. She played the tune again, this time singing the new lines.

Marlowe withheld any feedback, but Tess knew it was good. For some reason, bad choices and heartbreak always seemed to make for the best songs. She shook her head. Quite the opposite was true in life. That's why she preferred to sing the blues rather than live them.

She spent another hour drafting a couple of verses. They'd need work, but it was the most complete first run at a song she'd had in as long as she could remember. She stood up to stretch her shoulders and back, telling herself the creative surge didn't have anything to do with the time she'd spent with Sam.

Marlowe jumped down from the piano and meowed, his way of asserting it was time for dinner. Tess padded into the kitchen and filled his bowl. Deciding maybe she was a little hungry herself, she warmed up some gumbo and sat at the kitchen table with a magazine. She fished out a shrimp and offered it to Marlowe. "Thanks for your help, boy."

He accepted the treat, then rubbed himself on her legs. Tess leaned down to rub his ears. She picked up her phone and saw that Sam had sent the photos from their afternoon while she'd been at the piano. In addition to the pictures in the sculpture garden, Sam sent a few of the scenery from the park. She had a great eye, capturing angles and details that Tess wouldn't have noticed herself.

At the end, there was an additional photo of Tess. A candid shot, one she hadn't even realized Sam took. Tess was looking at something off in the distance; based on the location, she guessed it was kids on the playground. Tess stared at the photo. She looked...beautiful. Tess didn't think herself unattractive, but Sam had captured something more, something intimate.

I was tempted to keep this one for myself, but it seemed wrong. I hope you don't mind that I took it when you weren't looking. Looking forward to next time.

Tess looked through the images again, then reread the note. She started several responses, each time deleting the words and shaking her head. The noncommittal response seemed disingenuous, the personal one too precious. In the end, she settled for something in the vein of her new song.

Thank you for the photos. You're good at capturing the essence of things. It makes spending time with you all the more tempting.

Sam's reply came almost instantly.

High praise. Please know the feeling is mutual.

"What am I getting myself into, Marlowe?" The cat responded by jumping into her lap and nuzzling her neck. "Yeah, that's what I'm afraid of."

CHAPTER TEN

W orking in the library brought back fond memories of Sam's college years. Back then, there'd been as much making out in quiet corners as there had been studying. She didn't want to relive those days by any means, but thinking back on them gave Sam a pleasant mixture of nostalgia and appreciation of how far she'd come.

Classes at Tulane had resumed the week before, but the library remained relatively empty. By the time midterms arrived in March, she'd have most of her first draft complete. Her productivity had definitely improved with age.

Just this morning, she'd put in close to three thousand words. It was halfway to the goal she'd set for herself before meeting Tess for an afternoon walk along the levee. Although they'd yet to graduate to dinner, much less anything physical, Sam felt like things with Tess were getting more personal, intimate. While Tess's reticence had been frustrating at first, Sam had come to appreciate that they were becoming friends. It made her pause and appreciate the chemistry between them, the potential. In fact, it reminded her of more than a couple of her college relationships.

With thoughts of Tess now filling her mind, Sam hit save, stretched, and looked around. At the moment, no one else was in sight. She decided to take advantage and make a quick run to the restroom.

She was gone two, maybe three minutes. When she got back to her table, everything was exactly as she'd left it. With one glaring exception. Her laptop was gone.

Sam's eyes darted around. A guy who looked to be about twenty was walking toward her. "Did you just see anybody walk through here with a laptop?"

He didn't answer and she realized he had ear buds in. Sam waved her hands to get his attention. He pulled out one of them and Sam repeated her question.

"No, ma'am."

Even in a state, Sam bristled at being called ma'am. "Okay, thanks."

He kept walking and Sam looked around again, as though perhaps it had merely wandered off and would be sitting somewhere in the near vicinity. Of course, it wasn't.

She started cramming her things in her bag and tried not to panic. How could she be such an idiot? She'd been complacent and just a little bit lazy, that's how. She shook her head. It was the exact combination that got so many of her characters into trouble.

Sam walked the stacks near where she'd been working, poking her head into study carrels. She asked the few people she happened upon if they'd seen anyone or anything. No one had. And to make things worse, they all looked at her with a combination of sympathy and judgment—exactly the look she'd give to anyone dumb enough to leave their laptop unattended.

She loved that laptop. It had been through eight novels, three countries, and countless hotel rooms. She counted on it more than any woman she dated, and it had never let her down. And now it was gone.

Sam stored her work in the cloud, so things certainly weren't as bad as they could be. Still. All of the work could be accessed, along with personal information, financial records, and her email. All someone had to do was circumvent the initial login. Not an easy feat, but not an impossible one by any means.

What were the odds someone would do that? In all likelihood, the thief had seen it sitting there, swiped it, and was already en route to dumping it for some quick cash. People who did that sort of thing would wipe it clean and sell it online or in a pawn shop. In all likelihood, she had nothing to worry about.

Unfortunately, Sam made her living creating characters with far more sinister motives, not to mention skill sets. If someone wanted to cause her harm, stealing her computer had the potential to do a lot of damage, or at least stir up trouble. But she wasn't a character in one of her books. She was just a person in a library who'd been careless. And unlike the characters in her books, she kept a low profile. And she generally avoided making enemies.

Annoyed that she was talking to herself—in circles, no less— Sam gathered the rest of her things and tried to formulate a plan. She dismissed calling the police or even campus safety. They'd do little more than write up a report and give her a lecture. First up, call Prita. Then she'd worry about procuring a new computer and changing all her passwords.

She stopped by the circulation desk on her way out of the library to make sure no one had turned in a computer. Of course, no one had. As she walked to her car, she pulled out her phone. Prita answered on the second ring. "If you're calling to brag about something you're eating, I don't want to hear it."

Sam took a deep breath. "I wish. My computer got stolen."

"Son of a bitch. Where? How?"

Sam told her the story, then listened to Prita's lecture on how dumb it had been to leave her things unattended. She paused for a second and Sam cut her off. "You don't have to tell me. I know."

"Okay, okay. Game plan. Everything is password protected, right? The computer itself and then all of your files and accounts."

Sam confessed that, after the initial login, most of her passwords were stored. "Please don't yell."

Prita huffed. "I'm not going to yell. I'm pretty lazy about that stuff, too. Change your bank and credit card passwords first, then your cloud storage and email. I'm going to go into your Dropbox and pull all the manuscripts out completely just to be safe."

Sam felt infinitely better. "Thanks."

"I'll do your social media accounts, too, and text you the new passwords later."

"You're the best."

"I know."

"I'll call you later." Sam spent the next half hour in her car logging into every account she could think of. She saw no bogus charges in any of her accounts, no weird posts. Nothing seemed out of order. Sam let out a sigh of relief, then chuckled at herself for being paranoid. Feeling calmer, Sam went back to looking for a place to buy a new computer.

The Lakeside Shopping Center, complete with Apple Store, was only about fifteen minutes away. Perfect.

Two hours later, Sam was back at home and pulling her new MacBook Air out of its box. It was sleek and weighed probably half of what her old computer did. Maybe this whole thing was a blessing in disguise. She began the tedious process of downloading software and configuring it the way she wanted. Since the possibility of getting any more work done was clearly shot for the day, she picked up her phone to call Prita with an update.

Are we still on?

It took her a second to register the meaning of the text. Shit. She had a date with Tess and she was half an hour late.

She'd covered all the major bases, or at least she hoped so. She typed a hasty reply to Tess that she was on her way. She'd had enough of computer business anyway.

When she arrived at the levee, she found Tess on a bench, looking out at the water. "I'm so sorry."

Tess glanced up and offered a half smile. "I thought maybe you'd forgotten me. Or that something better had come along."

Sam shook her head. "Certainly not the latter. I may have temporarily forgotten, but I have a good reason."

Tess raised a brow.

Sam joined her on the bench. "It's been a hell of a day. My laptop got stolen this morning and I spent the rest of the afternoon replacing it and trying to make sure my accounts and everything else on it weren't compromised."

To Sam's relief, Tess's face immediately softened. "Oh, that sucks. I wasn't really pissed, but you're officially forgiven anyway. What happened?"

Sam rolled her eyes. "I went to the Tulane library this morning to work and I left my stuff for like two seconds."

Tess shook her head. "Sadly, that's all it takes."

"So I hear. I just ran to the bathroom. I knew it was lazy, but I didn't want to pack everything up. I had a great spot, too, and I didn't want to lose it."

"Is everything okay? I mean, considering?"

Sam shrugged. "Yeah. I had password protection on the computer and none of my bank or credit card accounts seem disturbed. I changed all the logins to be safe. That's what took so much time. I'm guessing someone wiped it clean to use themselves or sell."

"College campuses can be the worst for stuff like that."

"Well, it's over now. And it was a good excuse to buy a new computer, which I swear weighs half of what my old one did."

Tess smiled. "That seems to be the way."

"Right? I have a feeling that once I'm over my agitation, I'll like it."

"Are you still up for a walk?"

"Absolutely. Exactly what I need. I'm sorry again for almost standing you up."

"It's fine." Tess turned and punched her lightly on the arm. "Just don't make a habit of it."

They stood and headed east. At least Sam thought it was east. The way the river twisted and turned, she found it hard to get her bearings at times. They were in Algiers, on the opposite side of the river from the French Quarter—the same neighborhood where Sam had seen her sing. Perhaps Tess lived nearby.

The path looked well-tended and offered a great view of the city. One of the steamboats sat docked on the opposite shore. The brown water churned and flowed with a speed that always took Sam a bit by surprise. Not beautiful by traditional standards, but it had a unique appeal. She liked that about New Orleans.

"Is the water level low?" There had to be a hundred feet between where they stood and the water's edge.

Tess considered. "Actually, it's on the high side."

Sam had no idea where the levees breached, or were topped, during Katrina or any of the other hurricanes that had blown through over the years, but she had a hard time imagining the massive earthen dams giving way. She had vague images in her mind from the news, but she'd been living in San Francisco at the time and it had felt a world away.

They walked quietly for a little while, but then Sam could feel Tess's eyes on her. She glanced over and made eye contact. "What?"

"I feel like I've told you a lot about me, but I hardly know anything about you."

Sam's smile was casual and belied how little she'd shared about herself. "What do you want to know?"

"Where did you grow up?"

"Just outside of Philly."

Tess smiled. "I've never been there."

"The city is cool. We lived in the suburbs, though, so it felt more generic than anything else."

"I've never thought about it that way, but I guess you're right."

"I'm not complaining. We had a nice yard and I only had to share a room with my sister until I was ten. The schools were good and I got to play sports."

"Are you close to your family now?"

Man, the girl didn't waste time. "Sort of."

"You don't have to talk about it if you don't want to."

"It's not that."

Based on Sam's tone, Tess figured it was something. She wanted to get to know Sam, but that didn't need to include any deep-seeded vulnerabilities. "No, really. There are plenty of other things I can grill you about. Where did you live before you came here?"

Sam visibly relaxed. "Right before, I was in Dallas."

"And before that?"

"Rome, Dublin, and Vancouver."

"Wow." Tess had been to Dallas once, but otherwise had never ventured beyond the states along the Gulf Coast. Not that she'd ever minded. At least not all that much.

"I know. I consider myself very fortunate."

"So what's your home base? Where's *home* home?"

"Philadelphia, I guess. My parents are still there, and my siblings. I go there on holidays, so I'd say that's about as close to home as I get."

"But you don't have a house or a place somewhere you consider yours?" As far as Tess was concerned, the jetting around was only fun if you had a home to return to when you were done.

"Maybe one day. For now, I like not being tied down. Renting an apartment or a house feels plenty homey. Way better than hotels. And I just reconnected with my cousin who lives here, so I get to have some family close by, too."

Tess wasn't convinced. Her house wasn't fancy by any means, but it was hers, along with everything in it. Family was a more complicated matter, but still. "I guess we're just really different."

They made their way about a mile and half down the path before

Tess suggested they loop back. When they'd wound their way back to the bench where they started, Sam eyed her hopefully. "Bite to eat?"

Tess checked her watch. 5:30. "I don't know. It's awfully close to suppertime."

"But if we go dressed like this and we keep it casual, it's totally not a date."

Sam had taken to teasing Tess about her somewhat arbitrary definition of what constituted a date. Tess found the banter funny, mostly. "Well, when you put it that way. I'll say yes, but only if you let me buy this time."

Sam scowled, but agreed.

Tess gave her directions to a burger place nearby. And although the food came in paper-lined plastic baskets, they lingered in the high-backed booth for over two hours. By the end, Tess would have been hard-pressed to argue that they'd not been on a date. She mulled this over as they made their way to the parking lot.

"I'm sorry we have two cars," Sam said.

"You're okay to drive, aren't you?"

"Yes, yes. That's not what I meant."

Tess chuckled. "Just checking."

She'd been pretty sure she knew what Sam meant, but wanted to check. To her mind, having two cars was a safety net. It meant no close, shared space. It guaranteed no one would be tempted to invite anyone in. For some reason, that practical barrier seemed suddenly important to maintaining the boundaries of friendship.

"Thank you for dinner." They'd parked next to each other, but Sam followed Tess to her driver's side.

"You're welcome. Thank you for letting me reciprocate."

Sam smiled and Tess felt her insides flutter. "It's what friends do, right?"

"Mmm-hmm." But friends standing a foot away weren't supposed to make her pulse race, and that's exactly what Tess's was doing.

"And thanks for the walk. It was perfect. I'm sorry again I was late."

"No worries."

Everything about Sam's body language screamed that she was on the verge of kissing Tess. In that moment, Tess realized how badly she wanted her to. The feeling of desire, of anticipation, made her breath catch. Sam seemed to lean in slightly, but instead of pulling away, Tess prepared for the onslaught to her senses. She'd just see what it was like. Maybe that would dispel the ever-increasing curiosity, get it out of her system.

"I'll see you later this week, then. I've got some catching up to do tomorrow, but I'll be around."

Sam's words broke the spell that had been cast between them. Tess blinked a few times, trying to regain her bearings. She wondered if she'd somehow imagined the frisson or if Sam intentionally backed away from it. Tess struggled to clear her mind and not give away where her thoughts had been. "That sounds good. You know where to find me."

"You're okay to get home?"

"Of course. I'll see you soon."

Tess got the sense that Sam was going to stand there until she left, so she climbed into her car and started the engine. After fumbling with the seat belt a couple of times, she backed out of the spot and offered a wave before pulling away. As she drove, Tess attempted to replay the last few minutes with Sam in her mind. For all she knew, Sam's interest in her had passed. Tess got the distinct feeling that Sam rarely wanted for company. It seemed unlikely she'd waste her time pursuing someone who'd shot her down.

Then again, Sam continued to invite her out. Even with the premise of getting local flavor, Sam seemed eager to spend time with her. And she asked as many questions about Tess as she did about New Orleans. And there was that spark. Even in her state of reluctant attraction, Tess refused to believe she'd fabricated the electricity between them.

She pulled into her driveway and sat for a moment. What was worse—being attracted to Sam or obsessing about it? Annoyed, both with herself and the situation she'd gotten herself into, she got out of the car and went inside.

CHAPTER ELEVEN

The next morning, Tess felt no more settled, and no less attracted to Sam. The almost kiss that she might have imagined seemed to give her mind carte blanche to imagine kissing and much, much more. Tess couldn't remember the last time she'd had a full-on sex dream. Until last night.

She got ready to meet Carly for breakfast, acclimating to the idea that she needed advice. Aside from the first lunch meeting, she'd yet to tell Carly—or Jenny, or anyone else for that matter—about the time she'd been spending with Sam. In her mind, talking about Sam made her significant. And she'd been so damn adamant that there was no significance at all in her having a meal with an insanely hot woman.

But they'd had lunch again, then dinner after the walk along the river. Nothing fancy, nothing formal, but also not the kind of meal one shared with a casual acquaintance either. When she shared a meal with Sam, even if it was just po'boys, it felt intimate. They talked about personal stuff; they lingered long after the food was gone. Not to mention the times Sam had come into the restaurant.

She rode her bike to the diner, trying to formulate what she would say to Carly. The worst part was knowing that Carly would tease her about getting sucked in by a nice body and some good conversation. No, that was the second worst part. The worst part was having no idea what advice Carly would give her.

If Carly told her getting involved with Sam seemed like a terrible idea, would she heed it? What if Carly told her to go for it? Part of Tess—the part below her waistline—thrilled at the idea. As much as she didn't want to admit it, she hadn't had much action over the last couple of years. Most of the time, she didn't mind, but feeling that surge of attraction made her realize how much she missed it.

Would she regret it, though? She had a feeling that hooking up with Sam would be entirely different than what Carly had referred to as Tess's occasional third-date sex. She didn't know why she had that feeling, but it was the one thing coming in loud and clear.

At the diner, she locked up her bike and went inside. Carly was just being shown to a booth by the windows. Tess walked over to join her. "Hey."

Carly glanced up at the greeting and grinned. "Woman. How are you?"

"Fabulous. Happy to see you. Starved."

"In that order?"

Tess smiled. "Starved might be at the top of the list."

Carly shook her head. "It's good to know where I rate."

"You know I'm kidding."

"I do. But I also know how many pancakes you can put away."

"I do like pancakes. I'd been thinking about an omelet, but now you've gone and put that in my head."

"You're welcome."

The waitress came over and smiled at them. "Morning, girls. Can I start y'all with some coffee?"

"You absolutely can, although I think we know what we want." Carly glanced at Tess and Tess nodded.

"Sounds good. What can I get y'all?"

"Coffee, OJ, two eggs over easy, and whole wheat toast." Carly tucked her menu back behind the napkin dispenser. "Oh, and turkey sausage."

"Yes, ma'am. And for you?" She looked at Tess.

"I'll have coffee as well, pancakes, and a side of sausage, not turkey."

The waitress grinned. "Two, three, or five pancakes?"

"Three."

"You can get five. I won't judge. If I had your metabolism, I'd eat like a horse, too," Carly said.

"Three is fine. Thank you."

With their orders in, Tess sighed. No point in dragging it out. "So, do you remember me telling you I had lunch with that woman who came into the restaurant?"

Carly thought for a moment. "The one who asked you out, but you turned down?"

"Yes. She played the hospitality card, so I introduced her to Willy's."

"Nice."

"It was nice."

"And?"

"And we've gotten together twice since."

"I see."

"And she comes into the restaurant practically every other day. It's all been cool. She flirts, but isn't aggressive about it. She's interesting and smart and really nice to look at."

Carly laced her fingers together and leaned forward. "And?"

Tess was saved from having to give an immediate answer by the arrival of their food. She applied butter and syrup to her pancakes with intense focus. Carly didn't speak; she merely sat there patiently. Tess set down the syrup bottle. "And last night I really thought she was going to kiss me."

"Did she?"

"No."

"And you were disappointed."

"Yes."

Carly took a bite of her toast and smiled. "I love it."

Tess scowled. "What do you love?"

"Let's see. One: you've met a woman who gets you all hot and bothered. Two: she's clearly into you enough to keep coming around even though you turned her down."

"Yeah, but now I don't know what to do."

"Of course you do."

"Do I? It doesn't feel like it."

Carly pointed her fork at Tess. "You kiss her. At this point, you making the first move is the last thing she's expecting. She'll be caught off guard and it will be totally hot."

Tess's stomach tightened with a mixture of anticipation and nerves. "I don't know if I can do that."

"Has it been so long you've forgotten how? I could give you a refresher. Becca probably wouldn't mind."

Tess rolled her eyes. "Are you enjoying making fun of me?"

"Immensely."

Tess huffed. "That was a rhetorical question."

"You should have specified that beforehand." Carly shrugged in a way that was more playful than dismissive.

"Do you think I'm a hypocrite?" Tess cringed, both wanting an honest answer and afraid of what it might be.

Carly's face softened. "Of course not. You're probably the most genuine person I know."

"You don't have to say that."

"I'm not just saying it. You practically ooze integrity."

"But I've always sworn off getting involved with people who are just passing through."

"Yeah, but not in a judgy way. And you've never judged anyone else for it, either."

"I've been a little judgy."

"Okay, maybe a little. But it's okay to change your mind. It's not like you squawk about it. I'm probably the only one who knows you feel that way."

Tess shook her head. "And Sam."

Carly nodded sympathetically. "I'm sorry, my friend. I can't help you there."

"I don't want her to think I don't mean what I say." She hated women who played cat and mouse. It was so fake.

"Or that she's attractive enough to sway you from your principles."

Tess's shoulders slumped and she hung her head. "Shit. I hadn't even thought about that. This is a terrible idea."

"When did you become so obsessed with what everyone thinks about you?"

Tess folded her arms and scowled. "I'm not obsessed."

Carly raised a brow. "So what's really the problem?"

Carly had hit the nail on the head. The problem with Sam was that she was attractive enough to sway Tess from her principles. Whether or not Sam knew it was almost beside the point. The fact of the matter was that she'd let herself get swept up in this woman like a giddy teenager.

It went against every reasonable, rational tendency she had. If she threw her reservations to the wind, would she end up regretting it?

Even with that question hanging in her mind, that fear, she couldn't seem to help herself. Sam stirred things in her—things she'd not felt in a long time and a few she didn't recall feeling ever. "I don't know."

"Do you want to know what I think?"

The way Carly phrased the question told Tess she didn't want to know. Not in the least. "I asked, didn't I?"

"I think you're afraid of losing the upper hand."

"What?"

"The upper hand. You have it. You know it. She knows it. You're afraid that if you give in, you'll lose it."

Ridiculous. For one thing, she didn't think of relationships like that. Like they were some sort of weird power dynamic. And she certainly wasn't some uptight control freak who needed to call all the shots. "I don't know what you're talking about."

Carly didn't say anything. She just stared at Tess blandly.

"Okay, maybe I know what you're talking about, but I don't think I'm like that."

Again, no words. Only a subtle lift of the brow.

"Okay, for the sake of argument, let's say I might occasionally have those tendencies. I don't see how they apply here."

Carly folded her arms across her chest. "Before we go any further, can you state, out loud, that you're attracted to her?"

Tess sighed. "I'm attracted to her."

"Really attracted to her."

Tess rolled her eyes. "Really attracted to her."

"Thank you. And she's attracted to you, yes?"

"Yes."

"You know this for a fact. She has said as much."

"She keeps asking me out, so I'm going to go with yes."

Carly nodded. "Yet you've held her at bay. You've agreed to hang out with her, but pooh-poohed any romantic involvement."

"Pooh-poohed?"

Carly lifted a finger, pointed at Tess's eyes, then her own. "Hey. Focus."

"Sorry. Yes, I've dismissed the prospect of taking things to the next level."

"But you're pretty sure she's still interested?"

Tess flashed back to her interactions with Sam over the last couple of weeks. On more than one occasion, Sam looked at Tess like she wanted to swallow her whole. "Yeah."

"That means you have all the power. You get to decide if anything happens between you."

She hated when Carly was right, which was most of the time. "I can see that."

"It also means that if you give the green light, and things happen, you're back on a level playing field. No more upper hand."

Tess scowled. "You make it sound like I'm toying with her. And that I like it."

Carly's face softened. "Not at all. I think she's got you feeling unsteady. Seeking higher ground is instinct."

The metaphor packed a punch. It made Tess think back to the fights she had with her family about returning to New Orleans after Katrina. She'd refused to accept a life she didn't want for the security of a safer and more stable place. "But higher ground isn't all it's cracked up to be."

Carly shrugged. "For some people it is. You've just never been one of those people."

Except when it came to relationships. Tess nodded. "You're right."

"Usually. Do you feel better?"

She did. She also knew what she was going to do. "You know what? I do."

❖

Tess arrived at work the following day hoping that Sam would come in. She didn't want to put herself out there via text where she couldn't gauge Sam's reaction. And she wanted to act before she lost her nerve. She started setting up her station, chatting up Gary so she wouldn't start spinning hypothetical conversations in her mind.

A handful of lawyers came in right when they opened and Tess was relieved to have something to do. She focused so much on her work, in fact, she didn't even see Sam sidle up to the bar.

"Fancy seeing you here."

The sound of Sam's voice made her jump. Her knife slipped and she poked it right into the fleshy part of her palm, causing her to drop both the knife and the oyster and let out a small yelp.

"Oh, my God. Are you okay?"

Slightly mortified, but fine. Tess retrieved her things and set them in the sink, got out a clean knife. "Yeah. I wear steel mesh gloves for a reason."

"I'm so sorry. I didn't mean to startle you."

"It's fine. Clearly my mind was on another planet."

"You're sure you're okay?"

"Promise." She lifted her gloved hand and wiggled her fingers. She finished the tray she was working on and slid it into the kitchen window. "You're here early today."

"I've got an appointment at NOMA this afternoon, so I thought I'd indulge in an early lunch." Sam didn't add that she hadn't wanted to chance missing Tess if she had the early shift.

"Do you want to start with oysters?"

Sam also didn't want to admit she was getting a little sick of raw oysters. But it seemed like bad form to sit at the oyster bar and not order any.

"You don't have to, you know. No one will fuss at you, or me for that matter."

Sam cringed, sorry that her mind had been so easy to read.

"Really. A customer is a customer. And it's not like people are clamoring for a seat."

"Okay. Maybe I'll take a day off. I'm actually kind of craving a shrimp po'boy."

"Coming right up. Something to drink?"

"A Coke, please."

Tess put in her order, then went back to shucking. Sam learned that Tess often shucked for the kitchen when things were slow. Even though they ordered quarts of shucked oysters wholesale, they supplemented that with the less-than-perfect specimens that came still in the shell.

Sam had grown quite fond of watching her work. It had an almost hypnotic effect on her, watching the fluid, repetitive motions. She'd let herself slip into a bit of trance when Tess spoke. "What did you say?"

"Really?" Tess had her hands on her hips and an exasperated look on her face.

"I'm sorry. I was watching you and completely missed what you said."

Tess chuckled and Sam wondered what was so funny about that. "I said that I've been thinking and maybe we could have a real dinner sometime."

Sam knew better than to ask Tess to repeat herself a third time. She let the meaning of Tess's words sink in, hoping they meant what she thought they did. "Real dinner, huh? I'd love to have dinner with you."

"I know lunch has certain limitations. Seems like we might have more possibilities with dinner."

Her expression told Sam that Tess meant exactly what Sam thought she meant—that the possibilities had nothing to do with food. "I couldn't agree more."

"We've been talking about Cuban food, but we haven't had that yet."

"We haven't." Sam wracked her brain for ideas. The only Cuban food she'd discovered so far was a tiny place with counter service and exactly three tables. The food was amazing, but not what she had in mind for Tess.

"You know, if you have some personal specialties, I could just come over to your place."

Sam nodded slowly, attempting to rein in the dozen different directions her imagination was running. Yet the look on Tess's face remained unchanged. Sam had no idea what switch had been flipped, but she was pretty certain that, once again, Tess's words had little to do with dinner. "That would be…great. You name the night."

"I've got the early shift again tomorrow. Or next Tuesday."

"Tomorrow would be great. Seven okay?"

"Seven is perfect. I can't wait."

"Tess?"

"Mmm-hmm?"

Sam opened her mouth to say something, but there weren't any words. Her train of thought, or lack thereof, was interrupted by the arrival of her lunch. She mumbled her thanks to the waiter who dropped it off and returned her gaze to Tess, who looked at her expectantly. "Nothing. I'm…I'm looking forward to tomorrow night."

"Likewise."

A group of four women took seats at the other end of the bar and Tess moved down to greet them and take orders. Sam watched her shift effortlessly into her restaurant banter. She picked up her sandwich and tried to think of the last time a woman left her speechless.

Sam had no idea when or why Tess had changed her mind, but she wasn't going to waste the opportunity. All she had to do was figure out how to serve Tess an exquisite Cuban meal and make it seem like she'd done the cooking. She was about to have a very busy afternoon.

Sam finished her lunch and paid the check, scribbling her address on the receipt for Tess before she left. Rather than calling Villa Habana, the Cuban place Elisa had introduced her to, Sam decided to drive over and talk with Amarita in person. She timed it just right and arrived as the last of the lunch crowd cleared out.

Amarita looked her way and offered a warm smile. "Hola, Samara. How are you today?"

"I'm great, Amarita. How about you?"

"Good, good. Are you here for lunch?"

The po'boy had been good, but Sam now regretted having eaten. "Not today. I need your help."

Amarita chuckled. "Oh? What is it you're needing?"

"I'm trying to woo a woman."

Amarita's chuckle became a hearty belly laugh. "Why do I have a hard time believing you ever need help in that department?"

The compliment-slash-admonishment reminded Sam of her grandmother and made her laugh as well. "This one wants me to cook her Cuban food."

Amarita nodded. "Ah. I see. Let me guess. The reason you come here two times a week is not because you like my pretty face."

Sam flashed a smile. "It is a very pretty face."

"You're smooth with words, but not the stove."

"Guilty."

Amarita turned back toward the kitchen. "Miguel. Come out here and cover the register. I need to talk to someone."

Without waiting for a reply, she walked out from behind the counter and waved for Sam to follow her to one of the small tables in the corner. Sam did so and said, "Thank you so much."

They sat down and Amarita looked Sam up and down. Again, Sam felt like she was getting the once-over from her grandmother. Amarita folded her arms over her chest. "So, you want me to teach you or you want me to make you up some things you can serve her, pass off as your own?"

"Well, she's coming over tomorrow, so…"

"So you want me to cook for you."

The comment made Sam realize that, while she meant it in a complimentary way, Amarita might find such a request insulting. "It's not that I don't want to give you credit…"

Amarita laughed again, easing Sam's worry. "Child, I don't need the credit. I got a full restaurant every day and a man at home who knows how good he has it."

"So, you'll help me?"

"I'll help you all right. What do you have in mind?"

Sam grinned. "Well, it should be good, but nothing too complicated. I don't want her to get suspicious."

Amarita wagged a finger at her. "Or think you should be cooking for her every night of the week."

"Right. You are a very smart woman."

"Well, I sure didn't get where I am by being stupid."

They talked over options, decided on a few traditional dishes that weren't too labor intensive. After, they chatted about other things. Sharing a secret, it seemed, had made them friends. Sam learned all about Amarita's three children, four grandchildren, and the one on the way. Amarita asked questions, getting Sam to talk about her family far more than she was used to. Sam got so caught up, she almost forgot about her appointment at the museum. She stood to leave, making apologies along with her good-byes.

"I'll see you tomorrow, around three," Sam said.

"I'll have everything ready, including instructions for warming and finishing everything."

"Thank you again. You're a life saver."

Amarita waved a hand in dismissal, but added, "If this doesn't get her, she's not worth getting."

Sam bent down and kissed her cheek. "Don't worry. I'm pretty sure it will."

Sam was halfway out the door when Amarita called to her. "I expect a full report."

CHAPTER TWELVE

Tess knew from the address alone Sam's place would be something. When she pulled into the driveway of the huge house, complete with towering columns and a wide porch, it was worse than she feared. Worse. Probably not a fair way of looking at things. Just because people with a shitload of money made her uncomfortable, she wasn't one to judge.

Tess shook her head and chuckled to herself. This whole thing was a bit reckless. Now that she'd decided to indulge in it, she might as well enjoy the ride—and the spectacle. She got out of her car and started up the walk, hoping her choice of jeans and an off-the-shoulder sweater came across as casual sexy and not casual frumpy.

Her finger hovered a few inches from the bell when the door opened. Sam stood in the doorway, wearing khaki pants and an olive green button-down. The look was casual, but as usual, everything fit just right and looked, well, expensive. Tess resisted the urge to sigh. Did she have to be such a sucker for a well-dressed dyke?

"Welcome to my casa. Come in, come in."

Tess did sigh then, but it was with a smile. Yep, total sucker. And, in the moment, she didn't even mind. Maybe being reckless had its perks. "Thanks."

They stepped into the foyer and Sam closed the door behind them. The proximity gave Tess a whiff of whatever cologne Sam wore—something woodsy and clean. Again, it straddled that line of masculine and feminine perfectly. Tess eased out of her coat and took in the space. Glossy floors and soaring ceilings, a mirror so large it would take up an entire wall in her living room.

"Some of the decor is a bit fussy for my tastes, but the space and location are perfect. And of course I wanted something furnished."

Tess nodded. That Sam had such a knack for reading her mind was disconcerting. "Beggars can't be choosers, right?"

"Something like that."

The foyer opened to a huge living room with a marble fireplace, a massive Oriental rug, and a pair of matching plush sofas. Above the fireplace, a flat screen TV was mounted to the wall. It was tuned to a Latin jazz radio station and the music wafted through the room from speakers hidden from sight. "Nice."

"Thanks. Dinner's just about ready. Are you hungry?"

"Starved."

"Excellent."

Sam escorted her to the formal dining room. One end of the table, which seated twelve, was set with plates and wineglasses, candles, and several covered dishes. "Wow."

"You requested a Cuban feast, didn't you?"

"I don't think I specified a feast, but I'll take it."

"There are a couple of things still in the kitchen. Have a seat and I'll be right out."

Tess pulled her eyes away from the table and looked at Sam. "You didn't have to go to all this trouble."

Sam flashed a smile. "It's my pleasure."

"Is there anything I can do to help?"

Sam smiled. "Tonight, I serve you. Help yourself to wine. I'll only be a minute."

Sam disappeared into the kitchen and Tess looked around. In addition to the massive table, the room held a matching sideboard and china cabinet. Crystal vases held bouquets of silk flowers and the cabinet was filled with stemware and decorative bowls and items that looked expensive and utterly impractical. Tess knew the city had its fair share of opulence, but it never occurred to her that it could be had in a rental. No different from fancy hotels, really, but she'd just never thought about it.

Sam returned, carrying a bowl and a basket filled with some kind of bread. "Are you sure you're only feeding the two of us?"

"I finally got you to agree to have dinner with me. I wanted to make sure I didn't disappoint."

Tess shook her head. "I have a feeling you rarely do."

"I do what I can. Wine?"

"Sure."

Sam poured two glasses, then pulled out one of the chairs. "Please, sit."

Tess did, surprised by how comfortable the chair was. She'd always thought upholstered chairs in a room designed for eating were silly, but perhaps she'd have to reconsider. Impractical or not, it felt luxurious and she liked it.

"Have you eaten a lot of Cuban food?"

Sam's question pulled Tess off her random train of thought. "Not a lot. Street food, mostly—sandwiches and fried plantains."

"This is more the stuff your grandma would make. Although there are fried plantains because they're awesome."

"I couldn't agree more." Tess surveyed the spread. "What else did you make?"

Sam removed lids and started gesturing. "Picadillo, rice and beans, empañadas, avocado and tomato salad."

"It all looks amazing."

Sam smiled. "Please, dig in."

Sam watched Tess fill her plate. She followed suit, hoping she'd heated and finished everything the right way. When Tess started eating, Sam held her breath. No cringing, no weird faces. Sam relaxed enough to try her own plate. Not that she should be surprised, but everything tasted perfect, just like at Amarita's. Tess finished the food on her plate and helped herself to seconds, making Sam smile.

"Everything is delicious, but this," Tess pointed to the picadillo, "is spectacular. What's in it?"

Shit. Sam looked down at her plate. "Beef and olives and raisins."

Tess laughed. "I can tell that much. What are the spices? I'm ashamed to admit I've never dabbled in Cuban cooking."

"Um…" Sam couldn't believe she'd neglected to prep for questions. Such a rookie mistake.

"You're not one of those super secret recipe types, are you?"

"Yes. Yes, that's exactly what I am." Sam nodded with more emphasis than was necessary.

Tess raised a brow. "Why are you being weird all of a sudden?"

"I don't know what you're talking about." Sam wondered whether it would be better to confess or have Tess think she'd turned into a total freak.

Tess narrowed her eyes. "Did you cook all of this?"

Sam looked at her sheepishly. "Sort of."

"Sort of?"

"Cooking transpired." It wasn't a lie. She'd used the stove. The oven, too.

"I think if you're using the word 'transpired,' you're doing something wrong."

"I had some help." Sam had to laugh at herself. She made up stories for a living and yet couldn't seem to spin a plausible tale that involved her being adept in the kitchen.

Tess crossed her arms. "What kind of help?"

"The kind of help I'd get from my grandmother if she lived close by."

Sam hoped the mention of her grandmother might buy her some leeway, but Tess looked unfazed. "Does that mean someone else did all the work?"

"Please don't hold it against me. Everything we're having is authentic Cuban food, just like my grandma makes. I just…I don't know how to make any of it."

"Sam." Tess sounded scandalized.

"Don't be mad. When you mentioned coming over, I panicked. I wasn't going to let a silly little detail get in the way."

Tess laughed then, a deep belly laugh that had her bent over and clutching her stomach.

"Does that mean you aren't mad?"

Tess wiped her eyes. "I'm not mad."

"No?" Sam believed her, but she thought Tess might be withholding something.

Tess tipped her head to the side. "I actually think I like this better."

"What?"

"You not being able to cook, flubbing the perfect scheme. It's not smooth."

Sam cringed.

"It's a good thing. I thought at first you might be too smooth. This is more appealing, more real."

"Oh." That was a first.

"It makes it much easier for me to ask you to pour me another glass of wine, show me your place."

Sam topped off Tess's glass, then her own. "This," she gestured around her, "is the dining room."

Tess stood. "Lovely."

"Like I said when you got here, it's a bit fussy."

"I promise I won't judge you for the decor."

"I appreciate that. The kitchen is right through there."

Tess grabbed a couple of the bowls from the table. "Let's wrap up the leftovers while we're there."

"Good idea." Sam followed her lead, wondering if Tess was fastidious about leftovers or if she didn't anticipate them returning to the dining room for a while. She hoped it was the latter. Tess led the way through the swinging door, but stopped short. Even with her incompetence, Sam knew enough to know the kitchen was stunning. "It's nice, right?"

Tess turned around to face Sam. "Do you not cook Cuban food or do you not cook at all?"

Sam offered a weak smile. "I make coffee. And eggs."

"Seriously?"

She scooped food back into the containers it came in. No point in hiding them now. "And pasta. I make pasta."

"So you can boil water."

Sam's shoulders slumped. "Yeah."

Tess shook her head, glanced around the kitchen again. "What a waste."

"Maybe you could teach me a few things." Tess raised a brow. Sam stacked the containers in the fridge and turned back to Tess. "No, really. I'd love to learn a few Louisiana specialties."

"We'll see. For now, you're not done giving me the tour."

Sam took Tess through the rest of the downstairs, feeling oddly pleased that Tess seemed to approve of her work setup in the office. She led the way upstairs, pausing only briefly in each of the guest rooms. In the master, Tess made a playful comment about the size of the bed before taking it upon herself to check out the bathroom.

"Holy shit."

Sam barely made out the words; Tess had clearly spoken them to herself. "I know, right?"

She joined Tess in the spacious room, complete with marble floors and counters, a corner jetted tub, and a shower big enough for two. Or maybe four. It wasn't the most luxurious bathroom Sam had ever had, but it made the top five.

"Sorry. I didn't mean to say that out loud."

"It's okay. I felt the same way when I walked in the first time." Even if that wasn't entirely true, Sam wasn't about to admit it.

Tess looked back at Sam and her eyes sparkled with mischief. "If I'd known you had this, I would have come over sooner."

Sam struggled to think of a clever—and not entirely inappropriate— response. She'd hoped Tess might stay, but she wasn't going to press her luck. As much as she enjoyed the pursuit, pressure wasn't part of her game. She found herself wondering what had shifted to turn Tess from hesitant—if not suspicious—to interested. Tess walked back to Sam, stood close enough for Sam to reach out and touch her. Sam wanted to, but didn't.

"You're trying to figure me out, aren't you? Why I've had such a sudden change of heart?"

Tess clearly had her number. Normally, that might bother Sam, but tonight it felt like part of the foreplay. "Something like that."

"I could confess that I haven't had much going on in the love department lately. And that I find you...intriguing."

"But you wouldn't want to do that."

"Obviously. I could say that you've proved yourself to be irresistible, but surely that would go right to your head." Tess inched closer.

"Surely." Sam had no idea where Tess's logic would end up, but she sure was enjoying the ride.

"I guess it's a matter of principle."

Sam raised a brow. "Do tell."

"Well, on principle, you're the kind of person I don't get involved with."

"I do hope there's a 'but.'"

Tess's eyes danced in a way that made Sam want to scoop her up, toss her on the bed, and ravish her. She resisted. Barely. "But, also on principle, I'm adventurous. A seize-the-day sort of woman."

"I see."

"My best friend Carly convinced me that pretending we didn't have a spark was worse than dating against type." Tess took Sam's wineglass, then set them both on the counter.

"Remind me to get Carly's number so I can call her up and thank her."

Tess closed the remaining space between them. Because of their height difference, she had to look up to maintain eye contact. "Did you want to do that right now?"

Sam reminded herself to breathe as Tess ran a finger down her torso, between her breasts, stopping right above her belt. "Nope."

"Good, because I had other things in mind."

"Thank God." Sam bent her head and covered Tess's mouth with hers.

Tess wound her arms around Sam's neck, sliding her fingers into Sam's hair in a way that drove Sam mad. Tess's mouth was eager and warm. She traced Sam's bottom lip with her tongue, then took it gently between her teeth. Sam allowed her hands to drift down past the curve of Tess's lower back to her ass.

Tess broke the kiss and Sam shifted her hands. Maybe that was too much. She was on the verge of apologizing when Tess leaned back and smiled at her.

"Has anyone ever told you that you're a great kisser?"

Sam scrambled to come up with a clever, if not dishonest answer. She must have made a face though because Tess broke into a laugh.

"Never mind. I don't want to know."

"I—"

Sam was saved from a bumbling answer by Tess kissing her again. "I'm kidding. Now, are you going to take me to bed or am I going to have to beg?"

In lieu of a verbal answer, Sam took Tess's hand, leading her back into the bedroom. She spun around so she could wrap her arms around Tess's waist.

"Much better." Tess smiled while undoing the buttons of Sam's shirt.

After undoing the buttons on her sleeves, Sam slid her hands under the hem of Tess's sweater. Her skin was warm and smooth, making Sam long to put her mouth everywhere at once. Tess lifted her arms so Sam could remove the sweater. Underneath, she wore a ridiculously sexy black lace bra. Sam paused for a moment to appreciate the view.

Tess shifted her weight slightly, posing, but in a subtle way. Without breaking eye contact, she unbuttoned her jeans, slid the zipper down. The way she pushed them down, swaying her hips just so, made Sam feel like she was being treated to a striptease. When the jeans were gone, she realized Tess was wearing a lace thong that matched the bra. Sam sighed. She was such a sucker for sexy underwear.

"You're still wearing an awful lot of clothes." Tess's playful comment snapped her back to reality.

"I can rectify that." Sam slid her shirt off, then pulled the undershirt over her head. She undid her belt, then stopped, realizing how intensely Tess was staring at her.

"Here, let me help you with that." Tess tugged at the button of Sam's chinos, slid a hand inside.

Sam's abs clenched at the touch. The light brush of fingers sent her into overdrive. Just as quickly as Tess touched her, her hand moved away to slide Sam's pants and underwear down. Sam helped by kicking them the rest of the way off.

With gentle pressure, Tess guided Sam backward. When the back of Sam's legs bumped the edge of the bed, she sat down. Tess stood between her legs and, with the adjustment in height, Tess now had to bend down slightly to kiss her. Sam roamed her hands over Tess's body. Despite being short, Tess still had plenty of curves, and Sam enjoyed the way they seemed to mold to her touch.

When Tess's palms pushed against her shoulders, Sam lay back. Tess crawled onto the bed with her. Sam tried to roll over so she could focus her attention on Tess, but Tess once again pressed a hand to her shoulder. Assertive without being forceful, the gesture took Sam by surprise.

Not only was Sam accustomed to taking the lead, she was used to giving pleasure before she received it. But Tess was on top of her, straddling her hips. Her hands toyed with Sam's breasts—massaging, caressing, and turning her nipples into pebbled bundles of nerves. All the while, her body undulated, driving Sam completely insane. Just when she thought she couldn't take any more teasing, Tess moved to one side, brushing her fingers along Sam's thigh and between her legs. At the first touch, Sam bucked. She couldn't recall ever feeling so out of control of her body's response to another woman.

Before Sam could analyze it, Tess's fingers began to slide over her.

Light and quick, the touch made Sam squirm and ache for the firmer pressure that would make her come. Tess continued to tease, however, interspersing her light circles with more forceful strokes that promised release, but kept it at bay.

Sam lost track of how long they continued like that. Tess used her free hand to massage Sam's nipples, pinching and tugging them gently, taking her closer and closer to the edge. The whole while, Tess kissed her, exploring Sam's mouth with her tongue.

When Tess eased her lips away, Sam opened her eyes. She saw the top of Tess's head moving down toward her breast. "Tess…"

Tess shifted so that her gaze met Sam's. She offered a knowing smile before dipping her head and taking one of Sam's hardened nipples into her mouth. As she did so, she slid her hand lower and eased into Sam.

"Fuck." Any thought Sam had of forming a coherent sentence vanished. Tess's mouth and fingers worked in unison, stroking, filling, and coaxing Sam toward climax. She closed her eyes and rode the pleasure, her body following Tess's lead. When she crested, the orgasm rocked her. She continued to shake after it ended, fighting to regain her senses.

She finally opened her eyes and found Tess smiling at her, one hand between Sam's breasts and the other still between her legs. There was a look of satisfaction in Tess's eyes that bordered on smug. Sam found it ridiculously appealing. "Damn, woman."

Tess smirked and eased her hand away, leaving Sam with a strange feeling of relief mixed with emptiness. "I'm going to take that as a compliment."

"That would be putting it mildly. You're incredible, and I'm not saying that only because I've been wanting you from the moment we met." Sam shifted to her side and looked Tess up and down. "Even though I have been wanting you. I haven't been able to get you out of my mind."

"Is that so?"

"Oh, yes." Sam traced a finger down Tess's side, over the slight swell of her hips, and along her thigh. "I'm going to show you just how crazy you've made me."

"Mmm." Tess rolled to her back, giving Sam a full view of her breasts and torso.

"You are so beautiful."

Tess smiled. "You're just saying that because I gave you an incredible orgasm."

Sam grinned. "The orgasm was beyond incredible, but that has nothing to do with how gorgeous you are."

Tess started to say something, but Sam didn't wait to see if it was a protest or agreement. She covered Tess's mouth, trying to pour into her even a fraction of the passion Tess stirred in her. From mouth to neck, neck to breast, Sam explored Tess's upper body with her lips and tongue.

Tess writhed beneath her. As much as Sam wanted to tease, to draw out pleasing her for as long as possible, Tess's response to her filled Sam with urgency. Almost as much as she'd wanted her own release, Sam ached to feel Tess come undone.

Sam slipped her fingers into Tess, finding her hot and wet. She felt Tess clamp around her. She kept her movements slow at first, both wanting to give Tess a chance to acclimate and not wanting her to come too quickly. Tess's body began to undulate, setting a steady pace and taking Sam deeper. It was beautiful to watch and Sam found herself mesmerized by the way she moved, the soft moans she made each time Sam filled her.

When Tess's breath quickened, and her sounds grew more urgent, Sam turned her hand slightly so that her thumb could brush over her hard center. She watched Tess's hands fist in the sheets, the rise and fall of her hips, the light sheen of sweat on her breasts.

"That's it, beautiful. Come for me."

Tess's body arched and held, suspended for a moment like a perfect statue. She let out a sound somewhere between a scream and a moan. It was a primal, unguarded sound that made Sam's insides clench all over again.

Sam shifted so she could pull Tess against her. She loved the way Tess continued to quiver. Sam lifted a hand, running it through Tess's hair until her breathing returned to normal.

"Tess?"

"Mmm-hmm?" Tess didn't move and the sound was muffled by Sam's breast.

"Did you really decide to sleep with me as a matter of principle?"

Tess lifted her head at that. She offered a wry smile.

"I like your principles. Will you stay the night?"

"I will." Tess tucked her head back into the crook of Sam's shoulder. A moment later, she mumbled, "It's a matter of principle."

Sam laughed and pulled Tess close again, relishing how perfectly Tess's body molded against hers. She fell asleep with a smile on her face.

CHAPTER THIRTEEN

Tess woke with the awareness of Sam's body pressed against her back. She opened her eyes and took in her surroundings. If it was possible, the bedroom was even more beautiful in the daylight. It had all the luxury of the first floor without feeling so overdone—high ceilings and soft gray walls, simple, modern curtains and a gorgeous wood and wrought iron bed. Tess sighed. She could get used to a room like this.

She lay for a minute, letting flashes of the night before play through her mind. Sam had been surprised, but not turned off, by Tess's assertiveness. She didn't always have to be in control, but Tess didn't want to be with anyone who only had one way of doing things. If this was going to go anywhere—even as far as another date—Tess had to feel like they were on equal footing. Carly could say whatever she wanted about Tess having the upper hand, but she hadn't seen Sam's place. A woman with as much money as Sam was probably used to getting exactly what she wanted.

She shifted lightly to see if Sam was awake. The arm slung around her pulled her in closer and Sam moaned. "Don't go."

"What if I only go as far as the bathroom?"

Another squeeze. "I suppose."

Tess extricated herself from the bed and padded to the bathroom. She took advantage of the moment alone to center herself and to make sure she didn't look too frightful. No raccoon eyes, fortunately, but her hair stood out at shocking angles. She tried to tame it with her fingers before returning to the bedroom.

Sam was where Tess had left her, but she was awake and looking right at her. "Can I interest you in some breakfast?"

"It depends. Are you going to cook it?"

Sam made a pouty face that was way cuter than it should be. "I told you, I know my way around eggs."

Tess nodded. "Right."

"Scrambled or fried?"

"As tempting as that is, I should go."

Sam seemed genuinely disappointed, which was sort of nice. "Let me guess. Hair washing?"

Tess smiled. "I will wash my hair at some point today, but no. I'm working the lunch shift and I have a gig tonight."

Sam perked up. "A gig?"

"I sing on the side."

Sam propped herself up on her elbow. "Like in a band?"

"I am in a band, but tonight is a fill-in spot."

"What do you mean?"

Telling Sam might mean she'd want to come. Tess decided in a split second she was okay with that. "A lot of the hotel bars and lounges have live music. Usually it's a regular group or duo, and sometimes I fill in if the singer needs a night off or is sick or something."

"Ah. So that's what you're doing tonight?"

"Yeah, at the Riverside Hilton. They recently opened a second bar and I think they're trying to pull people in."

"I'd love to hear you sing."

Sam's tone was so earnest, Tess couldn't help but smile. And it might be fun to have Sam in the audience. "You're welcome to come tonight if you want."

"Yeah?"

"I do two sets. The first one starts at eight. And since it's a hotel, there's no cover."

"I'll be there."

"Great." It shouldn't surprise her that Sam would want to see her perform, but the enthusiasm, the sincere interest, caught her off guard. Sam seemed to be both the cool kid and the nerd. Maybe those things went together in some places, but that hadn't been the case in her experience. Given Tess's dating record over the last few years, maybe that was a good thing.

"Can I confess something?"

Tess braced herself. Confessions the morning after first sex were rarely good. "Sure."

"I saw you sing."

Okay, not what she was expecting. "You did?"

"I stopped by the restaurant one day last week and you weren't there. I sat at the bar and had a conversation with Gary, who told me about your band and where you played."

Of course he did. Gary had exactly zero filters. "And you came? I didn't see you."

"I sat in the back. You were amazing, like knock-my-socks-off amazing. I thought about sticking around at the end, but I decided it might make me seem like a creeper."

Tess couldn't decide how she felt about that. "You know, if I had seen you and you left without saying hi, that would make you seem like even more of a creeper."

Sam frowned. "I didn't think of it that way."

Tess laughed. Even if she didn't like the idea of Sam watching from the shadows, her being worried about coming across as creepy made up for it. "I'm teasing you. Although you should have said hi."

"I promise I will next time."

"Good. Consider yourself officially invited."

Sam smiled and looked relieved. "Are you sure I can't talk you into some breakfast? I promise it'll be delicious. And quick."

"I'm good, really. Thank you for the offer, though."

"Can I talk you into anything else?" Sam wiggled her eyebrows in a playfully suggestive way.

"Tempting, but then I'd definitely be late to work."

"Are you always so responsible?"

Tess thought about the question, the myriad of implications it could have. Sam wasn't looking for an assessment of Tess's life choices, but Tess couldn't keep her mind from going there. She shook off the weight of those thoughts and smiled. "Mostly."

Sam looked her up and down and returned the smile. "That's hot."

Tess shook her head, but laughed. She finished pulling on her clothes, then crawled onto the bed so she could kiss Sam good-bye. "I'll see you tonight?"

"Can't wait."

Tess let herself out and drove home. She'd just made it in the door when her phone pinged with a text from Carly.

Well?

Tess thought for a minute. *Exceeded expectations.*

She shed her clothes from the night before, then climbed into the shower. By the time she emerged, Carly had texted her four more times—one asking for specifics, one asking her if she was still at Sam's, an ellipsis that meant Carly was being impatient, and an assertion that clearly Tess and Sam were still at it. Tess contemplated letting Carly dangle, but she didn't want her actual night—which had been pretty awesome—to pale in comparison to Carly's imagination. She texted back with her real whereabouts and a promise to dish sooner rather than later.

❖

Although tempted to linger in bed, Sam had work to do. And the more she got done during the day, the better she could feel about spending her evenings on more enjoyable things. And her selection of enjoyable things had just expanded nicely.

She put on a pot of coffee, but instead of bothering with eggs, she went with leftovers from the night before. Since she was alone, she ate them cold and right out of the container. A bachelor habit for sure, but she didn't see anything wrong with it, especially if her overnight guest didn't stick around.

She took her second cup of coffee into the office. She stared at the screen for a moment, wondering if it was too late to work a femme fatale into the storyline. It might be interesting, especially if she turned out to be the distraction that led to Clayton's downfall. Sam would need to backtrack a little so the woman could make an appearance earlier in the novel, but not much else would have to change. Sam jotted a few notes before turning her attention to the scene in progress.

She worked at home until mid-afternoon. Going to the library had lost its allure. Still, she was quickly approaching the halfway point in the manuscript. Not only was she happy with the progress she'd made, she knew what still needed to be written. After getting stuck that one time early on, the story started to flow even better than she could have anticipated. The introduction of Victoria, who turned out to be a lounge singer, had been exactly what she needed to pivot the plot and keep it moving. She'd never say so out loud, but it almost felt like the story was writing itself.

She decided to run a few errands and grab some food before getting ready to go out for the night. With her work done for the day, Sam indulged in thoughts of Tess. Images and memories from the night before blended with the anticipation of seeing her onstage. She could only imagine, but an upscale hotel bar would be a very different venue from the—what was the name of it?—the Old Point where she'd seen her perform the first time. Sam wondered if the room would be small enough for eye contact. She wondered if Tess would look at her when she sang.

Sam walked out of the house with a spring in her step. She decided to start with a snack and drove to Brew, the coffee shop she'd discovered only a few blocks from her house. She ordered a latte and chocolate glazed donut the size of her hand, making a mental list of the places she needed to stop. She'd hit the post office first, then swing by to see Amarita before heading to the grocery store.

Coffee in hand, she walked out, passing a middle-aged guy carrying a bouquet of flowers. She should get flowers to thank Amarita for her help with dinner. She didn't remember seeing any, but there had to be a florist close by.

She was almost to her car when she saw the slip of paper. Sam felt mildly perturbed, more because she thought she'd heeded the posted parking restrictions than anything else. Even still, she wasn't about to let a ticket ruin her mood.

She pulled the piece of paper from under the windshield, realizing the paper was too thick to be a parking ticket. Maybe it was an advertisement or flier for something. She unfolded it and, as she read the words neatly typed on the page, felt the hairs on the back of her neck stand up.

I know what you did and I know who you are. I'll tell the world. We'll see who's sorry then.

A shiver ran through her and Sam rolled her shoulders to shake it off. She looked around, as if she might see whoever left it lurking nearby. Of course, she saw no one. That wasn't entirely true. A man who looked to be in his eighties was making his way down the sidewalk with a pair of toy poodles. Sam felt fairly confident he wasn't her guy.

She looked down at the note again. Maybe it was a mistake. Perhaps whoever left the note had meant it for someone else. Silver Audis weren't a dime a dozen or anything, but hers certainly wasn't the only one, especially in this neighborhood. Or maybe they thought she was someone else entirely. Maybe it was a prank.

Sam shook her head. That might be the weakest line of reasoning she'd ever come up with. And that was saying something. She pulled out her phone and looked up the number for the NOPD. After explaining the situation, the dispatcher told her to stay put. Half an hour later, a cruiser pulled up. One officer remained in the car while the other one climbed out and strode purposefully toward her. "Are you Samara Torres?"

"That's me." She relayed the same story she'd told the dispatcher.

The cop nodded, but looked only mildly interested. When she was done, he looked at her. "You got an angry boyfriend?"

Sam bristled at the insinuation. "No."

"Done anything you should be worried about?"

Seriously? Sam knew this wasn't the most serious incident in the world, but still. "No."

The cop nodded, scribbled a few notes. "What about secrets?"

The only secret Sam had was Sid. Not only did it seem unlikely that was the secret in question, Sam felt disinclined to confide in this guy who clearly didn't take her seriously. "None that would rise to this."

He took the note from her, looked at it for a moment, handed it back. "Maybe it's not for you."

Sam swallowed her anger. "Maybe. Can I get a copy of the report at least? I'd like a record in case it is for me and it happens again."

"Sure." The cop, who'd never even bothered to introduce himself, went back to the car. Sam watched him talk with his partner, type something into the laptop mounted on the dash. After what felt like an inordinate amount of time, he returned with a slip of paper. "There's a summary here. You can get a full copy using this number." He pointed at the top.

"Thanks." Sam sighed.

The cop's face changed; disinterest morphed into compassion. "Look, it's probably nothing. But it might be something. If anything else happens, you call us. It's patterns that we worry about."

Sam didn't feel any better, but she appreciated that he made the effort. "Thanks."

The cops left. Sam folded the piece of paper and stuck it in her jacket pocket. Whatever the situation, obsessing about it wouldn't get her anywhere. Besides, she had things to do. She pulled out her phone and found a florist on the way to Villa Habana.

When she walked into the restaurant half an hour later, she found Amarita at her usual spot behind the register. Sam presented her with the bouquet of hydrangeas, to which Amarita said, "I take it you had a good night."

Sam laughed. "Something like that."

She stuck around for lunch, but resisted lingering. Part of her wanted to pick up flowers for Tess, but it seemed weird to bring them to the show. She'd hold off for now, wait for another occasion. When she got home, Sam slid off her jacket. The note from her car fell to the floor. Sam unfolded the paper and read it again.

I know what you did and I know who you are. I'll tell the world. We'll see who's sorry then.

Now, several hours removed from everything, Sam felt more convinced that it couldn't possibly be for her. On top of all the reasons she'd already worked through, she could count on one hand the number of people she knew in New Orleans. She started to wad up the paper, then stopped. This would be great in a book, especially if it wasn't an actual threat, or at least not one intended for the protagonist. Effective distraction, mildly menacing—in other words, perfect. Sam chucked. Inspiration came in all forms. She left the note on her desk and went upstairs to get ready.

CHAPTER FOURTEEN

Tess enjoyed her occasional performances at the hotels around the city. Although she loved the Old Point specifically because it remained a spot for locals, singing for tourists—whether they were on vacation or in town for a conference—had its charms. Whether it was because they were generally more relaxed or half in the bag, they were almost always in a good mood and thrilled that decent live music could be had for free.

It also gave Tess a chance to dress up. She'd scored a number of great cocktail dresses and gowns at consignment shops and store closeouts, but didn't have much occasion to wear them. Tonight, knowing Sam would be there, she pulled out her favorite, a strapless green one with art deco detailing that made her feel like she belonged in a speakeasy. She added a couple of vintage gold bangles and the heels she saved for truly special occasions. Even if her feet protested before the end of the night, Tess decided it would be worth it.

When she got to the hotel, she didn't see any sign of Sam. She ordered a club soda from the bar and chatted briefly with Charlie, the piano player. They'd worked together before, so all she had to do was hand him the list of songs she had planned. She worked the room for a few minutes, chatting up the audience. Doing so made the show feel more intimate. It also gave her the chance to see if there were any special celebrations to note.

Tess was in the middle of a conversation with a couple from Cleveland when Sam walked in. It took all of her effort to keep her attention focused on their story about visiting New Orleans for the first time on their honeymoon twenty-two years ago. After congratulating them on such a successful marriage, she moved to the next couple. For some reason, the idea of talking to Sam before she sang made her nervous, so she kept to the front of the room, stopping at the last few occupied tables and then ducking into the tiny dressing room behind the bar.

She jotted a note for Charlie with a couple of additions to the set list. He nodded when she handed it to him. "You got it, doll."

He went out to take his seat at the piano and Tess took a moment to center herself. Although she'd avoided talking to her ahead of time, the moment Tess stepped up to the piano, her eyes locked on Sam. She told herself it was because Sam was the only person in the audience she knew. It had nothing to do with the fact that she could still feel Sam's hands, her mouth, on her. Even with the low lighting, she could tell that Sam returned the gaze. She tried to ignore the flush in her cheeks and forced herself to break eye contact. She glanced over at Charlie, gave him a small nod.

The music began, the lights in the bar dimmed slightly, save the one right above her. For a brief moment, she closed her eyes, settling into the rhythm. When she opened them, she was careful to look away from where she knew Sam sat, then gave herself over to "Stormy Weather."

The play list at the hotels consisted of standards. Always. She wound her way through the work of Etta James and Lena Horne, Edith Piaf and Dusty Springfield. Even though she'd sung most of the songs a hundred times or more, Tess never grew tired of them. As far as she was concerned, they were standards for a reason.

As the first set neared to a close, she scanned the tables nearest the piano for the woman she'd talked with before the show. Although she didn't take requests per se, there were occasions when a patron would make arrangements with her ahead of time to dedicate a song to someone. Mostly, they were celebrations of birthdays and anniversaries, with the occasional divorce thrown in. Tonight's special request came from a woman named Donna, for her husband, who was turning sixty. She'd tipped Tess a hundred dollars, more than twice what she typically saw for such a favor. Tess intended to give Donna her money's worth. If she gave Sam a little show in the process, well, that wouldn't hurt anyone.

She made eye contact with Donna, gave her a wink. "We're going to close out the first set with a special dedication to a gentleman who is celebrating a very special birthday."

Tess launched into her version of "You Make Me Feel So Young." She made her way over to where Donna and her husband sat. She sang directly to him, trailing a finger down his arm. He turned a dozen different shades of red, much to the delight of his wife and the couple sharing their table. Tess liked to think she had a gift for reading people, being able to sense just how thickly she could lay it on without crossing the line into unpleasant discomfort. She had Bill in the sweet spot and the audience seemed to be enjoying it almost as much as he did. Despite wanting to see Sam's reaction, Tess feared doing so would break her focus, so she resisted looking over.

She finished the song and the room burst into applause. Tess smiled and took a quick bow. She announced they'd be back in a few minutes, then slipped back to the small room behind the bar. It was hardly more than a coat closet, but it gave her a place to leave her things and to regroup during the break. They only took about fifteen minutes between sets, giving her just enough time to sip some water and check her makeup. Satisfied she still looked put together, she decided to take advantage of her hidden position and peer out at Sam.

A waitress stood at the table, partially blocking her view. Sam's body language, however, made it clear that some pretty heavy-duty flirting was taking place—in both directions. The waitress turned and Tess realized it was Jaelyn, whom Tess had gotten to know slightly when her performances at the Hilton became more regular. Tess rolled her eyes. Jaelyn was perhaps the single most flirtatious woman in all of New Orleans, which was saying something.

Tess always found her annoying, but tonight she felt full-on loathing. It had nothing to do with jealousy. Jaelyn was ridiculous, not to mention clichéd. She wasn't even a lesbian. That she had Sam eating out of her hand felt…dirty, maybe? Cheap? Unsure of whether she was more agitated by Jaelyn's behavior or Sam's, Tess huffed and turned away.

"What's wrong? You swallow a stinkbug?"

Tess hadn't heard Charlie come up behind her. The sound of his voice made her jump a mile. "What? No, nothing's wrong."

"You just about ready, then?"

Tess rolled her shoulders, willing herself to shake off being startled and the funk that had crept over her. "Let's do it."

Although telling herself she wouldn't, Tess couldn't resist looking over to where Sam sat. Jaelyn was long gone and Sam's eyes were fixed squarely on Tess. Tess decided the perfect cure for her vexation was to do a little flirting of her own.

She worked the room even more than usual, singing to men and women alike. She winked, let her hand brush a shoulder here and there. At one point, during her rendition of "Fever," she made her way over to Sam's table. Tess made eye contact with Sam and held it, then slowly walked around her, grazing her fingers along the back of Sam's neck. She had the pleasure of watching Sam swallow and shift in her chair. Tess smiled before turning and walking slowly back to the piano.

When she finished the show, Tess returned to the dressing room to catch her breath and down another glass of water. She didn't know if Sam would stick around, but Tess hoped she did. Any lingering annoyance about Jaelyn dissipated in the adrenaline and satisfaction of a good performance. She checked her makeup and the rest of her appearance, then headed out to the bar.

Charlie remained at the piano, providing a nice accompaniment for the patrons sipping cocktails and getting chummy at tiny tables and in high-backed booths. Sam, it appeared, hadn't moved from the table in the corner. She made her way across the room. As she got near, Sam stood.

"That was amazing."

Tess smiled. "Thank you."

"No, I mean really amazing."

Tess expected a compliment, but Sam's enthusiasm made her smile. "I really thank you."

"Is there anything else you need to do? May I buy you a drink?"

"A drink would be lovely."

"What's your pleasure?"

Tess raised a brow at the question. Something about Sam's expression made Tess think she meant more than her cocktail preference. But first things first. "Tanqueray martini, with a twist."

Tess sat and Sam signaled to a passing waiter. After putting in the drink order, she turned her attention to Tess. "How long have you been doing that?"

"What? Singing?"

"Well, singing like that."

"I got my first club gig when I was seventeen." God, those had been the days. "My cousin hooked me up with the manager and I got paid under the table because I was a minor."

Sam thought about her life at seventeen. Her parents had barely allowed her to date at that age and rigidly enforced a ten o'clock curfew. Not that she'd minded, since they still believed her to be straight at the time. The strict rules had saved her from many awkward make-out sessions. Sam imagined Tess walking around the French Quarter at night, singing in some dimly lit bar. The idea stirred up an uncomfortable mix of emotions, so she quickly set it aside. "And you've been doing it ever since?"

"Mostly. Sometimes it's only once or twice a month. Every now and then, I have two or three in a week."

"And that's on top of being in a band?"

"Yeah. The band is what I love. We play every other week, rehearse on the off weeks. And they're my friends, you know? Practically my family."

The waiter returned with Tess's drink, giving Sam a moment to plan her next move. "You should be in the recording studio."

Tess eyed her over the rim of her martini glass, then set her drink down slowly. "I've never been interested in that."

Sam nodded. "I know it can be cutthroat. You just need to get the right connections so you don't have to deal with the hassle of auditions and demos and stuff."

Tess smiled, but it looked to Sam like more of a grimace. "That's not it."

"I have a friend who works for a label based in Philly. I'd be happy to introduce you."

Tess's jaw tightened. "I appreciate the gesture, really. I'm not interested, though. It's not what I want."

Sam tried to find a hidden meaning in Tess's words. Tess seemed plenty confident, so that couldn't be it. "You could make so much money. You wouldn't have to work at the restaurant anymore. You could sing full-time."

"I like working at the restaurant. I like singing how and when and where I want. I don't do it for the money, or so someone will notice me."

Sam lifted her hands defensively. "I get it. It's so competitive and there's a ton of pressure. I'm pretty sure you could write your own ticket, though."

Tess sighed. "Look, I'm sure you mean it in a good way, but I don't want to write my own ticket. You aren't listening to me."

"Okay, okay. Sorry. I did mean it in a good way. You could be a star."

Tess drained the rest of her martini and stood. "That's just it. I don't want to be a star. Thank you for the drink, and for coming to the show. I hope you enjoy the rest of your night."

Without looking back, Tess walked to the door near the piano—the one she'd emerged from not twenty minutes prior—and disappeared. Sam remained at the small table, staring at it. She replayed the conversation in her mind, trying to figure out where it had gone awry. She'd only been trying to pay Tess a compliment. She sighed. Maybe mentioning her contact in the industry came off as conceited.

Sam settled the tab and headed to her car. She continued to rehash the conversation, trying to look at it from different angles the way she might do a character study. Perhaps Tess had a bad experience that made her so adamantly opposed to a career in music. Failure, rejection, even a romance gone sour could have that effect on a person.

The writer in Sam desperately wanted to get to the bottom of it, to solve the mystery. The woman in her—the one who'd spent the night with Tess—knew it was none of her business. She and Tess got along great and their sexual chemistry was even better, but that's where it ended. If anything, it meant the last thing she should be doing was sticking her nose into Tess's life.

Reasoning with herself did little to quiet the questions in Sam's head. When she got home, she powered up her computer with the intention of doing some work before bed. Instead, she found herself looking for traces of Tess online. She found her Facebook profile, but both her posts and photos were set to private. There weren't any news stories or other mentions in the basic search results. Sam had enough research experience to know she could dig deeper. An hour at the local library would likely turn up all sorts of details. That would be crossing a line, though. She'd already managed to stick her foot in her mouth once.

Feeling restless, she decided to make a dent in her email. She started with the generic account, breathing a sigh of relief that there were no new messages from Francesca. She switched to her work folder, answering questions about the upcoming cover design and promising Prita that her page proofs had been submitted on time. When she opened her author account, one with a red flag caught her eye. Peg had added a note to the flag:

Fifth email from this account in the last week. Getting a little weird. Just wanted you to be aware. See sent folder for my replies thus far.

Sam opened the email and skimmed it. It certainly wasn't the most threatening email she'd received. It actually wasn't threatening at all. She agreed with Peg, though. It had a weird energy. She'd gotten intimate fan mail before—rambling personal histories, family secrets, even some sexual fantasies. This one had an unsettling personal feel, like whoever had written it knew her. Knew her, not the vague public bio that she'd crafted for Sid.

Sam read through the previous emails and Peg's replies. They'd gone from the friendly and appreciative tone Peg typically used to increasingly detached and brief. Sam resisted the temptation to craft a firm, cease and desist type of reply. She knew from experience that sort of response only encouraged more weirdness. She typed a quick note to Peg, giving her the okay to ignore any further correspondence.

Feeling more restless than when she'd started, Sam picked up her phone to call Prita. Sam filled her in on the last couple of days—sleeping with Tess, managing to aggravate her not twenty-four hours later, the note on her car, the thoroughly unsatisfying experience with the police, and the weird emails. She concluded with a loud sigh, then, "And how are you?"

"Fine. Can we back up to the part where you became a magnet for trouble?"

"Right? I don't think I've had this much random drama in a single week since I was in college."

Sam expected Prita to laugh. Instead, she seemed worried. "It's weird that it all happened at once."

"Yeah, but the Tess stuff and the weird stuff are unrelated."

"Are you sure?"

"Yes." Sam's response was immediate, but as she processed it more fully, she grew even more convinced. "Yes, the note was right after we slept together. And the emails have come in over the last couple of weeks. Not only was Tess not irritated with me until tonight, she has no idea who I am."

"I'm not accusing, I'm just asking. It's interesting that this all started when you arrived in New Orleans."

"Aren't you supposed to be making me feel better?"

Prita sniffed. "Am I? I didn't get the memo."

Sam rolled her eyes. "How about you tell me what's going on with you? Distract me."

"Okay." She launched into a story about her only other client, another writer whose identity she refused to disclose. Usually, Prita didn't talk about him, or her, very much. She joked that she didn't want Sam getting any ideas about ways to make her life more difficult. But when Sam needed a lift, Prita came through. Tonight's story detailed a full-blown tantrum over a promotional event that took an ugly turn.

By the time they hung up, Sam was in considerably better spirits. Satisfied that she'd done enough to free up her morning the next day, she turned off her computer and went to bed. Once there, however, her mind returned to Tess. As she flopped around, adjusting the covers and flipping her pillow at least a dozen times, the image of Tess refused to leave her brain.

The tiff they'd had at the bar did little to temper her desire or her imagination. One minute, she envisioned Tess in that gorgeous dress, promising things with her eyes. The next, she conjured Tess naked, straddling Sam and giving her a knowing smile. When Sam finally fell asleep, the knowing smile followed her, but kept any kind of satisfaction at bay.

CHAPTER FIFTEEN

Seventy degrees in February wasn't unusual for New Orleans, but wasn't the norm, either. So when it happened, Tess tried to spend as much time as possible outside. After all, endless days of temps in the nineties wouldn't be far behind. She texted Carly, then picked up a couple of salads, a bag of Zapp's Voodoo chips, and a giant cookie from the deli near her house.

She rode her bike to the ferry, opting to stand outside on the brief ride across the river and bask in the sunshine. Carly's office was only a few blocks up Poydras Street, so they met at Lafayette Square. Surrounded by a combination of high-rises and historic buildings, the park was one of her favorites. By the time Tess pulled up, Carly had already procured their favorite bench. Tess pulled the food from her bike basket and joined her.

"I love when you bring lunch. I don't know anyone else who would buy me both a salad and potato chips."

Tess shrugged. "It's the next best thing to salad and French fries, right?"

Carly popped a chip in her mouth. "Right."

"So how are you liking your trial run as boss?" Carly's supervisor at the advertising agency where she worked as a graphic designer had just gone on maternity leave and Carly was chosen to take on some of the managerial responsibilities in her absence.

"I'm not really the boss, but still, kind of strange."

"How so?"

Carly chuckled. "Some of the stuff I'm doing is pretty high level—making decisions and looking at things beyond my department."

"That sounds reasonable."

"It is. It's challenging, but I like it and I think I'm pretty good at it."

"What's strange about that?"

"Nothing. It's that the other half of my job feels a lot like babysitting."

Tess started to laugh, but she had a mouthful of salad and started to choke. She took a sip of her iced tea. "Babysitting?"

Carly nodded. "I knew there was bickering in my department. I mean, there's some in every department, right? But I swear at least four times a day someone comes into my office to complain about or rat on someone else."

Tess made a face. A few times in her life, usually after a long, late, hectic shift, she considered trading it in for an office job. The feeling always passed and she never seriously considered it. Listening to Carly, Tess felt a wave of gratitude that she'd never taken the leap. "Ugh."

"Yeah. I guess it's good they're so quick to treat me like the boss. Sometimes internal promotions cause their own drama."

"That's true. And even though I tease you, you know I think you're great and will kill it."

Carly smiled. "Thanks. Although, for the record, I'm not sure 'kill it' is ever a phrase middle managers want to hear."

Tess laughed in earnest then. "I'll remember that."

"Now, if I recall, we weren't actually here to talk about me."

Tess tried to look offended. "We're always here to talk about you. Your professional success is very important to me."

"I never said it wasn't. But I don't think any amount of office gossip or drama can stand up to what you've been up to the last couple of days. Spill."

"Well…" Tess took her time closing up her salad container and pulling out the giant cookie.

Carly's eyes got big. "Is that white chocolate macadamia?"

Tess broke it in half, handing the slightly larger piece to Carly. "Only the best for you, big boss lady."

"Thank you." Carly accepted the cookie and took a bite. "Mmm. Now, I mean it. Spill."

"We had dinner, followed by amazing sex. I stayed over. I invited her to my show."

"And did you go home with her again?"

Tess frowned. "No. She pushed my buttons and I left."

"You managed to have sex and your first fight within twenty-four hours of each other?"

"It wasn't a fight."

Carly raised a brow.

"It was a disagreement."

"Okay. Which do you want to tell me about first?"

Tess sighed. She'd been so perturbed, she hadn't thought about the sex all day. Which said something about how perturbed she was. "She told me I should be in a recording studio."

"Mother of all insults, how dare she?"

Tess scowled. "I'm serious."

"I am, too. Tess, you have an amazing voice. A lot of people think you should be in a recording studio. Hell, I kind of think you should be in a recording studio."

Tess relented, at least a little. "I know it's a compliment. But when I clearly state that I'm not interested in doing that, I think people should respect it and not try to convince me I'm wrong."

"How hard did she push it?"

"Hard enough that it ended the conversation."

Carly's face softened. "I'm sorry. I know it's a touchy subject. Does that mean you're done?"

Tess considered. She'd stopped seeing people for this reason before. Usually, though, it was because she felt like they were more interested in the idea she might get famous than they were in her. There was even that one woman who insisted the only thing Tess needed was a good manager. The woman, of course, turned out to be a manager. The whole thing left a bad taste in her mouth.

"Tess?"

"Huh?"

"I asked if that meant you were done with Sam?"

Tess thought back to the conversation in the bar. In truth, Sam had been more enthusiastic than pushy. And while there definitely was some arrogance in her whole "I know somebody" bit, she probably did know somebody. Even without knowing exactly what Sam did for a living, Tess knew for certain that Sam was successful and well-traveled. She was exactly the kind of person who would also be well-connected. Tess looked at Carly. "No."

Carly raised a brow. "I take it the sex was really good, then?"

"It was. That's not the reason I'm going to see her again, but it most definitely was."

"I hope that's not all you're going to give me."

Tess smiled. "She fake made me dinner."

"What is fake dinner?"

"No, no. The dinner was real. She fake made it. I asked for Cuban food and I arrived to this gorgeous feast. When I started asking questions about how stuff was made, she got all awkward and then confessed that she ordered it all."

"That's kind of weird."

Tess lifted a shoulder. "Maybe a little. It was actually kind of sweet. She can't cook at all, but wanted to impress me."

"Aw, you really do like her. That's the kind of thing that would usually make you roll your eyes."

Tess scowled. "That's not true. You make me sound like a bitch."

Carly ate the last bite of her cookie and brushed the crumbs from her fingers. "Not at all. You're genuine, a 'what you see is what you get' kind of person. You don't have patience for pretense. That doesn't make you a bitch."

Tess folded her arms over her chest and sighed. So not only had they argued, now here she was dissecting the parts of her time with Sam that had gone well. "Maybe I should—"

"Whoa, hey. Settle down, lady. I feel like you're about to chuck it all to the wind."

"Maybe I am."

"Let's back up a minute. Before I got you overanalyzing everything, you were happy with how your date went, yes?"

Tess smiled at Carly's authoritative tone. She wondered if it was the same tone Carly used to mediate the office bickering. "You sound like such a manager right now."

Carly wagged a finger. "Don't try to distract me with compliments."

"Sorry. Yes, the date was perfect. The conversation was good, the food was good, the sex was…better than good."

"Okay. See, we can work with that. So then you had a fight—"

"Disagreement."

"You had a disagreement about whether or not you should pursue a music career. Now what?"

Tess unfolded her arms, but sighed again. "Now, I think I have to apologize."

Carly reached over and squeezed her hand. "It's okay. It builds character."

"I think I have enough character, thank you."

It was Carly's turn to shrug. "I can mediate, if you want. Turns out, I'm quite good at it."

Tess laughed. "I appreciate the offer, but I think I've got this one."

"Good. Because as much as I'd love to bask in the sunshine all afternoon, I should get back."

"Have to set a good example for the underlings, right?"

Carly shook her head. "You know, technically I'm still an underling."

"A technicality, my dear, that will soon be remedied."

They said their good-byes and Carly headed back to her office. Tess sat for a moment, enjoying the sunshine and the flow of people around her. Even if things with Sam didn't go any further, Tess wanted to apologize. Otherwise, their conversation—along with the fact that she walked away from it—would continue to bother her. And if things with Sam did go further…

Tess shook her head. For as long as she could remember, she'd wanted to find a woman who wasn't overly complicated, who loved New Orleans as much as she did, and who got her. From everything she could tell, Sam didn't fit any of those criteria. And yet.

And yet Tess couldn't remember ever being more attracted to a woman. It wasn't just a physical attraction, either. Tess felt drawn to Sam on a deeper level. She couldn't define it more concretely than that, but she also couldn't deny it.

Tess shook herself out of her reverie. She needed to head to work herself. If she had any luck, Sam would come in to the restaurant and she'd be able to apologize casually. It wouldn't need to be a whole thing. "Fingers crossed," she said as she started the ride to the restaurant.

❖

By eight o'clock, there was no sign of Sam, and Tess had to accept the fact that she'd need to adjust her plans. She had the option of waiting it out, giving Sam another day to drop in. It didn't sit well with her, though, in part because Sam might not drop in. The longer it played out, the bigger a deal it would become. And it was such a passive way of doing things. Tess hated being passive.

She took advantage of a lull at the bar to take her shift break. She stepped out back where a couple of the kitchen crew were having a smoke and pulled out her phone. A text from Sam waited on her screen.

Sorry about last night. My enthusiasm sometimes crosses the line into pushy meddling. Hope we're okay and that I see you soon.

The text had been sent right before her shift started and she'd missed it. Tess smiled, in part because Sam apologized first and in part because the tone felt exactly like what Tess was going for. She took a minute to craft her reply.

No worries. I'm sorry, too. It's a sensitive subject for me. Obviously. Working tonight, but early shift tomorrow.

Sam read Tess's reply and smiled. When she hadn't heard back from Tess, she'd hoped Tess was working, but feared Tess might be ignoring her. Knowing it was the former, combined with Tess's response, was a relief. Sam might not want to admit just how much of a relief—or how much of the day she'd spent thinking about Tess—but there it was.

"Is that from her?"

Sam glanced up from her phone to find Elisa looking at her expectantly. Sam was at a martini bar in the Lower Garden District with Elisa and a few of her friends for drinks. She'd been filling them in on how badly she stuck her foot in her mouth. "It is."

"Well?"

"She apologized back."

There was a chorus of hoorays and raised cocktail glasses.

"She also said she was off tomorrow night."

"You have to ask her out," Laura insisted. Laura was a patent attorney who reminded Sam of a woman she'd dated in New York.

"I know."

"Do it now," Elisa said. "We want to know what she says."

"I am, I am," Sam assured her while she typed her reply to Tess.

Go out with me tomorrow night? Real date?

While she waited for a reply, Sam began to formulate a plan in her mind. Not that she hadn't enjoyed all of the time she'd spent with Tess over the last few weeks, but they'd yet to have what Sam considered a real date, a fancy date. Sam was an expert at fancy dates.

The conversation around her returned to talk of Mardi Gras. A couple of the women, Chloe and Mia, were in the Krewe of Nyx, which Sam had learned was one of the newer, all-female Mardi Gras krewes. The second her screen lit up, however, everyone stopped talking and looked at her again.

Since we've already slept together, I suppose a real date is in order. Ideas?

Sam grinned at her phone screen. Oh, she had ideas all right. "She said yes."

Another chorus of hoorays and raised glasses.

Plenty. Let me do some research and I'll get back to you.

"Are you in charge of planning?" Laura asked.

"It has to be nice," Elisa said.

"What are you going to do?" Chloe asked.

Mia leaned forward and rested her chin on her fist. "Where are you going to take her?"

Sam lifted her hands. "Ladies, have no fear. Spectacular dates are my specialty."

The women laughed. A few of them commented that they wished they could find a man, or woman, with such a talent. Sam plied them with questions about some of the hottest spots in town—from swanky nightclubs to restaurants. With a list in hand, she stepped outside to make a couple of phone calls and, within a few minutes, she'd secured a private table at the nicest Latin dance spot in town and dinner reservations at a four-star restaurant nearby. She set a reminder to order flowers in the morning and returned to the bar.

Back at the table, Elisa and her friends insisted on knowing what Sam had cooked up. She offered an overview of her plan, which earned her nods of approval. Sam didn't need the reassurance per se, but it was still nice to know she hadn't lost her touch.

Chloe leaned over and put her hand on Sam's arm. "If it doesn't work out with her, you give me a call. I'll go out with you."

"Me, too, and I'm not even a lesbian," Mia said.

They lingered over a second round, discussing their best and worst first dates. Sam won the worst category with her story about the woman in St. Louis who hit on her in the hotel bar, but turned out to be straight, married, and looking for a "butch type" to do a threesome with her husband.

"I thought that only happened in movies," Elisa said.

"Bad movies." Chloe shook her head.

Mia made a face. "Of the porn variety."

Sam lifted her hands in defense. "I swear it's the truth."

"Did you do it?" Mia asked.

All eyes trained on Sam. "No! I'm pretty open, but I'm not that open."

That earned her peals of laughter. When their glasses were drained, Sam insisted on paying the tab to thank them all for their moral support. They parted ways and Sam headed home in an excellent mood.

Being able to talk up just about anyone was a skill she'd honed for the research portion of her work. As a result, she often made casual acquaintances in the cities where she lived. It rarely went beyond that, though. Being welcomed into this circle of friends was new for her; she liked it. Between that and the promise of another date with Tess, New Orleans was quickly becoming one of her favorite cities to date.

CHAPTER SIXTEEN

Tess studied herself in the full-length mirror on the back of her bedroom door. Sam had asked her if she liked to dance, then told her to dress up and be ready by six. Although not big on surprises, Tess did enjoy an adventure. And she loved a reason to get gussied up.

She spent more time than she cared to admit getting ready. After several wardrobe changes, she settled on a dark purple dress. It had an almost modest neckline but left her entire back exposed, save a couple of crisscrossing straps at the base, right above her rear end. She had no idea what kind of dancing Sam had in mind, but Tess could imagine Sam's hand on her bare skin and it sent a shiver of anticipation through her.

When Sam knocked on her front door at six on the dot, she opened it with a smile. The smile quickly became a sigh. Sam always looked sharp, but tonight she wore a dark gray vest and pants with a black shirt open at the neck. And she was carrying a bouquet of hot pink roses.

It took a moment for Tess to find her voice. "You sure clean up nice."

Sam flashed a smile that made her look even sexier, if that was possible. "Thank you. You look pretty delectable yourself."

Tess stepped back so Sam could enter. When Sam passed her the flowers, Tess was pretty sure she blushed. She couldn't remember the last time she'd blushed. "You didn't have to get me flowers."

"Which is exactly why I did."

"Let me put them in some water and we can go." Tess turned to walk to the kitchen. Sam made a noise that sounded like something between a groan and a whimper, then quickly coughed. Tess, pretty sure she knew what caused it, looked over her shoulder and offered Sam a slow smile. "Are you okay? Can I get you some water?"

Sam cleared her throat and returned the smile. "I'm good. Thanks."

In the car, Sam headed back over the river, but didn't say anything about their destination. "I can't believe you won't tell me where we're going. I'm the local. That's supposed to be my move."

"I have to have a few tricks up my sleeve."

Tess drummed her fingers on the console. "Do I get a clue?"

"You already did. I asked you if you like to dance."

"Around these parts, that doesn't narrow it down too much."

Sam showed no signs of showing her hand. "We're having dinner and then I'm sharing something near and dear to my heart."

"Okay. Is it a one-time thing or a standing destination?"

"What?"

"Is it like a concert or like a club?" Tess gestured with one hand, then the other.

"You really don't like surprises, do you?"

Tess huffed. "Of course I do. I like solving puzzles more."

Since it didn't seem like Sam was going to give her anything else, Tess decided to change the subject. "So, I really am sorry for biting your head off the other night."

Sam gave her an easy smile. "You didn't. And like I said, I can come on a little strong sometimes."

It would have been easy to let it go at that, but Tess knew there was more to it. "I've had some issues with people thinking they know what's best for me."

Sam chuckled. "I actually know what you mean."

Tess nodded, feeling better. "Family?"

"Yes. You?"

"Definitely family, but also a woman I dated once. She worked in the music industry. I think she was more interested in my potential career than in me."

"Ah. Well, my apologies for stirring that up."

Tess waved her hand. "I think we just agreed to call it even."

"Agreed."

With the air cleared, Tess sat back and enjoyed the ride. Sam drove them to the warehouse district and pulled up in front of a restaurant Tess hadn't heard of. After handing her keys to the valet, Sam guided

Tess inside. They were seated in a high-backed booth and, almost immediately, greeted by a waiter dressed all in black. He rattled off a few specials, including the chef's tasting menu, which consisted of five courses of the chef's choosing.

"Are you feeling adventurous?" Sam asked.

Tess's only hesitation was how much it cost, but she reminded herself that dinners like this were probably par for the course with Sam. "I am."

"Is it okay if I order a bottle of wine as well?"

"That would be perfect."

Sam placed their order, then chatted up the sommelier like they were the oldest and dearest of friends. Tess told herself one more time not to worry about money and settled in for the meal of a lifetime. The wine, a twenty-year-old red, was exquisite. The food—nothing she'd ever consider ordering from a menu—was as beautiful as it was delicious, right down to the lavender lemon pots de crème.

After dinner, they walked out of the restaurant to find the car waiting for them. Tess enjoyed watching Sam drive; the casual confidence of her hand on the gearshift made Tess think of all the other things Sam could do with her hands. Again, they pulled right up to the door and Sam handed her keys over to a valet. Tess might not want to admit it, but it was the sort of thing she could get used to.

"I hope you like it."

Tess turned her attention back to Sam and smiled. "What's not to like about a swanky night on the town?"

Sam nodded, glad she'd gone with her first instinct. She wasn't all about the flash, but she definitely felt like some evenings called for opulence. "We're just getting started."

When they walked in, the music had already started. Several dozen couples moved around the dance floor. Others crowded around the bar and occupied small tables with votive candles on them. Sam kept her eyes on Tess's face to watch for her reaction. Only when Tess smiled did Sam realize she'd been nervous.

"I've never been salsa dancing."

"But you're adventurous, right?"

"You bet I am."

Tess's eyes sparkled with glee. It was enough to tempt Sam to drag her back to the car and take her home. All in good time. She took Tess's hand and led her through the crowd to an empty table near the edge of the dance floor.

Sam felt her hesitate. Tess pointed to a small tent card with black script letters. "It's reserved."

Sam released Tess's hand to pull out one of the chairs. "For us."

Tess looked incredulous.

"Don't you know I earn my living attending to details?"

Tess shook her head, but smiled and sat down. "You've said something along those lines once or twice."

"May I buy you a drink?"

"You always do. How about I buy you a drink?"

"No, no. I insist. When you plan the date, you can buy the drinks. Deal?"

The look on Tess's face made Sam think she'd taken the statement as a challenge. It was sexy as hell. "Deal."

"Martini?"

"No, I'm feeling adventurous, remember? Surprise me."

It seemed like Tess had flipped a switch. Any traces of hesitation and reluctance were gone; even the playfulness of their first night together paled in comparison to this. Tess exuded a bold, up-for-anything energy. Sam didn't think she could find Tess any more attractive, but somehow Tess had managed to crank the dial a little higher. Perhaps having to work for it made it all the more appealing.

Sam caught the eye of a waiter and ordered traditional daiquiris. She'd learned the hard way to be specific in a town known for its frozen, glow-in-the-dark concoctions. When the drinks came, Sam raised her glass in a toast. "To dates done right."

Tess clinked her glass to Sam's and took a sip of her drink. "Excellent choice."

Sam smiled. "Thank you. I thought we could watch for a little while, but I'm hoping to get you out on the floor with me."

"I'd certainly hope so."

It was fun to watch Tess study the people dancing. She watched their feet first, then her gaze traveled up to take in the movement of arms and postures. She ran her finger around the rim of her cocktail glass, an absentminded gesture that made Sam think of the things Tess could do with her fingers. After three songs, Tess nodded and asserted that she was ready to give it a try.

Sam took her hand and led her to the floor. She took a minute to show Tess the basic steps and Tess got the hang of it almost instantly. "I thought you said you'd never done this before."

Tess offered her a playful look. "I haven't, but I know enough other kinds that this is just a variation. You lead me and I'll follow."

Sam swallowed. She knew Tess was referring to the dance floor, but she couldn't stop her mind from racing ahead. She thought of Tess, willing and pliant, and all the things she wanted to do with her. The fact that she could feel Tess's skin, warm and smooth under her hand, didn't help.

As they moved back and forth across the room, Sam's thoughts were trapped in a vicious cycle. One second, she was absorbed in the moment—the thrum of the music and the voice of the singer, pleading to his love in Spanish. The next, she was so aroused the only thing she could think about was getting Tess home and naked and under her. She wondered if Tess felt the same way. Or if the sinuous way Tess moved against her was specifically designed to drive Sam out of her mind.

They stopped once to finish their drinks, but when the band stopped for a break, Sam didn't think she could take it anymore. "You want to get out of here?"

Tess looked at her with bedroom eyes. "I thought you'd never ask. My place?"

The drive to Tess's took an eternity. Every red light in the city conspired against her. Sam shifted uncomfortably in her seat as Tess stroked her thigh.

"Do you want me to stop?" Tess asked.

"No." Sam glanced down at Tess's hand, imagining where it would be and what it would be doing in a matter of minutes. "Yes." She swallowed hard. "I mean no."

A few minutes later, Sam pulled into the driveway and put the car in park. Before she could unfasten her seat belt, Tess was climbing out of the car. Sam hurried to catch up, coming up behind Tess as she unlocked her front door. She placed her hands on Tess's hips, barely resisting the urge to pull Tess against her.

After what seemed like ages, the door opened and Tess grabbed her hand, pulling them both inside. Sam closed the door behind them, then turned Tess so that she could press her body against it. Tess tipped her head to the side, giving Sam access to her slender neck. Sam took full advantage, kissing and nibbling her way up to Tess's earlobe.

Tess pulled at the buttons of Sam's vest. Sam released her hold long enough to shrug her arms free. She let it fall to the floor while Tess went to work on her shirt.

Tess couldn't remember the last time she'd been so turned on. She wanted Sam with a desperation that clouded her vision, took up all the space in her lungs. She channeled that energy into Sam, into the vortex that threatened to consume them both.

She tore at the buttons of Sam's shirt. Her fingers trembled, making her clumsy. Instead of a bra, Sam wore a tight black undershirt. Her nipples strained against the fabric. Tess brushed her thumbs over them, causing Sam to moan.

Sam's mouth covered Tess's. The kiss was hot, possessive. Sam's hands crept under the hem of Tess's dress, grabbing her ass. She stopped moving suddenly and leaned back far enough to lock eyes with Tess. "What are you wearing under this dress?"

Tess arched her brow and struggled to keep her tone light. "Perfume."

"Fuck."

Tess started to laugh, but Sam's mouth claimed hers. There was an almost frantic urgency to the kiss. Tess eagerly took Sam's tongue into her mouth, matching the intensity with her own. She was trapped, pinned between Sam's body and the door. It was a delicious feeling, knowing that she drove Sam as crazy as Sam drove her.

Sam's left hand stayed on Tess's ass while her right moved around the front of her thigh. Tess shifted her legs to give Sam access. Before she could say anything, Sam's fingers were plunging into her. The speed and the force of it took her breath away. "Oh, God. Sam."

Sam slid her left hand down the back of Tess's thigh, lifting her leg slightly. The change in angle allowed Sam to go deeper. Tess pushed back with each thrust. The pressure of Sam's whole hand against her exaggerated the sensation of being filled over and over. The combination drove her over the edge. Tess came violently, her whole body bucking against Sam. She sagged against her, fighting to keep her legs steady.

Before she could gain her footing, Sam lifted her off the ground. Tess wound her arms around Sam's neck, her legs around Sam's waist.

"Bedroom?" It was as much command as question.

Tess angled her head in the right direction. "That way."

Sam carried her across the living room and through the doorway to her bedroom. The orange glow of a streetlight came through the curtains, providing just enough light to illuminate the bed.

Sam lowered her onto it without breaking contact. Tess hadn't expected her to be so strong. Tess trailed her hands down Sam's arms with a new appreciation for the well-defined muscles.

"Why aren't you naked yet?" Tess asked. It was half joke, half demand. She wanted to see Sam's skin, to feel it under her hands.

Sam let out a ragged laugh. "I could ask you the same question."

Tess moved her hands to Sam's stomach, tugging the undershirt up and over Sam's head. She sat up just enough for Sam to ease the straps of the dress from her shoulders. She lifted her hips so Sam could work the dress down her torso. Sam slid it down her legs and dropped it to the floor, then removed Tess's shoes.

Tess propped herself on an elbow and pointed to Sam's pants. "Off."

"So demanding," Sam said, but obeyed, stripping off the rest of her clothing.

Tess had a witty reply on the tip of her tongue, but Sam dipped her head and pulled one of Tess's nipples into her mouth. Words became moans, the need to be clever subsumed by a much more basic need. Tess once again wrapped her legs around Sam's waist, pulling Sam against her. She needed the weight of Sam's body, the heat and friction of it.

Sam pressed a thigh between Tess's legs. Tess loosened her grip so she could grind against it. She felt herself climbing higher, hurtling toward another orgasm. She was almost there when Sam abruptly shifted. Tess opened her mouth to protest, but all that came out was a whimper.

Before she could formulate an actual sentence, Sam slid down the length of her body. The next thing she knew, Sam's mouth was on her, her tongue gliding over Tess's swollen clit. Sam kept her strokes light, but fast. Tess's whole body quivered, held on the precipice of release. "Please," she panted over and over. "Please."

Sam adjusted the pressure only slightly, breaking the thread and pushing Tess over the edge. Tess's entire body bowed. Sam stayed with her, holding her tongue in place and making the orgasm go on and on. Tess cried out, the sound echoing in her ears so loudly she thought the neighbors might hear.

As Tess began to come down, Sam moved back up her body. She wrapped an arm around Tess and pulled her close. Tess rode out the aftershocks, letting her toes uncurl and her muscles relax. She stretched the rest of her body and rolled onto Sam. "That was hot."

Sam traced a finger along her jaw. "It certainly was." She smiled with more than a hint of smugness.

Tess took it as a challenge. She braced herself over Sam, holding her face a few inches away. "You seem awfully satisfied with yourself."

Sam tipped her head slightly. "If your orgasm was half as good as how you sounded when you came, then yes, yes I am."

"Let me see if I can show you how good it was." Tess leaned forward, pulling Sam into a kiss. She traced Sam's lips with her tongue, teasing Sam's mouth open then plunging in. She felt Sam's body tense, heard her moan. When Sam's arms wound around her, Tess grabbed her wrists. She placed them over Sam's head and looked into Sam's eyes. "Don't move."

Sam nodded. Tess smiled and then set about driving Sam completely mad. She licked and sucked, nibbled and bit her way down Sam's torso. She reveled in the way Sam's body twisted under hers. Once, Sam's hands slid down and wound into Tess's hair. Although she loved the sensation, Tess stopped what she was doing. When Sam lifted her head and opened her eyes, Tess made a stern face. "I said no touching."

"Sorry." Sam placed her hands back over her head.

Tess smiled at how quickly Sam did her bidding and continued her way toward Sam's center. She could feel the heat emanating from Sam; the scent of Sam's arousal made her insides tighten. She teased Sam a little more, brushing her lips over the soft, dark curls.

Sam continued to squirm. Finally, she said, "Tess, you're killing me."

Tess pressed her tongue into Sam, finding her swollen and hard. Tess sucked the nub between her lips, matching each gentle tug with a circle of her tongue. Sam moaned and moved against her, whispering her name. Each time Tess thought she was getting close, she changed her rhythm or altered the pressure. Sam's moans of pleasure melded with groans of frustration. Tess continued, relentless. She could do this all night.

Only when Sam's noises started to sound more like whimpers did Tess change her tactics. With long and forceful strokes, she drove Sam up and over. Sam's body went rigid and then collapsed into a soft heap. Tess crawled up the length of her, appreciating that Sam's hands remained linked over her head. She kissed Sam again, enjoying the way their tastes melded on her tongue.

Tess smiled, indulging in a little smugness of her own. "I take it back. That," she paused for effect, "was hot."

CHAPTER SEVENTEEN

Sam woke to sunlight filtering through the lightweight curtains on the windows. She stretched and smiled, relishing the fact that her body felt likc it did after a really good workout. The disappointment of realizing she was alone dissipated with the realization she was in Tess's bed. Tess couldn't have gone far.

Sam pulled on her undershirt and pants from the night before, then went in search of Tess. She opened the door and was greeted by the aroma of coffee and frying bacon. Tess stood at the stove, barefoot and wearing a baggy men's shirt with the sleeves rolled up. Sam couldn't decide whether the sight or the smell was more enticing.

"Good morning."

Tess turned and smiled. "Barely. I was beginning to think I'd have to send in the cavalry to wake you up."

Sam scratched her temple. "You could have just opened the door. If the smell of coffee hadn't done it, the bacon would have."

Tess laughed. "Good to know. The bacon needs a minute still. Coffee?"

"Yes, please. Is there anything I can do to help?"

Tess poured a cup and handed it to her. "It's just about done, but thanks. Cream and sugar are on the table."

Sam took a seat and added cream to her coffee. She wondered if the chrome and Formica table reflected vintage style or a frugal practicality. "You didn't have to make breakfast, but I love that you did."

Tess set a plate of bacon on the table, followed by a mound of scrambled eggs and a jar of what looked like homemade jam. When she opened the oven and pulled out a pan of biscuits, Sam thought she might actually drool. Tess set the pan on a cast iron trivet and took the other seat. "I'd have done it whether or not you were here, to be honest, but I'm happy to share."

Sam helped herself to a biscuit. "I wouldn't have pegged you for the big breakfast type."

"When I work evenings at the restaurant, I don't usually get a real supper, so I have to make up for it."

"I thought you were off today."

Tess shrugged. "Habit."

"Fair enough. What kind of jam?" Sam pointed to the jar.

"Persimmon."

Sam was unfamiliar with it, but had never met a jam she didn't like. She spooned some onto her biscuit and took a bite. "Mmm."

"My Mawmaw's recipe."

"Really? Did you make it?"

Tess piled bacon and eggs onto her plate. "Does that surprise you?"

Sam, impressed with Tess's appetite, filled her own plate. "Only because I can't imagine doing so myself."

"It isn't hard."

"I say any activity that comes with a chance of botulism counts as hard."

Tess nodded. "That's fair. But jam and pickles are pretty safe. It's your green beans and such that you have to look out for."

"I've always felt that way about green beans."

Tess snickered.

"And rhubarb." Sam pointed at her for emphasis. "I don't trust a vegetable whose stalks you eat but whose leaves can kill you."

"Well, when you put it that way."

"I do. But I've recently come to embrace collard greens, so I feel like I've earned some goodwill in the produce department."

Tess shook her head, but cracked another smile. "Vegetable diplomacy?"

"Exactly." Sam finished the biscuit and reached for another. "The jam is good, but your biscuits are to die for."

"Those are my Mawmaw's recipe, too."

Sam thought about her own grandmother's cooking, as well as

the debacle of pretending to cook for Tess. She should plan a visit specifically to get some lessons, especially while Abuelita was still in good health. "Is she still alive?"

"She is. There are some days I think she might outlive us all."

Sam knew the feeling. "Does she live nearby?"

"A couple hours away. I try to go see her once a month or so."

"That's really sweet. I'm sure she appreciates it."

Tess nodded. "She does, but I do, too. I'm probably closer to her than anyone else in my family."

Even though Sam didn't see her grandmother nearly as often, she could relate. "It's easier with grandparents sometimes, isn't it?"

Tess took a bite of her eggs and nodded. "It sure is."

"Not to pry, but are you not close to your parents?"

Tess made a production of applying butter and jam to another biscuit and Sam wondered if she shouldn't have gone there. But then Tess set down her knife and said, "It's not like we're estranged or anything."

Sam couldn't help but smile. She'd say the exact same thing about her own parents.

"We talk every few weeks. I see them and my brother at holidays. This is actually the house I grew up in." Tess motioned around herself. "We just have different priorities, want different things."

"I understand. It's like they want what's best for you, but their definition of that is nothing like yours."

"Exactly. I'm exactly where I want to be and doing exactly what I want to do, but my parents still act as if I ran away from home and joined the circus."

"Which is ironic, since you're the one who's home."

"Right?" Tess smiled then and Sam was glad she'd asked.

They finished breakfast and cleaned up. Since Tess had practice with her band in the afternoon, Sam resisted the urge to linger. She gathered up the rest of her clothes and slipped on her shoes. Tess walked her to the front door. Before she opened it, Sam leaned down and kissed her. "I had a great time last night. Thanks for going on a real date with me."

If Sam wasn't mistaken, Tess blushed. "Thank you for such an extravagant date. I hope you don't feel like you have to go to such lengths, but I had a great time, too."

"I'm not extravagant all the time, but it can be fun. Speaking of, how would you like to be extravagant with me again next Tuesday?"

Tess offered her an apologetic look and shrugged. "Sorry, but I've already got a date for Valentine's Day."

Sam tried to ignore the clenching sensation in her stomach. She looked at Tess, whose eyes held mischief. What the hell was that about? "You do?"

"I'm afraid so. His name is Dustin and, I don't know, I guess I just found him irresistible."

Sam tried to reconcile the words coming out of Tess's mouth with the woman she'd gotten to know, the woman she'd slept with not twenty-four hours ago. Was it a joke? Sam didn't find it very funny. She didn't have a problem with bi women; she'd dated more than one through the years. But in her book dating several people at once was the sort of thing you mentioned. "I'm sorry. I don't understand."

Tess broke into a full smile then. "I mean, I have to feed him and change his diapers, but otherwise, he's a total charmer."

Oh. A baby. Sam wondered whose baby it was, but that mild curiosity was a vast improvement over the sickening feeling of a moment before. That made it easier to play along. "I don't know. I think the feeding can be quite fun under the right circumstances. Exactly how old is this Dustin, anyway?"

"Six months, give or take a week."

"I see. Let me guess, you met him online."

Tess let out a snort, then laughed. Sam found it satisfying to know she'd been able to take Tess's little joke and run with it. "You're cute," she said.

Sam shrugged. "I know. Really, though, how did you get roped into babysitting on Valentine's Day?"

"I didn't get roped in. I volunteered. First, because he really is irresistible and I don't get to see him enough. Second, I adore his mamas and I don't think they've gone on a real date since he was born."

Sam considered. Maybe this was the universe's way of telling her spending Valentine's Day with Tess was a bad idea. Or maybe it was a perfect chance to hang out with Tess in a different way and get in a little baby time. She liked babies, and she'd hardly spent any time with one in the last couple of years. "Would you consider taking a wingman on this date?"

Tess raised a brow. "Wingman?"

"Wing-woman. Same difference."

"No, I knew what you meant. I'm having a hard time picturing it, though. You don't strike me as the baby type."

"Me?" Sam pointed both hands at herself, then made a sweeping gesture. "I love babies. Even more importantly, babies love me."

"Is that so?"

Sam nodded. "You might say they find me irresistible."

"Well, when you put it that way."

"So I'm in?"

Tess shook her head, but said, "You're in."

"Excellent."

"Let me check with Carly and Becca, though. They trust me, but they might want to meet you before signing on for babysitter with wingman."

"Or wing-woman."

"Exactly."

Sam smiled. "Call or text me later?"

"Sure."

"Have fun at rehearsal." Sam kissed her again and then opened the front door.

Since Tess still wore only a shirt, she stood behind it, leaning slightly so she could offer a wave good-bye. Once Sam climbed into her car, Tess closed the door. Marlowe sauntered into the living room from the kitchen. Tess scooped him up and carried him with her to the back of the house. Tess set him on the bed and headed to the bathroom for a shower. By the time she emerged fifteen minutes later, he was curled up and sound asleep in the middle of Sam's pillow. Tess chuckled; he didn't waste any time reclaiming his territory.

❖

Rehearsal wasn't until four. Instead of chores, which she should do, Tess pulled out the song she'd started writing after going to City Park with Sam. She read over the lyrics and chuckled. When it came to Sam, Tess had failed miserably in the resisting temptation department. Of course, she'd come around to thinking that might not be a bad thing.

Inspiration hit her and she scribbled down a third verse about the pleasure of giving in. She started at the beginning and sang all the way through. She sat for a moment and contemplated a fourth verse, sort of a moral of the story. No, leaving it open-ended was better. She had no regrets about sleeping with Sam, but it didn't mean she was quite ready to extol the virtues of letting her libido call the shots.

When she got to Jenny and Cedric's house, Tess showed them what she'd come up with. After getting the equipment set up, she took Zack's usual spot at the keyboard. She picked out the melody and hummed along. The next time through, Cedric strummed the chords Tess had written and Mo tapped her foot. She gave the seat at the keyboard back to Zack and let them put the pieces together. Then Tess sang along. By the time she'd run all the way through it, everyone was smiling at her.

"I know it's still rough, but what do you think?"

"Uh, not that rough," Cedric said.

Jenny nodded in agreement. "Yeah, it's pretty awesome already."

Tess smiled. "Thanks."

Mo said, "I think we can have it ready for next week. What do y'all think?"

"Absolutely." Cedric pointed a pencil at the piece of paper where she'd written out the music. "Tess, walk me through how you want to pace it and we'll start adding layers."

In less than an hour, "Your Spell" was a fully formed song, ten times better than what Tess had imagined in her head. In the end, Cedric set aside his guitar and pulled out the sax he played for a couple of their jazzier songs. Jenny slowed the tempo some and Mo came in with just the right bass line. The final result was more sexy than wistful; Tess loved it.

They ran through the rest of their usual set, then "Your Spell" a couple more times. Tess couldn't remember the last time she'd been so energized by a rehearsal. She didn't necessarily want to give Sam credit for the shift, but she couldn't deny that her creative juices were flowing more than they had in ages. That sort of thing didn't happen out of the blue, at least not for her. Maybe she'd be able to make the case for temptation after all.

They began packing up instruments, talking about the next show. When everything was squared away, Zack issued an invitation to his house the following weekend. "The deck is finally done and Laura is dying to christen it with a party."

"That's awesome," Jenny said.

"Yeah." Cedric snapped his guitar case closed. "Let us know what we can bring."

"I'll talk to Laura and let you know. I don't know if she's planned the menu yet or not."

"Would it be cool if I brought someone?" Tess asked.

All eyes turned to look at her. Jenny put her hands on her hips. "Like a date?"

Tess rolled her eyes. "No, like a third cousin. Yes, like a date."

Zack walked over and slung an arm around her shoulder. "Of course. The more the merrier."

Tess looked up at him. "Thanks, Zack."

Jenny waved a hand back and forth. "I'm sorry. Can we go back to the part where there's someone you want to bring as a date?"

Tess sighed, but good-naturedly. When she told Sam her band mates were like family, she'd meant it. They cared about her. And they were totally nosy. "It's nothing serious. We've been out a few times. She's only in New Orleans for a few months for work. I don't think she has a ton of friends in town."

"You're dating an out-of-towner?" Jenny's tone was incredulous.

"We hung out as friends a few times and it went from there."

"Wait." Mo narrowed her eyes. "Is 'Your Spell' about her?"

"No," Tess said, a little too quickly.

"Oh, my God, it is." Jenny's hands returned to her hips. "It totally is."

Tess took a deep breath. "Maybe a little."

Mo nodded slowly. "Well, if she's got you inspired enough to write sexy-ass songs, I approve."

Tess tipped her head deferentially. "Why, thank you."

Jenny wasn't quite as easily won over. "She just better not leave you singing the blues."

Both Mo and Zack groaned and Tess rolled her eyes. "Did you really just say that?"

Jenny shrugged. "I did. Don't change the subject."

Tess shook her head. "I think I can look out for myself, but I appreciate the sentiment."

Cedric said, "Well, we can't wait to meet her. I promise I'll keep Jenny from giving her the third degree."

"Hey!" Jenny punched him in the arm.

"Really, it's not a big deal. We aren't serious or anything, I'm just trying to be hospitable."

Zack nodded. "If you say so, that's good enough for us."

"Thank you."

"I don't know." Mo shook her head. "I'm not sure the welcome wagon usually makes a stop in the bedroom. Unless, of course, I completely misinterpreted verse three."

Four pairs of eyes trained right on her. Tess raised a shoulder. "Let's just say it's hospitality, with benefits."

Mo and Jenny erupted with laughter. Cedric joined in and even the relatively stoic Zack snickered. "That's a New Orleansism if I ever heard one," Zack said.

"Gives a whole new meaning to the Tourist Welcome Center," Mo added, leading to another round of laughter.

"All right. Are we done amusing ourselves at my expense?" Tess didn't mind being the punch line every now and then, but things with Sam were…What were they? Complicated. And whether she was more worried about being dismissive of where they might be going or jinxing them, she felt the need to tread lightly.

"Sorry, sorry." Mo lifted her hands. "I'll stop. I mean, technically, you started it, but I'll stop."

"Yeah, what she said." Jenny angled her head at Mo.

"I know, I know. I'm just kidding. It's fine. I'm fine." Tess said.

"Good." Cedric snapped the last case shut. "We really are excited to meet her."

"Well, don't get your hopes up too much. I haven't even invited her yet."

Tess walked out with Mo and Zack and waved her good-byes. On the ride home, she continued to hum their new song. Theirs, because it wouldn't have become what it did without all of their input. But even recognizing that, Tess would always have the thrill of knowing it started with her. She decided she should commit to spending more time writing. She'd never considered herself a fountain of ideas, but maybe she simply hadn't tapped into the right places.

Tess tapped on the steering wheel as she drove, willing a tune to come together in her mind. By the time she pulled into her driveway, she had to dig around in her purse for something to write with. She found a pen, but had to settle for the back of a piece of junk mail. She scrawled out what she had so far to make sure she wouldn't lose it, then went inside.

She fed Marlowe, then sat down at the piano. Marlowe joined her a few minutes later, clearly unimpressed by Tess's creative flow. When her phone beeped with a text from Sam, Tess realized she'd been at it for over an hour. She sent a flirtatious reply and stood up, rolled her shoulders.

She'd tapped into something, all right. Whatever it was—and whether or not it had anything to do with Sam—she liked it. All she had to do was figure out how to keep it going.

CHAPTER EIGHTEEN

Tess didn't really expect Carly and Becca to have a problem with Sam tagging along to babysit. She'd only wanted to give them the official say, without the pressure of knowing she'd already told Sam yes. What she hadn't expected was the level of excitement the plan stirred up. According to Becca, dates that included babies were serious business. Carly readily agreed and it took Tess nearly half an hour to downplay the significance of the whole thing—to them and to herself.

Sam offered to pick her up and Tess readily accepted. She'd never admit it because it made her feel old, but she hated driving at night. Besides, Sam had a nice car.

She went back and forth over what to wear. It was a date and she didn't want to feel like a slob, but she was spending her evening with a baby and wanted to be practical. She flipped through her closet again, as annoyed with herself as with her selections. Ultimately, she settled on leggings and dress with a busy pattern that she figured wouldn't show spills or stains.

Annoyed that she'd put so much thought into so many aspects of the evening, Tess stood by her front door, tapping her foot and checking her watch every fifteen seconds. Sam's car pulled into her driveway exactly one minute past the time Tess told her to arrive. Tess wasted no time, stepping out and pulling the door closed behind her. The second she opened the passenger door, Sam started spouting apologies.

"I'm so sorry. Am I late? I got stuck on a phone call with my editor. I hope you haven't been waiting too long."

So not only had she been hovering, she was scowling, too. She took a breath, forced her features to relax, and smiled. "You're fine. I was ready early."

"Okay. I just didn't want you to think I was shirking. I take babysitting very seriously."

The choice of words made Tess laugh. Why was she being high strung? She hated being high strung. "It's all good. We have plenty of time."

Tess gave Sam directions, then watched her as she drove. Even in jeans and a henley, she looked classy. A short while later, they pulled into Carly and Becca's driveway five minutes early. Tess took another deep breath, trying to will away any lingering nervousness.

"What a cute neighborhood. Great house, too."

Tess had always thought so. If she weren't so attached to Algiers, or if she ever had a family, Mandeville, with its 1950s subdivisions and spacious yards, would be near the top of her list. It struck her as odd that someone like Sam would find the old-fashioned ranch charming. "It feels about ten times bigger on the inside than it looks from the outside."

"Sounds just like the house I grew up in."

Tess filed that detail away. It had never occurred to her that Sam didn't grow up with money. She needed to be better at asking questions.

They climbed out of the car and Tess led the way to the side door. She had a moment of hesitation, but decided that using the front would be weird, even if Sam was with her. They found Carly and Becca in the kitchen, both looking gorgeous. Dustin sat in his swing, making enthusiastic gurgling noises.

After introductions and compliments, Sam said, "Thank you for letting me tag along with Tess. I don't get to see my nieces and nephews nearly enough, so I'm excited to get some baby time."

Carly offered Sam a warm smile. "Any friend of Tess's is a friend of ours. We appreciate you for sacrificing your Valentine's Day so we can get a little non-baby time."

"It all worked out well. I'm not sure Tess would have agreed to anything overly romantic anyway."

Carly and Becca both laughed. Tess put her hands on her hips. "Hey. I'm standing right here."

Carly leaned in and bumped her shoulder. "You can't protest if it's true."

Protesting would only draw more attention, so Tess changed the subject. "Where are y'all going?"

Carly smirked, clearly seeing Tess's plot. Fortunately, Becca either didn't notice or took mercy on her. "We're rocking it old school. Dinner at Galatoire's and then 21st Amendment for drinks and music."

Tess smiled. Becca had taken Carly to Galatoire's on their first date in hopes of impressing her. She could still remember Carly gushing about how fancy it was. "Nice."

"It does sound nice. Why haven't we done that?" Sam asked.

Tess had a pithy answer on the tip of her tongue, but Carly spoke first. "You totally should. It's one of the few famous places that earns its reputation."

Sam turned to Tess and pointed an index finger at her. "You let me know your next night off because we have a date."

Tess chuckled. "Fine, but first things first. These two have a date to get to and we're holding them up."

Carly shrugged nonchalantly. "We've got time. We cushioned a little so we'd have a few minutes to meet Sam."

Becca added, "Not because we don't trust you with Dustin. Tess is notoriously picky when it comes to the women she dates, so we were curious about who'd managed to capture her attention."

Sam looked at Tess with a raised brow. "Is that so?"

"She exaggerates."

"Not really," Carly said.

The look Sam shot Tess was pure mischief. "Fascinating."

Tess tried to change the subject. Again. "So, any special instructions? Bedtime?"

"No instructions, but he was in rare form this afternoon and didn't go down for his late nap until almost four. He's only been awake for about half an hour. He'll want a bottle soon. It's in the fridge. Tess, you know the drill. He'll probably be up for two or three hours before being ready for bed."

"Perfect. We'll have a great time."

"You'll call or text if you need anything?"

Tess patted Carly's arm. "We won't, but we will. Now, shoo."

Carly and Becca left and Tess scooped Dustin out of his swing. They took turns holding him, playing peekaboo, and talking nonsense.

Tess warmed his bottle according to Carly's instructions. Dustin went to town on it, so she figured she must have done it right.

"He's such an easy baby," Sam said.

"Right? It's almost enough to make me want one."

After finishing his bottle, Dustin remained all smiles for about twenty minutes. And then he wasn't. It started with a little fussiness and pushing away his favorite toys. Things went downhill from there. He cried. He shrieked. He thrashed. Tess didn't know what else to try. She regretted bringing Sam along. Not that she needed to impress Sam, but being unable to calm a six-month-old made her feel painfully inadequate.

"Will you let me try? Please?"

Sam had offered twice before, but Tess had thought it was more of a token gesture than a genuine desire. At this point, however, she just wanted a break. And to be more than two feet away from the wailing. "Be my guest."

Sam took Dustin from her more deftly than she expected. She positioned him on her shoulder and started rubbing his back while pacing back and forth. He didn't stop, but having a little distance helped Tess feel a little calmer. "Do you think we should call Carly and Becca?"

"I don't think so. Did he burp after his bottle?"

"Yes, he burped." Tess looked at her with a mixture of humor and exasperation. "I'm not an idiot."

"Just once?"

"Once that I could tell. Do you think that's what's wrong?"

Sam stopped rubbing Dustin's back and started patting it. "I don't know. But I do know gas is one of the primary reasons babies are miserable."

"I'm willing to try anything at this point. Let me get you a burp cloth in case he—"

Tess didn't get to finish her sentence. Dustin let out a huge burp, punctuated by a stream of spit-up. It covered Sam's shoulder and ran down the back of her sweater.

"Oh, God. Don't move."

"It's fine. It not the first time a baby has spit up on me."

Tess dabbed at the mess on the sweater and locked eyes with

Dustin. He blinked his big blue eyes at her, his lashes still wet from crying. Spit-up dribbled down his chin.

"Hey, cutie. You okay? You had a little upset tummy?" He continued to blink. After a few seconds, his face broke into a lopsided grin. "Sam, he smiled. You fixed him."

Sam lifted the baby from her shoulder and held him in front of her. "Is that true, Dustin? Did I fix you up right?" Dustin's response was to laugh and shake his fists in the air. Sam turned him around and settled him in the crook of her arm. "I'm going to take that as a yes."

"Let me get a wet cloth to wipe his face." Tess went to the kitchen sink and ran one corner of the burp cloth under a stream of warm water. She wiped Dustin's face and studied him for a moment. Other than the pink splotches on his cheeks, no one would have guessed he'd been screaming his head off not five minutes prior. "I can't believe you got him to stop."

"I'm just glad my suspicions were right. If that hadn't worked, I didn't have any other tricks up my sleeve."

Tess returned her attention to Sam's sweater. Despite her dabbing, a large splotch of milky white residue remained. "I'm afraid your sweater is a lost cause."

"No worries. That's what washing machines are for, aren't they, Dustin?"

Dustin let out an excited string of babble in response.

"See?"

"You're the baby whisperer."

"Not quite, but I've been around enough of them."

"Really?"

"Nieces and nephews, mostly. Some baby cousins."

Tess had been around her fair share, too. And she'd thought that she was pretty baby savvy. It bothered her some that Sam had so effortlessly one-upped her. It was petty, though, so she pushed it to the back of her mind and tried to focus on having the rest of the night go smoothly.

They sat on the sofa and played with Dustin's farm animal See 'n Say. When he started to rub his eyes, they changed his diaper again and put him in a pair of onesie pajamas with frogs on them. They each read him a bedtime story, then Sam offered to sit with him in the rocker in his room until he fell asleep. Tess went to the kitchen and called in the Chinese food they'd agreed to earlier. She was standing at the refrigerator looking at photos when Sam emerged.

"Please tell me there's General Tso's in my very near future."

Tess turned and smiled. "It'll be here in about half an hour. Did he fall asleep okay?"

"Out like a light."

"I'm sorry the evening turned out to be so stressful."

Sam walked over to her and slid an arm around her waist. "You have nothing to apologize for. Babies are work. A ton of fun, but also work. I knew what I was signing up for."

Tess shook her head. "You're full of surprises, you know that?"

Sam pulled away and looked at her quizzically. "I'm not sure if I should take that as a compliment or an insult."

"It's a compliment, I promise. It's not like I thought you were one-dimensional."

Sam raised a brow. "But?"

"But...I guess I didn't give much thought to who you were outside the context of the time we spend together. Does that make sense?"

Sam nodded. It did make sense. It reminded her of how she usually approached dating. For some reason, being on the other side left her feeling vaguely let down. Not wanting to say that, she settled for, "It does."

"Maybe it's because I don't know much about you outside of us."

"You know I like to eat. And dance." Sam did a little cha-cha in place.

Tess chuckled. "True. I don't really know about your work, though, even though it's clearly a huge part of who you are. I've not met any of your friends or your family."

That was Sam's usual M.O. She kept the focus on the other person—her likes and dislikes, her interests and hobbies. The women she typically dated either didn't notice or didn't care. "Does that bother you?"

"It doesn't or, at least, it didn't."

This was uncharted territory for Sam. She was saved, or given a reprieve at least, by the sound of the doorbell. "I'll get it."

Tess waved her away. "No, let me. You saved the day. The least I can do is buy your dinner."

Sam busied herself with getting out plates and pouring glasses of iced tea. She debated how to handle Tess's assertion. Suddenly her usual strategy felt like just that—a strategy. Tess deserved better than that. She checked on Dustin via the video monitor while Tess set out the food, then joined her at the table.

"I'm one of four."

Tess set down the carton of lo mein. "Excuse me?"

Sam finished chewing the dumpling she'd popped in her mouth. "Children. My parents have four children."

"Oh. Okay." Tess smiled. "Brothers or sisters?"

"Two brothers, one sister."

"And are they globe-trotters like you?"

Sam thought about how very settled the rest of her family seemed. She shook her head. "No, just me."

"Do you not want to talk about them?"

Sam had made the decision to open up. She wasn't about to backpedal now. "No, no. I'm happy to. My oldest brother is a middle school science teacher in the district where we grew up. My sister just finished medical school and is doing her residency."

"And the youngest?"

"He's still at home. A senior in high school. He was a surprise."

"Sounds very traditional."

Sam chuckled. "You don't know the half of it."

"Tell me."

Sam leaned back from the table. Maybe this opening-up thing wasn't so bad. "My family is very traditional and very Catholic."

"Ah."

Sam couldn't tell if Tess's response was one of general understanding or a more personal empathy. "It's okay. We get along okay. They're not quite sure what to do with me, I'd say."

Tess frowned. "Because you're gay?"

"They had a hard time when I came out, at least at first. Honestly, I think it's what I do for a living that they don't understand."

"What do you mean?"

"I think if I had a normal job and settled down with a nice Cuban girl and started a family, they'd be willing to overlook the gay thing." Thrilled, probably.

"They don't approve of your job?"

"I don't put my name on my work. For them, that means I don't take any pride in it, or in my heritage. There's nothing they can point to and say, 'Look, there is Samara's contribution to society.'"

Tess furrowed her brow. "I don't understand. You seem pretty successful to me."

Sam sighed. "It's less about being successful as it is doing the family name, and the community, proud."

"I get it. I think."

"I think it's an immigrant thing, at least in part. Proving that leaving home was worth it, proving that you deserve to be in the new place."

"That makes sense. I haven't had that experience, obviously, but you know a little of my family story. Having different priorities can make things hard."

Sam thought about what she knew of Tess and her family. It resonated. "Yeah. It's not animosity or anything. More like a missing connection, or lack of understanding."

"Exactly." Tess tipped her head to one side. "Do you think you'll ever settle down?"

Sam searched Tess's face. Often, when women asked that question, they had themselves in mind. They wanted to know if Sam would settle down with them. Not Tess, though. She seemed interested, but without pretense. "I'm sure I will eventually. I'm not going to be some eighty-year-old jet-setter. But I can't imagine wanting to do it anytime soon."

"It does seem to suit you." Tess's smile looked genuine, without judgment.

"What about you? Do you consider yourself settled?"

"I like to think of myself as settled, but not rigid. I can't imagine leaving New Orleans, but I would like to find someone, maybe get married one day."

Tess's tone and phrasing made it clear she didn't think of Sam as having anything to do with those hopes or plans. Usually, that would give Sam a sense of relief. For some reason, it made her sad, or wistful at least. She suddenly wanted to change the subject. "So, Mardi Gras is coming up."

Tess's face registered the shift in conversation, but she didn't acknowledge it otherwise. "It sure is."

"I'd love to celebrate like a local."

"Okay. What are you interested in?"

"What about Bourbon Street?"

Tess made a face. "If you go to Bourbon Street, you do so at your own peril."

"I'm sure it's rowdy, but it can't be all bad."

"Look, I like to drink. I'd go so far as to say I'm a happy drunk. And I like the company of happy drunks."

"But?"

"But for every happy drunk on Bourbon Street, there's one who's fall-down drunk and another who's throw-up-on-you drunk."

"I can see your point."

"And another thing. I don't need to see some frat guy waving his penis around for a ten cent string of beads."

"Ew." Sam didn't realize the tradition of flashing had spread to both genders.

"Exactly."

"Okay, then. So, what do locals do? How do you celebrate?"

Tess leaned back and looked Sam up and down. Sam got the feeling Tess was trying to gauge whether or not she was worthy of being let in on her plans.

"A couple of parties. Mostly parades."

"Tell me when and tell me where."

Tess folded her arms, but nodded. "Okay. Things start picking up next week. We can look at the schedule and pick a few. There will be dozens leading up to Mardi Gras itself."

Sam knew the Carnival season lasted more than a weekend, but hadn't realized it went on for the better part of a month. "Sweet."

"And speaking of parties, I meant to invite you to one some friends of mine are having this weekend."

Sam was pretty sure Tess didn't issue such invitations lightly. "I'd love to."

"It's Saturday, late afternoon. Not Mardi Gras themed, just a cookout. They've got kids, so it's a grill and hang out sort of party, not a drunken orgy." Tess shrugged. "Just so you know what you're signing up for."

Sam chuckled. "Contrary to whatever image you have of me, I'm really not a drunken orgy kind of woman."

Tess smirked. "Point taken."

"Wait."

"What?"

Sam scowled. She took out her phone and pulled up her calendar. "I have plans on Saturday."

"Oh. It's fine. Not a big deal." Her words said so, but the look on Tess's face made Sam think otherwise.

"I promised to go to this thing with my cousin. One of her work-slash-yoga friends is having a party."

"Oh, that's cool. I think it's great that you're reconnecting with her."

"Yeah." It was nice, even when it interfered with something Sam might rather be doing. "I'd still rather hang out with you."

"You can't cancel on her." Tess wagged a finger. "Don't worry, I'll drag you to something else to make up for it."

"Promise?"

"Promise. Are you going to come to the show at the Old Point next week?"

"Wouldn't miss it."

"It'll be a lot of the same people from the party. I'll introduce you around."

"I'll take it."

They cleaned up their dishes, putting the leftover food in the fridge for Carly and Becca, then moved to the couch. Tess pulled up the parade schedule and walked Sam through her preferred parades and festivities, including a couple that would run next week. Sam fought the urge to take notes, but only because she figured Tess would make fun of her.

Dustin didn't stir again and Carly and Becca got home a little after eleven. They joked about it being past their bedtime, so Sam and Tess said their good-byes. In the car, Sam glanced over at Tess, feeling desire, but also a hint of something more. Probably just a reaction to having baby time. "Come home with me?"

Tess's smile was slow and sultry. "I thought you'd never ask."

Chapter Nineteen

After Valentine's Day, Tess had two back-to-back closing shifts at the restaurant. Both times, Sam wandered in for a late dinner, leveraging her Jacuzzi tub to talk Tess into heading to her place instead of home. The second night, they didn't even have sex. If it felt like they were teetering on the edge of relationship territory, neither of them said anything and Tess specifically chose not to analyze it. She stayed the night after that, too, and more than made up for the night of abstinence.

The morning of Zack and Laura's party, Tess woke late, leaving her only a few minutes to linger in bed before having to get ready for work. Sam lay sprawled on her back and Tess curled up against her with her arm across Sam's chest and a leg thrown over her thigh. Sam stopped playing with Tess's hair and pressed a kiss to her temple. "Are you sure you have to go to work?"

Tess shifted her arm so she could poke Sam lightly in the ribs. "Yes. Not all of us can be independently wealthy."

Sam lifted her head and scowled. "Hey. I work."

Tess rolled on top of Sam, pushing herself up and straddling Sam's hips. She moved back and forth a little, eliciting a groan from Sam. "I don't think it's quite the same thing."

Sam continued to frown. "I might not punch a time clock, but if I didn't work, I wouldn't have any money. It's not like I'm a trust fund baby."

Tess nodded, not at all convinced. She still didn't understand exactly what Sam did for a living, but it was hard to imagine Sam earned enough doing it to support her lifestyle. "And what is it you do again?"

"I told you. I poke around interesting places and then sit at my computer most of the day."

Tess shook her head. "I'm not sure I buy it. How is that a job? Or, perhaps I should say, how is that a job that pays well?"

Sam turned quickly and, before Tess knew it, she was flipped onto her back and Sam was braced over her. "It's all just a cover for what I really do."

"Spy?"

"I prefer the title International Woman of Mystery."

Sam leaned down and kissed her, a slow, deliberate kiss that Tess felt certain aimed to distract her from the conversation they were almost having. She considered resisting. It was one thing when they spent an occasional afternoon together. Whatever was between them had morphed into something more. They were, at the very least, dating. Not that she needed to know all her secrets, but this felt silly.

Then again, did it really matter? At the end of the day, Sam was still just passing through. It was probably a good idea to keep things superficial. So if Sam didn't want to talk about her work, Tess wasn't going to pry.

Sam stopped kissing her and pulled back enough to look in Tess's eyes. "What? You don't think I'm funny?"

Tess smiled, willing away the questions and the doubts they stirred up. "Oh, you're plenty funny."

"And sexy, too?"

Tess rolled her eyes. "And sexy, too."

"So you'll let me have my way with you before you go to work?"

"Well…"

"I'm not going to see you all day."

"When you put it that way." Tess leaned up to pull Sam into another kiss. She hooked her legs around Sam's thighs and pulled her close. She smiled at Sam's moan of pleasure and skimmed her nails lightly along Sam's back.

Sam leaned back slightly and gave her a stern look. "Let's remember who is having their way with whom."

Tess looked at her through lowered lashes. "I wouldn't dream of standing in your way."

❖

When her shift ended, Tess hustled home. After a quick shower, she threw on a pair of shorts with a flowy peasant tank top and sandals. Knowing she'd be outside much of the day, she opted for just a little mascara and lip gloss before grabbing her keys and sunglasses and heading out.

The party was in full swing by the time she arrived, with cars filling the driveway and lining the street. She pulled up behind the last one, snagged the six-pack she'd picked up on her way, and went straight to the backyard. She unlatched the gate and let herself in. There was a rough circle of lawn chairs set up in the yard, another six or seven on the newly finished deck. Kids ran around the swing set, smoke wafted from the grill, and music came from speakers that had been set in the windows. It was, to her mind, a perfect afternoon.

Zack looked up from his position behind the grill and caught her eye. "You made it!"

"Wouldn't miss it." She lifted the beer. "Cooler or fridge?"

"I've got a cooler right up here."

Tess weaved her way through the chairs and up onto the deck, greeting people as she went. After taking one out for herself, she nestled the remaining bottles into the ice and closed the lid. Zack reached over with an opener to pop the cap, then clinked his bottle against hers. "Cheers."

"Cheers. The deck looks great."

"Thanks. We're really happy with it. I'm glad we ended up hiring a contractor."

"Yeah. Some things are better left to the experts."

Tess went inside to find Laura and grab a plate. In the kitchen, she waved a hello, then stopped short. "Sam?"

The person whose back had been to her turned. It was, in fact, Sam. Her face registered the same level of surprise Tess felt. "Tess."

"What are you doing here?"

"I'm at a party with my cousin, like I said when I told you I couldn't go to your thing. What are you doing here?"

"I'm at a party at my friend's house, the one I invited you to."

Laura gazed back and forth between Sam and Tess. "Wait. Tess, is Sam the person you're dating?"

"Yes?" Tess answered hesitantly, like it might be a trick question. She looked at Laura. "You know Sam?"

"We've met a couple of times. Elisa invited her for happy hour once, then started dragging her to yoga on Saturday mornings. You've met Elisa a couple of times, right?"

Tess looked at Elisa and nodded slowly. "I think she came with you to a couple of our shows."

Elisa, who stood next to Sam but had otherwise remained silent, spoke up. "Yes, that's how I know you. Sam, why didn't you tell me this was who you were seeing?"

Sam raised both hands in the air. "I didn't know you knew each other."

Everyone laughed and Laura shook her head. "Figures."

Elisa nodded. "Yep."

Sam furrowed her eyebrows. "What figures?"

Tess put a hand on Sam's arm. "For being a big city, New Orleans is a shockingly small town. Everybody knows everybody. If not that, they're somehow related."

"I see." Sam found that funny, but also disconcerting. That sort of thing still happened in her parents' neighborhood. For her, it was usually a matter of asking whose kid she was followed by an assertion that she sure had grown up. Most of the time, it left her vaguely uncomfortable—a strange mix of being both an insider and an outsider. This was different, though. Maybe, even, kind of cool.

Laura put her hands on her hips. "Tess, I thought you were seeing someone who didn't have any ties to the area."

Sam felt the need to come to Tess's rescue. "I didn't, or at least I didn't think I did when we met. My mom reminded me Elisa lived here and we recently reconnected."

"Nice." Laura nodded. "Tess, I think that makes Sam a local by extension. Or at least close to it."

Sam turned to Tess. "Is that a good thing or a bad thing?"

Before Tess could answer, Laura's husband came in from the deck. "Hey, looks like everyone's getting acquainted." When all four women laughed, he raised a brow. "What'd I miss?"

Laura excused herself to explain and help him get more burgers for the grill. Sam turned her attention back to Elisa and Tess. They didn't need introductions per se, but Sam wanted to give each of them some additional context. When they headed back outside, Sam got pulled into a fierce game of bocce. At one point she glanced over and saw Tess painting the toenails of one of Laura and Zack's little girls. Sam found herself in a conversation with Mo, who played bass in Tess's band.

"Not to be too stereotypical lesbian or anything, but our softball team is looking to pick up a couple of members. It's a super-casual league, no competitive streak or mad skills required."

Sam chuckled. Part of her wanted to say yes on the spot. She'd lettered in softball in high school—she was a lesbian, after all—and missed playing. But she had no intention of being around past the end of May. She hadn't found an apartment yet, but her sights were set on Barcelona. For the first time in as long as she could remember, the idea of the next new place didn't thrill her. Of course, Mo didn't need to hear all that. "Thanks. It sounds like fun. Let me know the specifics and I'll see if I can make it work."

As the sun began to set, someone got a fire going in the stone pit in the center of the yard. A guitar appeared, along with a panel of ridged metal Sam realized was a washboard and a harmonica. The music started and it felt like everyone sang along. Even without knowing any of the words, Sam got caught up in a refrain or two. And while part of her wanted to be near Tess, touching her, Sam enjoyed her vantage point on the opposite side of the fire. Tess's skin glowed in the warm light and her voice, while not louder than the others, seemed to permeate Sam.

As the party wound down, Sam pitched in with cleanup. Rather than a chore, it made her feel like part of the family. In one way, it made Sam miss her own family. It also made her long for something that she wasn't sure she'd ever experienced in the confines of her blood relatives.

People began to leave and Sam sought out Tess. She liked that they'd been at the same party, spent some time together, but also mingled separately. Even though they didn't officially come together, something about that dynamic felt fresh, different. It occurred to her that, maybe with the exception of New York, she didn't have a circle of friends like this anywhere. Maybe that was the yearning she'd felt earlier. As much as she liked her life, it did lack that strong sense of community. Until now, she'd not considered it all that important.

Not wanting to dwell on the things her life might be lacking, she focused her attention on trying to schedule her next date with Tess. She considered trying to convince Tess to come home with her, but settled for an invitation to join Tess and Carly and Becca for one of the upcoming parades. She stole a kiss in Laura and Zack's driveway, then rustled up her wards. She'd promised to serve as designated driver for Elisa and her friend Chloe and wanted to get them home before it got too late. After dropping them both off, Sam made her way home. Tess—and the new territory they seemed to be charting—continued to occupy her thoughts.

CHAPTER TWENTY

Sam was knee deep in Clayton's third murder when her phone buzzed and snapped her back to reality. The text from Prita made her scowl.

WTF were you thinking????

It wasn't unusual for Prita to question her judgment, but at least Sam generally knew the cause of her ire.

WTF are you talking about?

The only thing Sam got in reply was a link. She clicked on it and found herself at the site of one of those men's magazines that tried to be like *Esquire*, but always seemed to fall short in both polish and sophistication. The article in question boasted the headline "Sid Packett Knows What He Likes."

Sam skimmed the article, then went back and read it more thoroughly. In it, Sid was painted as a consummate playboy, a man who kept his anonymity, in part, to facilitate his love-'em-and-leave-'em philosophy of women. The artfully used quotes made Sid seem like a complete misogynist. And to top it off, the story included a sneak preview of Sid's next book, *The Ninth Informant*—information not yet public.

She didn't understand. The marketing division of her publishing house sometimes went out on a limb, but they'd never done anything without her knowledge or consent. And since all of that usually funneled through Prita, it made even less sense. She closed the article and dialed Prita.

"Seriously, what the fuck were you thinking?" Prita said in lieu of a hello.

"I wasn't. I mean, I didn't. It wasn't me."

The silence on the other end told Sam that Prita didn't know any more about this than she did. Eventually, she said, "You didn't talk with any reporter."

Exasperation briefly replaced confusion. "Of course I didn't. And even if I did, I wouldn't do it without telling you. And I sure as hell wouldn't say such asinine things."

"Okay, this makes no sense."

"No shit."

Prita huffed. "Well, where the fuck did it come from?"

Sam rolled her eyes. If she knew, they wouldn't be having this conversation. "Would the marketing guys do this? I know they're perpetually irritated that I refuse most of their suggestions."

"They sure as fuck better not have." Prita was easygoing with most things, but she took her role as a manager and agent very seriously.

"Yeah, but if they didn't, who did?" As much as Sam didn't like the idea of her publisher going rogue in trying to promote her work, the alternative seemed far more problematic.

"The million fucking dollar question."

Sam rubbed her temple with her free hand. "So what do we do?"

Prita let out a disgruntled sigh. "For the moment, you do nothing. I'm going to do some digging, starting with the ass wipe who wrote the article."

"Might I suggest not calling him an ass wipe from the get go?"

"Thank you, guru of diplomacy."

"You're welcome." The banter helped to keep Sam from focusing too much on the problem at hand, along with the feeling of powerlessness it generated. "Are you sure there's nothing I can do?"

"Not right now. I'm sure you have work to do. Focus on that."

"I'll have you know I'm running ahead of schedule."

"Even better. Keep it up and I'll be in touch."

"Yes, Ms. Mookerjee."

Prita ended the call without saying anything further. Sam couldn't help but laugh at how compartmentalized Prita could be. When the woman talked business, she was all business.

Sam flipped back to the article and read it again. Some of it actually made her cringe. Worst, probably, was the insinuation that Sid maintained his anonymity to enjoy the company of women without fear of having to fend off gold diggers at every turn. Sam assured herself it wasn't because that part may have a thread of truth in it.

She knew better, but she couldn't resist scrolling down and reading some of the comments. They were even worse than she imagined. A few people expressed disappointment, especially in light of the fact that Sid's work didn't have the anti-feminist undertones that many mainstream mysteries did. Others went with repugnance and indignation. Most off-putting, however, were the virtual high fives. A lot of guys, it seemed, were in complete agreement.

Sam let out a disgusted sigh and put down her phone. Even if Prita got to the bottom of this quickly, the damage had been done. Well, at least in one sense of the word. Plenty of people in the book business espoused the belief that all publicity was good publicity. The idea that an article like this might actually help sales left a bad taste in her mouth.

Did it matter? Should it? For the most part, Sam brushed off the assumptions and personality traits people ascribed to her alter ego. But this was different. Even though she didn't think of Sid as an extension of herself, it wasn't like he existed completely apart from her. And to have it seem like he owned and embraced things she found loathsome, well, felt wrong.

Sam glanced at the clock and realized she'd wasted almost an hour. While she saved her work and shut down her computer, Sam tried to shake off the unease that had settled in her stomach. Something in the back of her mind told her this wasn't a marketing snafu. Of course, she had no basis for that beyond a gut feeling. And as much as gut feelings helped her protagonists get to the bottom of things, she knew better than to rely on them in real life.

As she mulled it all over, Sam had another realization. She wanted to tell Tess about it. Not who she was, necessarily, but the fact that she had this weird and stressful thing going on. She wasn't generally one for confiding in people. She attributed it more to not having a need to confide instead of not having anyone she trusted. Sam wondered if her current feelings had something to do with Tess, or maybe more likely, just how infrequently stuff like this happened to her.

In either case, she didn't have the time or desire to process it. She tried to shake off her annoyance, along with the shadow of worry, as she drove to Tess's. After picking her up, they headed to one of the suburbs just north of the city called Metairie. Tess let Sam unload the cooler she had brought and pull it along behind them. Sam let Tess take the lead in scouting out and securing the best spot to watch the parade. She kept one eye on Tess, but took in the sights and sounds around her.

The crowd was big, but it didn't have the press of people that Bourbon Street did. She wasn't sure how she could tell, but the crowd felt more local, too. Maybe it was the diversity—old and young, black and white and everything in between. It surprised Sam to see so many kids. When Carly and Becca showed up with a sleeping Dustin nestled into a Baby Bjorn, it didn't even seem out of place.

She was surprised, too, by how many people dressed up. A few were in full costume—superheroes and princesses and someone in a full bear outfit. Those not in costume sported striped leggings and feather boas, jester hats and gold sequins. A lot of people wore masks.

"I feel underdressed," Sam said, half to Tess and half to herself.

Tess patted her arm reassuringly. "You'll feel better once you have some beads."

"Is that so?"

"Absolutely. A cocktail will help, too," Becca said.

"Well, you are the experts. I'm sorry. Let me rephrase. Y'all are the experts." That earned her a chuckle.

Tess opened the cooler. She doled out cans of beer and plastic water bottles she'd filled with sangria. "I threw in some soda in case you weren't drinking," she said to Carly.

Carly accepted a Sprite. "Thanks. Now that Dustin is eating some solid food, it's less of a headache to pump and dump, but I still try to pick and choose."

Sam took a beer and turned her attention to the parade that had just started. A few of the floats looked like what Sam expected when she thought of a parade. Others were little more than pickup trucks decorated with balloons and crepe paper, with people in costume piled into the back. The marching bands were full of energy, if not in perfect formation. And then there were what Tess called marching clubs—groups of men or women, every shape and size, in matching over-the-top outfits performing routines that were at once ridiculous and impressive.

On top of the spectacle of it all, there was so much stuff. Even with one hand holding a beer, Sam snagged cups, doubloons, and at least three dozen strings of beads. Tess had been right. They did make her feel more festive. They also helped her feel like she belonged.

By the time the second parade ended, Sam had a pleasant buzz. She also had to pee like nobody's business. She felt silly disclosing either of those things to Tess. "Now what?"

Becca slung an arm around her shoulder. "Now we eat."

Sam nodded. She could always eat.

Carly raised a finger. "And pee. I've had to pee since the second parade started."

Sam couldn't help but laugh. She appreciated knowing she wasn't the only one.

Carly and Becca walked in front, holding hands. Tess linked her arm through Sam's, resting her head briefly on Sam's shoulder. "Did it live up to your expectations?"

"More than. Way better than Bourbon Street."

"Well, no nipples, but no puke either."

"It's a trade-off I'm happy to take."

"That's good. I'm not sure we could be friends otherwise."

They walked a few blocks, ending up at a po'boy shop that looked to be the destination of at least half the people who'd been at the parade. They took turns going to the bathroom while the others held their place in line. Sam stood in one line, then the other, unsure of the last time she'd waited so long for a sandwich and the chance to pee.

When the number for their food was finally called, enough people had taken their orders to go that they were able to snag a booth in the corner of the restaurant. Sam took a bite of her fried oysters and let out a contented sigh. As was so often the case in New Orleans, the caliber and cleanliness of the establishment had little to do with the deliciousness of the food.

After eating, Carly, Becca, and Dustin headed home and Tess and Sam strolled back in the direction of Sam's car. Tess looked at Sam, who appeared to be lost in thought. And from the looks of it, they weren't good thoughts. "Did you decide this was too tame for you after all?"

"Huh?" Sam's startled expression confirmed Tess's suspicion.

"I asked if this was too tame for your expectations of Carnival. You've gone sullen on me."

"Oh, no. Not at all. I had a great time." Sam flashed a smile.

"Even if I believe you, you've got something on your mind. Care to share?"

Sam took a deep breath, but didn't speak.

"Hey, I'm not trying to pry. You don't have to tell me."

"You're not prying." Sam shook her head. "It's nothing major. Just some weird stuff going on with work."

"Oh." Tess felt oddly relieved. "Do you want to talk about it?"

"Actually, this afternoon helped me forget all about it. I think I'd rather hold on to that instead."

"Okay." If Sam didn't want to talk, Tess wasn't about to push her. She didn't borrow trouble—for herself or anyone else.

"So, do we get to do this again?"

"Darling, we're just getting started."

CHAPTER TWENTY-ONE

It hadn't taken much cajoling to convince Tess to stay the night.
Again. At this point, they were spending more nights together than
apart. Not that Sam was complaining. She'd even managed to talk Tess
into giving her a cooking lesson that evening.

After Tess showered and left for work, Sam took a quick shower
of her own. She wanted to get at least two thousand words in before
heading to the grocery store. She poured a cup of coffee and headed into
her office. Before opening the manuscript, she checked her email to see
if Prita had made any progress on the media debacle. Sure enough, an
update sat at the top of her inbox. The resolution, however, left much
to be desired.

Sam picked up her phone and dialed Prita's number. Although Sam
got a hello this time, it was clear from Prita's tone that she remained
displeased.

"What do you mean it came from my official email account?"

"It came from your account. The guy forwarded me the message."

"That doesn't mean anything. He could have easily made that up."

"Yeah, but I had Peg check your account and it was there, right in
the sent folder."

"I don't understand."

"It was sent from your account. Who has access to that password?"

"Peg and I do. No one else." Sam thought for a moment. "Do
you?"

"I don't. So unless Peg's gone rogue, I'm thinking you might have
been hacked."

Son of a bitch. "I don't imagine myself immune from such things, but if someone was going to hack into my email, is that really what they'd do?"

Prita sighed. "I'm sure stranger things have happened."

"Now what?"

"Now I negotiate with the magazine. They printed the story in good faith, and it's not bad enough to threaten libel, so I'm not sure how far I'll get."

"I appreciate you trying." Sam realized with a flash of guilt she hadn't asked about Prita at all during their last conversation. "How are you otherwise?"

"Good. I've started looking at investment properties in New Orleans."

Sam chuckled. "Where did that come from?"

"You seem to be enjoying it so much. I thought I might buy a place that I could use when I want and rent out the rest of the year."

"Like your condo in P-town?"

"Exactly. You've converted me to disliking hotels."

"Not a dislike per se, just a preference."

"Whatever. I might fly down before you leave to scope out a few. You up for a house guest?"

"If the house guest is you, always."

"I'll keep you posted."

"Thanks, P." Sam was about to hang up when a thought occurred to her. "Prita, you don't think this email thing is related to my computer getting stolen?"

"Huh. It seems unlikely. It's like you said—if someone got hold of your passwords, you think they'd try to milk it for money."

It made sense, but the wheels in Sam's head had already begun to turn. "Yeah, but then where did they get the book teaser? That was saved in my Dropbox, but not in my email."

"And I pulled everything out of your Dropbox. I mean, someone could have gotten to it before I did that, but they'd have to have known what they were looking for."

"Yeah. I don't like it. I'm going to go change all my passwords."

"I thought you already did."

Sam cringed. "I did it for all my bank and credit card stuff. I did my main email, but not that one. Which didn't seem entirely dumb at the time."

"I think that's how hindsight works."

Sam's jaw tightened. She hated that she deserved that. "Thanks."

"Sorry. Let me know if you need anything."

After hanging up, Sam logged into her account and started rifling through her sent mail. She saw the email to the editor of the magazine, but no other sent mail. Of course, that didn't mean anything, since sent mail was just as easy to delete as anything else. She changed her passwords, sending Peg a message to let her know.

Sam worked for a few hours, fine tuning a few of her early chapters and drafting the one leading up to the climax. At this point, Clayton had all but abandoned art forgery, getting both his sexual and creative satisfaction by killing women and then painting them before disposing of their bodies. With a compulsive need to increase the thrill, he set his sights on the daughter of the lead investigator—a twenty-two-year-old who was part ingénue, part femme fatale. The hubris, paired with Detective Boudreaux's tenacity, would be his undoing.

Satisfied with her work, and distracted from her email fiasco, Sam shut down the computer and headed to the store. As she roamed the aisles and filled her cart, she couldn't decide what amused her more— the length of the list for making one dish or the extensive notes Tess included to explain ingredients Sam might not understand. In the end, she laughed at herself, since even with the notes, she needed to seek out help with a few of the items.

❖

Tess had never been asked to give a cooking lesson before. When Sam asked for a gumbo tutorial, Tess couldn't decide if it was from a true desire to learn or wanting Tess to cook for her. In truth, she was fine with it either way. She'd been wanting to play in Sam's gorgeous kitchen. On top of that, Sam had offered to do all the shopping.

She finished up the lunch shift a little after three and headed to Sam's. When she got there, Sam greeted her with a kiss, but immediately retreated back to her office. "I just need twenty minutes to wrap up some work. Make yourself comfortable."

Since Tess had brought a change of clothes with her, she opted for a quick shower before getting started. Sam's bathroom was the most luxurious one she'd ever been in. The shower, which was separate from the tub, was huge. Not only did it have two main showerheads, it had those sideways sprayers. It was like being in a car wash, but in a good way.

By the time she got back downstairs, Sam had emerged from her office, eyes bleary and hair disheveled. Sam blinked at her a few times, as though she'd forgotten Tess was there, then ran her fingers through her hair a few times. Her vision seemed to focus and she offered Tess a smile. "Sorry I kept you waiting."

Tess regarded her with concern. "No worries. I helped myself to your shower. Are you okay?"

"I'm great."

"You look a little…haggard."

Instead of taking offense, Sam laughed. "In my line of work, that's a good thing. It means I've had a very productive day."

Tess nodded. "Okay, then."

Sam led the way to the kitchen. "I bought everything you had on the list. It's all on the counter except for what needed to go in the fridge."

"Thank you. I really could have brought things, but it was sweet of you to get them."

"If I'm going to learn how to do this, I'll need to have the ingredients around, right?"

Tess shrugged. "You have a point. That said, if you want to dabble in cooking, there are easier places to start."

"I'm going to take copious notes. I'm really good at notes."

She poked Sam in the ribs. "That's what I'm worried about."

"Hey. Don't be knocking my attention to detail."

"I'm not. Promise. Notes are great for baking. Cooking, though, it's more about feel."

Sam wrapped an arm around her, sliding her hand down Tess's back to cup her ass. "I'm pretty good at feel, too."

Tess swatted her hand away. "Again, I'm not sure those are transferable skills."

"No faith. How about you cook, I watch, then we'll see?"

Tess tried to keep her face stern, but couldn't suppress a smile. "We'll see all right."

She turned to the fridge. Inside, she found a bag of shrimp and a pound of andouille, along with the vegetables she'd requested.

Other than that, there were two bottles of wine, some beer, a bottle of hot sauce, and a handful of takeout containers. She pulled out the ingredients and looked back at Sam. "Do you cook at all? Like, ever?"

"I made eggs just yesterday. With toast."

"Seriously?"

Sam crossed her arms defensively. "I'm surrounded by dozens of extraordinary restaurants. I'm enjoying the local flavor."

Tess shook her head. "I don't even want to know what you spend on restaurants in a year."

"I make good money. I like to think I'm doing my part to help the local economy."

Exactly the kind of person who kept her gainfully employed. "Hard to argue with that."

"So what do we do first?"

"First, we make a roux."

"Sounds fancy. What's a roux?"

"Fat and flour."

Sam made a face. "Really?"

"You'd be amazed what a little fat and flour can do. But since we're learning, let's do some prep work first. It will make everything easier."

After watching Sam butcher a poor defenseless onion, Tess set her to peeling shrimp while she chopped the remaining vegetables. She put the shells on the stove with some water to make a quick stock, then had Sam slice the andouille. Normally, she'd do that while getting the roux going, but she wanted Sam to have her hand in each step of the process. Besides, they had all day.

When everything was set, Tess nodded. "Now, we make a roux."

She stationed Sam at the stove with a wooden spoon, stirring the mixture of vegetable oil and flour. "Just keep doing that. You want it to get good and brown without burning."

"How long does it take?"

"About two beers."

Sam raised a brow. "Huh?"

"The old Cajun adage is that a roux should be done in as long as it takes you to drink two beers. Really, it's about twenty minutes."

"I love a culture where time is marked by number of drinks consumed."

Tess loved the spirit of it, if not the logistics. "I personally gave up drinking that fast in my early twenties, but if you want to give it a shot..."

"I think I'm good."

"Well, then, we cook it until it's dark brown. Can you handle stirring duty?"

"Is that a trick question?" Sam looked offended.

"Not at all. You have to stir it constantly, so the bottom doesn't burn."

"On it."

"And even if you don't drink two beers, having one while you tend the stove is practically required."

"I like the way you think."

Tess went to the fridge and pulled out two bottles. She popped off the tops and handed one to Sam. "Cheers."

"Cheers." Sam sipped her beer, but kept her attention focused on the pot. The last thing she wanted to do was mess it up. Or get scolded for doing it wrong.

It took forever. Like, seriously, forever. Small areas began to brown slightly and Tess coached her to keep stirring so everything would brown evenly. Sam watched as the mixture went from pasty to the color of peanut butter. She asked Tess at least five times if it was brown enough. Each time, Tess shook her head. "Not quite yet."

Sam started to worry when it turned the color of chocolate and wisps of smoke wafted from the pot. Tess assured her it was all part of the process and ordered her to keep stirring. Just when she thought they were on the verge of burning the whole thing, Tess took the bowl full of chopped onions, garlic, celery, and bell peppers and dumped it into the pot. "Keep stirring," Tess insisted.

The whole thing hissed and steamed and Sam thought her arm might give out. Eventually, Tess poured in the shrimp stock they'd made and offered to take over. Sam happily relinquished the spoon and stepped aside. They added the sausage Tess had browned, more stock, and seasonings. Tess plopped the lid on and told her the whole thing needed to cook for an hour before they could add the shrimp.

Sam finished her beer and pulled two more from the fridge. "This is hard work."

"It is not. It just takes time."

"And work. You know your restaurant serves gumbo, right?"

Tess shook her head. "Not only is that expensive, it's never as good as homemade. You'll see."

Sam was far from convinced. "If you say so."

Tess showed her how to cook rice, teasing her for trying to boil it like pasta. Then they split a loaf of French bread, smearing it with butter and garlic before putting it in the oven to toast. Even if Sam never attempted gumbo again, she filed away that technique, sorry for all the years she'd eaten her spaghetti and jarred sauce without garlic bread.

By the time they sat at the kitchen island with two steaming bowls, Sam was starving. Tess picked up her beer and raised it. "To home cooking."

They clinked bottles. "To home cooking."

Sam picked up her spoon. Although it smelled phenomenal, she took her first bite with hesitation. "It tastes like gumbo."

Tess folded her arms over her chest. "What did you think it was going to taste like?"

"But it tastes just like the gumbo at the restaurant, if not better. And we made it."

Tess laughed. "That is the point."

"I had no idea it would taste this good." Sam honestly couldn't remember the last time she'd tasted something so delicious. "Is it really because we made it? Like victory being sweeter when it's hard won?"

Tess raised a brow. "Maybe. Or maybe it's the fact that you always have more control with smaller batches, both over the process and the ingredients. Not that the restaurant uses shoddy ingredients."

Sam nodded. "Maybe it's love."

"That must be it."

Sam indulged in a second bowl. She considered a third, but decided she'd end up regretting it. Tess doled the leftovers into containers while Sam did the dishes. According to Tess, it would taste even better the next day. As full as she was, she was already looking forward to it.

When they were done, Sam looked around the spacious kitchen. "Do you think we could do a party here? Maybe a Mardi Gras theme?"

Tess considered for a moment. "Like something fancy?"

"No, no. Definitely casual. I had such a good time at Zack and

Laura's. I'd love to do something similar. I don't have a huge yard, but there's plenty of space inside."

Tess nodded slowly and looked around the room. "How do you feel about being home base?"

"Home base?"

"Your place is like two blocks from the best parade routes."

Sam hadn't considered that. That could definitely be a draw. "Oh, like a place for people to meet up. Is there a pre-party? Like tailgating?"

Tess smiled. "Sort of."

Sam grinned. "I'm so in. Tell me how many people you think we can get to come, what I can serve. I'm sure there's no shortage of great caterers around here."

Tess raised a brow. "Caterers?"

"Well, I sure as hell can't put together a spread for dozens of people. And there's no way I'm asking you to."

"Honey, caterers are for weddings. And cotillions."

Sam crossed her arms. "Are you making fun of me?"

Tess shrugged. "Yes. I'm sure your heart is in the right place, but my people are not fancy people. You should know that by now."

"Right." Sam shook her head. Most of the women she dated would jump at the chance to host a fancy party with someone else footing the bill. "So what do we do?"

"Pick a day there are good parades and tell people what time they can show up. Everyone will bring their own drinks and something to eat. You don't need to put out food unless you want to. Mostly, people will appreciate the bathroom."

"Seriously?"

"You know the saying."

"*Laissez les bon temps rouler*?" The motto was splashed across every gift and souvenir shop in the state. Sam couldn't figure what letting the good times roll had to do with her bathroom.

"No, the other one."

Sam looked at her blankly. She didn't know any other ones.

Tess grinned. "Ain't no place to pee on Mardi Gras."

"Of course." She hadn't heard it, but she believed it.

Sam grabbed her tablet and pulled up the parade schedule. They settled on the Saturday before Mardi Gras proper, partially because

Tess knew she'd be able to get the day off and partially because that was the day of the Krewe of Iris. Sam was fascinated by the idea of an all-female parade on that large a scale.

Then they made a list of names. Sam realized she'd met a good number of Tess's friends, as well as some of her coworkers at the restaurant. Sam texted Elisa, both to invite her and encourage her to extend the invite to her friends. By the time they were done, the guest list had over fifty names.

"You're sure you're okay with this?"

Sam rubbed her hands together. "So sure. This is going to be awesome."

CHAPTER TWENTY-TWO

The morning of the party was unusually chilly and overcast. Sam sipped her coffee and looked out the kitchen window. "Will they have the parade if it's raining?"

Tess sat at the island with her own cup. "Honey, if they canceled a parade every time it rained, we'd hardly have any fun at all."

"Ah."

"You don't have to go if you don't want to."

"Oh, I still want to go. I'm just worried no one will come."

"Trust me, everyone will come."

Something in Tess's tone made Sam think there was a double meaning in her words. "Because…"

"Because a little rain doesn't scare folks around here from a good time." Tess paused for a moment, then shrugged. "And because you and your place have a certain exotic air."

"Exotic?" Sam frowned. New Orleans had one of the most melting-pot feels of any place she'd been. The idea that she might be some sort of ethnic novelty to Tess's friends did not sit well.

"Yeah, you're sort of this funky blend of local and tourist. And you live in a neighborhood that's way swankier than most of my friends."

"Oh." That made Sam feel better. Sort of.

Because people were due to start arriving by nine, they didn't dawdle. After getting dressed, Sam put out the king cakes she'd ordered from the bakery Tess recommended while Tess made another pot of coffee. When the doorbell rang, Sam hurried to answer it.

Elisa stood on the other side with her friends Mia and Chloe in tow. Their arms were full of plates and bags and bottles. One of them carried a slow cooker. Sam took as much as she could carry and led them back to the kitchen. She left Elisa to do introductions and went back to the door to greet the next guests.

Laura and Zack arrived without their kids. "I hope you know they would have been welcome," Sam said.

"We took them to a parade yesterday. Today they get to hang out with Mawmaw and Pawpaw while Mama and Daddy play." Laura lifted a bottle of vodka and a gallon of orange juice.

Sam took them from her and motioned for Zack, who was carrying two big platters of something, to follow her. Even though Tess had told her to expect it, Sam felt compelled to say, "You didn't have to bring all this."

Zack set down the food and shrugged. "Y'all are providing the space. The least we can do is bring snacks and booze."

People continued to arrive and Sam watched her counter fill up. Donuts and a platter of mini quiches sat next to trays of deli meat, rolls, and six different slow cookers filled with various dips and meatballs. The amount of food was shown up only by the amount of liquor. Some people brought bottles of whiskey or vodka with soda and juice; others brought jugs of brightly colored hurricanes. There were no fewer than four varieties of Bloody Mary.

"You weren't kidding," Sam said to Tess.

Tess smiled. "Around here, the only thing worse than showing up to someone's house empty-handed is not eating and drinking while you're there."

"Good to know."

Sam wandered the house. She introduced herself to people she hadn't met and accepted countless thank-yous and compliments for hosting the party. She'd always been turned off by the idea of tomato juice, but, at Tess's urging, tried a Bloody Mary. "Where have these been all my life?"

"I told you."

Sam's whole house took on a festive air. Even people who didn't know each other seemed to have become the best of friends. And even though it was barely ten in the morning, everyone seemed at least slightly buzzed.

About a half hour before the parade was scheduled to start, people began heading out to secure their spots. They devised a system where

Sam and Tess each had a key to the house, along with one floater that people could use to get in as needed. Much to Sam's amusement, everyone seemed to leave with a water bottle or travel mug filled with some sort of cocktail.

When the house was mostly empty, Tess appeared at her side with two large lidded cups. "Is one of those for me?"

"I took the liberty of pouring you a hurricane."

Sam grinned. "So thoughtful."

They walked the short distance to St. Charles Avenue. The crowd was larger than the parade they'd gone to in Metairie. Sam surmised there were still plenty of locals in the mix, but tourists seemed to make up at least half the press of people lining either side of the street. Sam chuckled, thinking how quickly she'd come to think of herself as a local.

"What are you laughing at?" Tess's inquisitive look made Sam guess she feared she'd missed something.

"Myself, I think."

Tess waited for her to elaborate.

"For all the places I've lived, this one might feel the most like home."

"And that's funny because..."

"It's not. I think I'm amused because it hit me in the middle of Mardi Gras. I find myself scanning the crowd, trying to pick out the tourists."

Tess smiled. "Well, you do fit in quite nicely."

"Thanks."

The first float passed by and Sam allowed herself to be absorbed by the moment. She waved her free hand in the air, catching beads and a few doubloons. During the short break between the Iris and Tucks parades, she headed home to use the restroom. Elisa's friends Mia and Chloe walked out as she was walking in.

"Thanks again," one of them said.

"Definitely. Great party," said the other.

Sam held the door for them. "My pleasure. Thank you for coming."

The house felt oddly empty after the morning's festivities, especially with so much food and drink still around. She hoped people would take things home with them at the end. Even with her appetite, she'd never be able to eat it all and she hated the idea of it going to waste. After using the bathroom, she refilled her cup and Tess's. It felt a strange to have a buzz at one o'clock in the afternoon, but really, if there ever was a time to, this was it.

When she opened the front door, something caught her eye. Laying on the ground, right in the middle of the welcome mat, sat a little doll. Thinking it might be a dog toy, Sam's eyes darted around in search of who, or what, might have left it. There was no sign of a person or animal, not even a rustling from the bushes. She bent down to take a closer look.

Son of a bitch. It wasn't a dog toy. It was a motherfucking voodoo doll. The black fabric had a cartoonish face painted on it and thick yarn stood in for hair. And sticking out of the chest, a single straight pin.

Sam stared at it for a long moment. She hesitated to pick it up, although she didn't know if the hesitation was tied to some inkling of black magic or the fact that her front porch suddenly felt like a crime scene. Ridiculous. She didn't believe in black magic. She wished she could say the same about the crime scene part.

What should she do? It was Mardi Gras. The police had their hands full. And the last thing she wanted was to ruin the party. Not to mention drawing a massive amount of attention to herself. Sam's shoulders slumped. She should bring the police into it. Just not today.

Sam stood, pulled her phone out of her pocket, and snapped a few photos. Then she closed the door, walked back to the kitchen, and pulled a baggie out of one of the drawers. She reopened the front door quickly, as though she might find the perpetrator looming on the other side. Of course, no one was there. Even with a parade in full swing a couple of blocks away, the side streets remained quiet.

She opened the baggie and turned it inside out like a mitt, picking up the doll and then wrapping the bag around it without touching it. She told herself it was proper protocol for handling evidence, should it need to become evidence at some point. For some reason, that proved more comforting than admitting she was freaked out by what the doll implied. She tucked the doll, baggie and all, in the drawer of the foyer table. She'd worry about it later. But she couldn't seem to take her eyes off it.

The sound of people approaching made Sam slam the drawer closed and lunge into the open doorway. Mo, the bassist from Tess's band, and the woman she'd brought with her stopped dead in their tracks. Mo's guest, Angelique maybe, let out a small shriek.

"Sorry," Sam said.

"You trying to give us a heart attack?" Mo asked.

Sam laughed. "No. I thought you were someone else."

"You trying to give them a heart attack?"

"No, I promise. Hope I didn't give you too much of a fright."

Mo narrowed her eyes. "You okay?"

"Yes. Absolutely. I was just heading back to the parade."

Mo nodded, but didn't look convinced. "We'll lock the door on our way out and see you back there."

"Sounds good." Sam jogged down the stairs. On the short walk back to the crowd, she scanned for anyone who might be lurking in the bushes or behind a car. The only thing she saw was a trio of people meandering down the street with Styrofoam daiquiri-to-go cups. They looked about as menacing as a litter of kittens.

By the time she rejoined the crowd on St. Charles, Sam had mostly convinced herself the whole thing was nothing more than a silly prank. Much like beads, voodoo dolls could be found in practically every gift shop in the Quarter. And Mardi Gras, much like Halloween, would be prone to antics meant to have a spooky effect. She didn't know if that was true, but it sounded reasonable.

The problem with that logic was just how many pranks and weird coincidences she'd been having lately. Like, more in the last two months than she'd had in her whole life. Was it something about New Orleans, more hocus-pocus in the air? Even if that was the case, it didn't make for a satisfying explanation. Maybe she'd find a way to casually ask Tess. Not today, though. Today was for drinking and eating and fun.

She met back up with Tess just in time for the second parade. Compared to Iris, with all her white-gloved riders, the Krewe of Tucks felt like a rowdy frat party. Well, that wasn't entirely accurate. Raucous for sure, but the irreverence included some sophisticated sarcasm. "I had no idea the parades would be so different," she said to Tess.

"Yeah. Each Krewe has a distinct personality. I think that's what makes it fun."

The Tucks parade culminated with the king's float, which turned out to be a giant commode. Sam felt a bit like the Pied Piper, leading the ragtag group back to her house. A few people lingered over another round of snacks or drinks, but most headed home.

"Will everyone get home okay?" Sam asked.

Tess nodded. "Between busses and designated drivers, everyone is covered."

"Good. Does that mean I get to drag you to bed now?"

"I was going to try to deal with that first." Tess tipped her head in the direction of the kitchen.

Sam waved her hand. "Just leave it. I warned the service I was having a party."

Tess tipped her head to one side. "Service?"

"The cleaning service. They come every other Monday."

"Cleaning service. Right."

Sam got the feeling Tess was judging her. "I'm not lazy or anything. It came with the house."

"Sure. Of course."

Tess still seemed dubious, so Sam decided to change the subject or, more accurately, change it back. "Weren't we talking about how you're going to let me drag you to bed."

"Right."

"So, may I?"

Tess rolled her eyes, but smiled. "By all means."

CHAPTER TWENTY-THREE

The price Tess paid for getting the Saturday before Mardi Gras off was working the next four days straight. The restaurant stayed packed and Tess worked extra hours to keep up with the waves of people in search of sustenance between parties and parades. It was a blessing and a curse, really. She was exhausted, but she'd raked in more in tips than she usually did in a month.

By the time she pulled off her apron at the end of her shift Wednesday, she was glad Carnival season was over. She was glad, too, to be heading to Sam's. And not just for her tub.

Tess walked out the back door of the restaurant, stopped short, and stared. She turned and looked behind her, as though someone or something might be behind her that would explain what she'd just seen. Just the door and the same dumpster that always resided against the far wall. She turned back to look at her bike, thinking maybe she'd imagined it.

No, no imagining. Her bike stood where she'd left it. Well, sort of stood. It had been toppled over, but was partially held up by the lock looped through the gas meter. Both of the tires were slit, ugly jagged cuts that appeared to be from a box cutter. The seat was cut, too, and the basket on the front handlebars had been ripped off. Deep scratches crisscrossed the paint on the frame.

After taking in the damage, Tess looked around again. Nothing else seemed disturbed, and there was no sign of who might have inflicted such destruction. Or why.

She stood for a moment, trying to decide what to do. Was it foolish to call the police about a bicycle? It wasn't like it had been stolen, though, or doused with spray paint as part of a stupid prank. And the drunken revelers were gone. Even in a city as rowdy as New Orleans, things settled down on Ash Wednesday.

Tess wasn't sure why, but this felt malicious and, somehow, personal. She shook her head. This was the last thing she wanted to do with her night. She pulled out her phone and searched the non-emergency number for NOPD. While she waited for the call to connect, anger and unease wrestled in her chest.

"New Orleans Police Department. Is this an emergency?"

"No. I need to file a police report."

"Okay. What is your location and the nature of your report?"

"I'm on St. Charles at the corner of Napoleon, behind Superior Seafood. I need to report a…um…vandalism."

"Are you currently in a safe location?"

Tess glanced around again. She'd thought so. "Yes."

She relayed the details of what she'd found when she'd attempted to leave work. It was a slow night, apparently, so a pair of officers patrolling nearby would head her way. The dispatcher encouraged her to wait inside until they arrived. Tess thanked her and hung up.

Although she'd stood in that spot hundreds of times and never felt anything but safe, Tess found her eyes darting around, her skin prickly with discomfort. She hated to give in to it, but the entire situation was beginning to overwhelm her. She knocked on the back door of the restaurant and waited.

T-Jacques, one of the restaurant dish washers, opened the door a crack. Seeing it was Tess, he swung it wide and smiled. "Y'all forget something?"

Tess shook her head. "Someone tore up my bike."

"What?"

T-Jacques's presence, all six feet four inches of him, dispelled the unease, allowing Tess to focus on the anger. "Seriously tore up. Like, obliterated."

"Child, that's terrible. Let me see."

They were looking at the mess when the police cruiser pulled up. Tess assured T-Jacques that she was fine and sent him back inside so he could finish his work. She introduced herself to the officers and told them what she knew, which was unfortunately, very little.

"Do you often leave your bike here?" the male officer asked.

"I work here, usually five days a week. I ride my bike more often than not."

"And is it always in the evening?" The female officer, who'd been writing something in a notepad, looked up.

"I probably do half and half, days and evenings."

"It seems more personal than passing vandalism. Not to mention that the damage was kept exclusively to your property. Can you think of anyone with a grudge against you? Anyone who would want to threaten you?"

Tess turned that prospect over in her mind for what felt like the hundredth time. "I really can't."

The female officer gave her a sympathetic look. "No angry exes? No persistent suitors you've recently turned down?"

"I'm a lesbian." Tess scowled. Not that lesbians weren't just as capable of doing fucked-up stuff, but she didn't have any of those suitors, either. "Wait, you don't think this could have anything to do with me being a lesbian?"

"That's unlikely, but there's no way of knowing for sure."

"Are you saying there's also no way of figuring out who did it? Or catching them?"

The male officer shrugged. "If you can't think of anyone, then probably not. Are there security cameras back here?"

"I don't think so." Tess's shoulders slumped. Even though she expected that, it didn't prevent the wave of disappointment. "So there's pretty much nothing you can do."

"We can give you a copy of the report. It's good to have in case something else happens. It will help establish a pattern."

Sure. A pattern. That's exactly what Tess wanted to think about.

"You can also use it if you decided to file a claim with your insurance company."

Tess raised a brow.

"Your homeowner's insurance. It usually covers all of your personal property."

"Ah. Thanks." Tess didn't bother adding that her deductible was close to three times the value of her bike. She took the slip of paper with the information on it and watched the officers leave. She went in to let T-Jacques know she was leaving the mess there and would deal with it in the morning.

"You need a lift, Miss Tess? I get off in an hour."

"I'm just going a couple of blocks tonight, but thanks. You have a good night."

"You, too. I'm sorry about your bike."

"Thanks, T-Jacques."

Tess walked the short distance to Sam's place. Having her bike ruined sucked. It wasn't like she couldn't afford to replace it, but she'd grown attached to it. It had taken her a lot of places. She almost laughed, realizing it was how most people probably thought about their cars.

What bothered her most, though, was what the officer had said—more personal than a passing vandalism. It did feel personal. And yet, she couldn't think of a single person who harbored such ugly feelings toward her. That seemed more disconcerting than suspecting someone. If she didn't know who it was, how could she stop it from happening again? If someone really had it in for her, would they stop there?

Tess willfully set those feelings aside. She was being dramatic. It was far more likely this was a passing act of vandalism. Kids on a dare or someone strung out. Unfortunately, there was a lot of that in New Orleans. She'd pick petty crime any day over the more violent alternatives, but it still sucked.

By the time she arrived at Sam's, Tess had essentially talked herself out of it being anything nefarious. She focused on how pointless the whole thing was, a fact that made her angry. She stomped up the front steps and banged—perhaps a little too forcefully—on Sam's door.

When Sam opened the door, her face reflected a mix of confusion and concern. "Are you okay?"

"Sorry."

"No need to be sorry. I just wasn't sure it was you at first. Is something wrong?"

Tess rolled her eyes. "Oh, you know, just some punks tearing up my bike."

"What?" Sam's eyes widened. "Wait. Come in and sit down. Then tell me what happened."

Sam took Tess's hand and led her inside. They walked into the living room and sat on the sofa, Sam never breaking the contact. It was a tender gesture, almost enough to distract her. But when she glanced up from their laced fingers, Sam was looking at her expectantly. Tess took a deep breath and launched into the story.

By the time Tess finished relaying the whole thing, most of her anger had dissipated. In its place, a lingering sense of disappointment. "I understand that there's crime in the city, just like any city. I'm lucky this is one of the few times I've been personally affected by it and that it wasn't me who was attacked."

Sam studied her. "Is it me you're trying to convince, or yourself?"

Tess sighed. "Both, I guess. Robbery is one thing, you know? I can at least understand the motivation behind it."

"And this feels senseless."

"Senseless and brutish. I mean, did some kid—or adult—get a thrill from that? Was it some kind of dare? It just leaves me with a really negative vibe, on top of having my bike ruined." Tess rolled her shoulders. "I'm being dramatic."

"You aren't." Sam thought back to the one time she'd been mugged. She'd only had about fifty dollars on her, but the experience left her on edge for weeks. "You don't have to be physically assaulted to feel violated. Your job and how you get back and forth, those things are an ingrained part of who you are. Someone messed with that. It would be weird if it didn't get under your skin."

"Thanks. That makes me feel better."

"What can I do? Do you want a glass of wine? A hot bath?"

"I'm okay."

"No, seriously. Let me pamper you a little."

Tess seemed incredulous, but agreed. "I'd love both a glass of wine and a bath. You don't have to draw it for me, though. I'm not five."

Sam shook her head. Perhaps more than any woman she'd been with, Tess resisted anything that resembled being taken care of. It wasn't like she dated clingy types, either. Sam gravitated to women who valued their independence but appreciated the indulgence of having someone spoil them a little. She couldn't help but wonder if Tess actively disliked it or was simply unused to it. Either way, Sam wanted to show her that it didn't make her needy or weak. "Okay. You head on up. I'll join you in a minute."

Sam went to the kitchen and poured two glasses of wine. She walked into the upstairs bathroom to find candles lit and Tess surrounded by an almost comical number of bubbles. Apparently, she had no problem pampering herself.

"I already feel better," Tess said.

Sam handed her the wine. "Good. Can I get you anything else?"

Tess took a sip. "No, but you could keep me company."

Sam smiled. It might not be the coddling she was going for, but she'd take it. She settled herself on the closed toilet seat. "My pleasure."

"Can I confess something?"

"Of course." Sam leaned forward and attempted to ignore the flutter of anticipation in her chest.

"I added the bubble bath without thinking about the fact that you have a jetted tub. When I did remember, I turned it on and almost flooded the bathroom with bubbles. Apparently, you're not supposed to do that." Tess shrugged and lifted her hands. "Who knew?"

Sam smiled and shook her head. "Sorry I didn't warn you about that. It's a lesson I learned the hard way at the Ritz Carlton in New York."

Tess grinned and scooted herself a bit lower into the frothy water. "I'm so glad it's not just me."

"Yeah, I managed to cover the floor with a good six inches of suds. I sopped it up the best I could, took a shower, and left a huge tip for the housekeeping staff the next morning."

Sam sat with Tess for a while. Tess asked her about her day and Sam rattled off a few details about her work, including her field trip to a cemetery and the mountain of email she'd tackled. Part of her wanted to tell Tess more. The book was going so well, it was hard not to be able to celebrate it with someone. Even more than that, though, Sam wanted to share that part of herself with Tess. It was the first time she'd felt that way. It left her unsettled, but strangely hopeful.

Before Sam could follow that train of thought any further, Tess sat up. "Okay, I'm getting wrinkly. I feel a ton better, though. Thank you for suggesting this."

"I'm glad it did the trick."

"Wanna dry me off and have your way with me?"

Sam stood and grabbed a towel from the rack. "Absolutely."

Tess snickered. "I was kidding about the dry me off part."

"I don't see why."

Tess shook her head. "How about you go warm up the bed and I'll be there in a minute?"

Sam sighed. "If you insist."

"I do."

Tess pulled the plug from the tub, stood, and took the towel from Sam. Any consternation Sam felt about Tess's stubbornness vanished as Sam watched water and bubbles slide down Tess's body. "Do you have any idea how beautiful you are?"

Tess wrapped the towel around herself. "You're just trying to get me into bed."

Sam didn't have a problem with playful banter, whether the end goal was a moment of flirtation or getting a woman to sleep with her. Tonight, though, it didn't feel right. She wanted Tess to understand it was more than that. Of course, Sam had no idea what "more" meant, or what she wanted it to mean. She tried to shake off her frustration and focus on the moment. "Always. That doesn't make you any less beautiful."

"Flattery will get you everywhere."

Sam smiled, but the feeling didn't fade. "I'm sorry about your bike."

Tess hugged the towel around her middle. "Thanks."

"I'm glad you weren't there when it happened."

Tess placed her hands on her hips. "Are you implying I couldn't fend off some hoodlums?"

Sam realized what had been nagging her since Tess arrived and told her what happened. It didn't feel like the work of punk kids. And if that was true, Tess could have been in real danger. "I hate the thought that something might have happened to you."

Tess lifted her chin. "I can take care of myself."

Sam frowned. "It's not about that."

Something in her tone must have registered, because Tess's face softened. "Hey, it's okay. I'm okay."

Sam chuckled and shook her head. "I'm supposed to be the one making you feel better."

Tess smiled. "You did. You do."

Out of the tub, Tess stood almost a full head shorter than her. Sam had never thought of Tess as small or frail. Yet, in that moment, she wanted nothing more than to gather her up and keep her safe from anything and everything that might threaten her. Sam gave into the urge to cup Tess's face in her hand.

Tess leaned into it, but her face maintained a questioning look. "What is it?"

Sam struggled to find the right words. "I know you weren't in danger, but…"

Tess stepped back, breaking the contact, and took a deep breath. "I know."

She could have let the conversation end there. Tess wasn't looking for reassurances or emotional declarations. Hell, Sam didn't know if they'd even be welcome. But something shifted in her and she couldn't—or at least didn't want to—let the moment pass. "I know we haven't really talked about feelings, but I need you to know that you matter to me."

Tess didn't say anything at first. Sam searched her face for some sign of reaction. She realized how far out of her comfort zone she'd drifted and, for a brief moment, wanted nothing more than to take it back.

Tess took another deep breath. Then, in what felt like slow motion, she reached out and took Sam's hand. "You matter to me, too."

With her free hand, Sam loosened Tess's towel and let it fall to the floor. In the intensity of Sam's gaze, Tess shivered. "Are you cold?" Sam asked.

Tess shook her head. How could she be cold with Sam looking at her like that? Without saying anything else, Sam clasped Tess's hand more firmly and led her from the bathroom to the bedroom. She stopped a few feet from the bed and turned, placing her hands in the curve of Tess's torso. Tess worked her hands into the waistband of Sam's shorts and pushed them down, then tugged Sam's shirt over her head.

Sam guided them toward the bed. But instead of nudging Tess onto her back, or falling back and pulling Tess with her, Sam paused. She ran a finger along Tess's jaw to her chin. Tess tipped her head back so she could look into Sam's eyes. Tess saw the passion she'd come to expect, and the desire. Something else shone there, however. It was gentle, questioning almost. Tess had to fight the urge to squirm under the fervidness of it.

Slowly, gently, Sam eased Tess back. Sam followed, bracing herself over Tess. Sam kissed her, a lazy exploration of her mouth that left Tess breathless and aching. Tess wound her hands around Sam's neck, scraping her fingernails through the short hair.

Sam let out a small moan, then pulled back and looked at Tess. She lifted one of Tess's hands, then the other, over her head. She managed to hold both of Tess's wrists with one hand and Tess realized that she was gently, but expertly, pinned. "This time, you're the one who has to stay put."

The softly spoken command did more to arouse Tess than the kiss. Sam trailed her fingers from Tess's knee to her hip, up her side and back down again. Unlike their usual sex, Sam seemed determined to draw out every touch. As much as Tess loved the heat and need and urgency, something about this captivated her. She let her head fall back and gave herself over to wherever Sam wanted to take her.

After another languid kiss, Sam's mouth traveled back and forth between her breasts. Lazy circles with her tongue gave way to sucking, interspersed with just the right amount of pressure. The sensations traveled directly from Tess's nipples to her clit and made her whole body pulse with need. Sam remained there, relentless. Tess wondered if she might have an orgasm without even being touched. Just when she didn't think she could take any more, Sam shifted.

"Remember, no touching." Sam slid down Tess's body and settled between her legs. The anticipation, the need, was so keen that Tess struggled to keep still. Even then, Sam made her wait, placing feather-light kisses on the insides of her thighs.

"Please." She'd never been one to beg, but something in Sam's touch was unlike anything she'd experienced before. It stirred something in her, made her desperate for release. But more than that, too.

After what felt like an eternity, Sam moved so that her mouth covered Tess's throbbing center. Tess's entire body tightened in response. Slowly, softly, Sam began to move. Her tongue stroked Tess with just enough pressure to make her ache for more. But rather than driving her higher, Sam seemed to draw her out. Rather than a volcano erupting, the orgasm felt like gliding effortlessly into a warm and welcoming ocean.

"Sam." Tess half spoke, half sighed Sam's name again and again. Sam moved up her body, brought Tess's hands down to her sides, then gathered Tess into her arms.

"I'm right here," Sam whispered.

The weight of Sam's arm draped over her and the warmth of Sam's body lulled Tess into a trance. She felt satiated, but she also felt safe. Tess allowed herself to sink into it.

She stayed like that a long time. Although she didn't fall asleep,

Tess completely lost track of how much time had passed. She summoned the strength and coordination to roll onto her side. Sam was propped on an elbow, watching her. "I'm so sorry."

Sam furrowed her brow. "Why are you apologizing?"

Tess smiled. "I sort of left you hanging. I think I lost track of time."

"That means I'm doing something right. Besides, we've got all night."

"And I intend to use it." Tess shook off the haze that had settled around her and wiggled down the bed until their earlier positions were reversed. Despite Sam's professed lack of urgency, Tess could tell she was turned on. "You have an amazing body. Have I told you that before?"

Sam chuckled. "Thanks."

Tess slid her arms around Sam's legs. "Seriously. I think you have the sexiest thighs I've ever seen."

Without waiting for a reply, she leaned forward and took Sam into her mouth. Sam was swollen and hard; it took all of Tess's self-control not to nudge her right over the edge. Instead, she focused on the way Sam's body moved, the way it responded to her. She focused, too, on the feelings Sam had stirred in her. Tess did everything she could to channel them back to Sam and to give Sam an inkling of what Sam had given her.

After, they lay with limbs twisted up together and the sheet pulled loosely around them. Tess contemplated asking Sam if the sex had been different for her as well. She didn't know what to call it, though, or even if she could adequately explain it. She wasn't sure she wanted to make a big deal out of something that might be nothing. Instead, she traced Sam's breastbone with her fingers, enjoying the way Sam's bronzed skin contrasted with hers.

"Would you like to take a day trip with me?" The idea popped into Tess's mind and she asked the question without thinking it through.

"Absolutely. Where are we going?"

Tess couldn't help but smile at Sam's willingness to try just about anything. "I try to visit my grandmother once a month or so. She lives in a little town a couple of hours away. You've been talking about wanting to see Louisiana beyond New Orleans."

"I have."

"And I think you'll like my Mawmaw."

"I'm sure I would. When?"

Tess smiled. "I switched shifts with someone so I could be off on Friday. That means we could visit and go listen to zydeco music."

Sam grinned. "I can't wait."

CHAPTER TWENTY-FOUR

Before she left Sam's, Tess dashed off a quick text to Carly. They'd planned a lunch date for the following week, but Tess was feeling like she could use a dose of predictable, reliable conversation. When Carly agreed, and didn't seem suspicious about the last-minute invite, Tess took Sam up on her offer of the house's laundry facilities to wash her work pants and the change of clothes stuffed in her bag from the day before. She told herself it was practical, not domestic, to wash a few of Sam's things to make a full load.

Sam offered Tess both a ride and the use of her car for the morning, but Tess declined. As much as she'd love to get behind the wheel of Sam's gorgeous Audi, today was not the day for it. By the time she'd folded everything and dressed, Sam was squirreled away in her office working. Tess couldn't fathom what could possibly be so thrilling about her work, but Sam barely grunted a good-bye when Tess poked her head in to say she was leaving.

She met Carly at their usual spot, taking the streetcar instead of her bike to get there. When she relayed the details of the night before, Carly offered the perfect blend of sympathy and outrage. She said, "It's so pointless. Their mamas should've raised them better than that."

"Sam said the same thing, if not in the same words." Tess paused for a moment, then added, "She was very sweet after."

"Sweet? Do tell."

"She brought me a glass of wine while I took a bubble bath."

"Aw, that is sweet."

"And then we had incredible sex."

Carly grinned. "Even better. I love that she's brought out the vixen in you. You'd become downright tame."

Tess wouldn't have used the word "vixen" necessarily, but Carly had a point. As her sex life had grown increasingly sporadic, it had also become more predictable. Being with Sam had definitely shaken her out of a rut. Even with that in mind, though, last night had been different. Sam had been...tender. It was no less satisfying than their other nights together, but it affected her on a level that their previous times together hadn't. She wanted to relay that fact to Carly, but wasn't sure she had the right words.

"What is it?"

"I'm...it's...the sex. Not to be cheesy, but if I said it felt more like making love, do you know what I mean?"

If Carly wanted to laugh, she did an excellent job of covering it up. Instead, she tipped her head to the side and studied Tess. "I do."

"Maybe it's because I was kind of emotional? And I let her take care of me. I don't usually do that."

Carly shrugged. "Maybe."

"You think it's something else?"

"Only you can know what you're feeling, but the same thing happened with me and Becca."

"What do you mean?"

"I mean we'd been dating and the sex was great and then it was like a switch flipped. We were in bed together and I got this tightness in my chest and for a second I thought I might be having a heart attack. And then I got super emotional and cried."

Tess squinted at her. "You never told me that."

"Yes, I did. Becca panicked because she thought I was breaking up with her. When I finally calmed down, I told her I loved her."

"Oh." Tess remembered the story. At the time, her focus had been squarely on the fact that her best friend—the one who'd sworn off serious commitments—had fallen head over heels in the span of five weeks. Her mind leapt from that to the connection Carly seemed to be making. "Wait."

Carly lifted both hands in the air defensively. "I'm not saying you're in love with her."

"It sort of sounds like it." It was Tess's turn to panic.

"I'm only saying that there are different kinds of sex. I get it. I'm agreeing with you."

Tess didn't believe her. Carly was smart. And savvy. And she knew Tess better than probably anyone else. Hell. Tess took a deep breath. "I invited her to go to Breaux Bridge with me."

Carly raised a brow. "You're taking her to meet your Mawmaw?"

Admitting this didn't help her cause. Of course, that assumed her cause was still downplaying her involvement with Sam. "God, it's not that big a deal."

Carly folded her arms; she meant business this time. "You value her opinion more than what your parents think."

"So?" Tess's tone came across as petulant, but at this point, she wanted Carly to say it out loud. If Carly said what Tess was thinking, she wouldn't have to.

"So, I'm just saying you might be talking about it all casual, but you wouldn't be doing it unless you were at least a little bit serious."

Tess mulled over Carly's assertion. When she invited Sam, she hadn't meant it like that. She wanted Sam to experience another side of Louisiana. Right? It wasn't like she was bringing Sam to meet her family. She certainly hadn't framed it that way. They weren't that serious. Even though Sam had listened and been sweet and taken care of her. Even though the sex they'd had after left her with a warm glowing feeling that had yet to dissipate. Tess sighed.

"Well, you can't change your mind and uninvite her now."

"What?"

Carly shook her head. "I can see your wheels turning and I'm sorry I said anything. It doesn't have to mean anything you don't want it to mean."

Tess slumped her shoulders and shook her head. "No, you're right."

"I usually am. What am I right about?"

"I am taking her home to meet Mawmaw."

Carly smiled. "I think that's nice. And not only because it makes me right."

"Nice except for the fact that Sam's a serial dater who'll be jetting off to her next adventure in a month or two."

"Maybe this time she won't."

Tess rolled her eyes. "I don't think it works like that."

"Do you know that or are you assuming?"

"Ugh. Could we not have this conversation?" Why had she been so anxious to talk to Carly again?

"Yes, if you promise me one thing."

Tess closed her eyes. "What's that?"

"Promise me you won't shut down because of what you think may or may not be the case."

Tess opened one eye and looked at Carly with suspicion. "Have I really become that pathetic?"

"You're not pathetic at all."

Tess opened her other eye and looked squarely at her best friend. "I am if I need that kind of pep talk."

"You're cautious."

Tess scoffed. "I think that may be the first time anyone has used that word in reference to me."

Carly didn't laugh. "I know living in New Orleans still feels like an act of rebellion sometimes."

Tess sighed. For the first four or five years after Katrina, her parents used words like "impetuous," "stubborn," and "impractical" to describe her. "Selfish" had been thrown in, too. They'd stopped eventually, but more because they knew they weren't getting anywhere than the fact that they'd changed their minds. Even though the dust had settled from that time, the scars remained. "It wasn't supposed to be."

"But it was. I get it." More than a lot of people, Carly did get it. After the storm, the company she worked for relocated to Baton Rouge. When they decided not to come back, Carly quit. Finding a job in the city meant both a pay cut and starting her pursuit of a management position from scratch.

"I know."

"So when I say you're cautious, I mean you've had to find ways of balancing that out."

"And you're saying I do that with relationships."

"I think you choose women that won't demand too much. That way you don't have to compromise or disappoint."

"I hate it when you're right."

"And dating Sam in the first place was a compromise, so she's already working with a handicap."

"What are you suggesting?"

"Only that if you're enjoying the ride, there's no need to get off."

"That's a terrible metaphor."

Carly circled her hand over her head as if she were riding a bull in a rodeo or, perhaps more accurately, doing a cheesy dance approximation of it. "It's a great metaphor, which is exactly why you hate it."

Sam stared at the computer screen and smiled. The first draft was done. In the ten or so years she'd been writing, Sam didn't think she'd ever pounded out a complete draft in under three months. Not only was it done quickly, it was good. Sure, it needed work. First drafts always needed work. But the story was tight and the characters were some of the most nuanced she'd ever written. On top of that, she'd moved beyond gritty and managed to capture a level of darkness she'd never written before.

Sam's first instinct was to tell Tess. The desire to confide in Tess had been growing over the last few weeks. At first, she'd pushed it aside. When the feeling didn't go away, Sam began to think in earnest about what it would mean to open herself up in that way. Just because she never did, it wasn't like it equated to a marriage proposal or anything. Whether or not she and Tess stayed together—romantically or even as friends—Sam felt a connection to her that went beyond anything she'd ever felt with a woman she dated. And she trusted Tess.

Maybe she could do it. It wasn't like it had to be some grand reveal. And it would be nice to have someone besides Prita and her immediate family know. It might be the sort of thing that would help her stay connected to Tess even after she left town. She liked the idea of Tess in her life.

Feeling even more buoyant than when she'd typed "THE END," Sam decided to take a walk and pick up a late lunch. She contemplated stopping by to see Tess, but decided against it. She wanted their next time together to be special, and loitering at the bar while Tess tried to work was not that.

She walked away from St. Charles and toward the deli she'd discovered the first time she'd wanted to avoid hovering around Tess. Since the lunch crowd had long cleared out, Sam chatted with Miss

Louella while she waited for her food. She stuffed a generous tip in the jar next to the register and headed home with a spring in her step.

Sam walked up the sidewalk with her po'boy in hand. It smelled so good, it took a considerable amount of willpower not to tear into it before getting home. She noticed a manila envelope sticking out of the small metal mailbox to the right of her door. It looked out of place, given that she could count on one hand the number of times she'd received actual mail since moving in. She unlocked her door and grabbed it, making a beeline for the kitchen.

She set everything down on the island, then turned to the fridge for a Coke. She sat down and unwrapped her sandwich so she could take a bite. She sighed with pleasure, then turned her attention to the envelope.

Sam flipped it over and realized there was no writing or postage on the front. Weird. Maybe it was something from the rental agency. She pulled out the contents and felt a chill wash over her.

The envelope was full of pictures. Of her. At least twenty of them, each black and white and printed eight by ten. The first few were shots of Sam out in public—getting coffee, running in City Park, coming out of Villa Habana. As Sam flipped though, the images became more intimate. There was one of her on the phone in her living room, one of her having drinks with Elisa and her friends. The last few made her chest tighten. They were photos of her with Tess. One at Tess's restaurant, one from the night they went dancing. The last one was a shot of Sam and Tess in Sam's kitchen; they were kissing and Sam's hand was up the hem of Tess's skirt, cupping her ass.

Sam grabbed the envelope and stuck her hand inside, thinking there might be a note of some kind. Nothing. Nothing written on the back of the photos. Nothing at all to give her any indication who'd taken the photos, or why.

She flipped through them again, trying to piece together a message or motivation. The only theme was her; the only clear communication was the fact that someone had been watching her. In her experience, only two kinds of people did this kind of watching—private investigators and stalkers.

Sam shook her head. As far-fetched as both of those scenarios seemed, Sam had to accept the fact that one of them might be true. And since most private investigators went out of their way to stay hidden, Sam was left to face the chilling notion that she had a stalker. Who, or why, remained a mystery.

At this point, she knew she needed to get the police involved. Despite her interaction with them regarding the note on her car, she figured now they'd take her seriously. Unfortunately, that would come with lots of snooping and questions about Sam—her life, her past, the people she knew. She picked up the phone and called Prita. As soon as she said hello, Sam launched into what she'd just discovered. When she finished, there was silence on the other end. "Prita?"

"Fuck."

Sam's heart rate escalated even further. "You're supposed to make me feel better."

"Yeah, I'm not sure I can do that. This is bad."

"I know I need to call the police. I just need to figure out what I'm going to say to them. Do I tell them who I am?"

Prita sighed. "I don't know."

Prita always knew what to do. As an agent, as a businesswoman, as a friend. Sam's anxiety went up another notch. "My instinct is no. No one here knows. It probably has nothing to do with Sid."

"Unless this and the stolen computer and the book leak are related."

"Shit." As much as the recent events had put her on edge, Sam had considered Sid's drama and hers as separate matters. "You think?"

"Maybe. I think it's weird that all this is going down at the same time."

"When you put it that way." Sam's sigh held the trace of a growl. "What are we going to do?"

"Give me a day to think and look into some things. Either way, I think you have to get the police involved. Sid's reputation is one thing. Your safety is another."

Sam nodded, then realized Prita couldn't see her. "Okay. I'm going on a road trip with Tess tomorrow. Let's talk when I get back, then I'll bring them in."

"Sounds good. In the meantime, keep your guard up. Lock your doors."

Sam swallowed. When her mother said that sort thing, she didn't think anything of it. Now she had to accept the fact that there might be a legitimate threat to her. And not some general, unspecified danger, either. Even without knowing the who or the why, Sam could no longer pretend it wasn't personal.

She set down the photos and glanced at the po'boy she'd been so looking forward to. With a detached sigh, she folded up the butcher paper and tossed it in the trash. For the first time in as long as she could remember, Sam had completely lost her appetite.

CHAPTER TWENTY-FIVE

By the next morning, Sam had worked out what, and how much, she would tell police. Since she'd likely been targeted, at least initially, at random, she wouldn't lead with her alter ego. If their investigation made it seem like Sid was part of it, she'd fill them in. Having a game plan didn't lessen the unease that had taken root in her chest and the pit of her stomach, but it helped her feel more in control. For the moment, though, she tried to set it aside so she could focus on her day with Tess. She had a feeling Tess hadn't made the invitation lightly. Even if the premise was showing off some of Louisiana's small-town charms, it came with meeting Tess's grandmother. And, as she and Tess had discussed, grandmas were a big deal.

When she pulled up at Tess's house, Tess hovered in the driveway. At first, Sam thought something was wrong, or that maybe she'd thought better of issuing the invitation in the first place. But then it occurred to her to ask Tess if she wanted to drive and she was greeted with a big, slow smile. Sam switched over to the passenger seat, Tess climbed behind the wheel and, after a few adjustments, they were off.

Sam enjoyed watching Tess drive her car. Although she'd waited for Sam to extend the offer, she clearly enjoyed it. Sam couldn't blame her. She'd picked out the Audi in Dallas as a short-term lease, but she'd liked it so much she extended the terms and had it sent to New Orleans. With the sunroof open, Tess's hair flipped and twisted in the wind. Combined with her oversize sunglasses, the look reminded Sam of a carefree road trip in a movie from the fifties. Sam figured Tess would balk at being called glamorous, but in that moment, she channeled movie star.

They followed I-10 west, through Baton Rouge and over the Mississippi River. Shortly after leaving the capital, the land around them gave way to swamp. Trees grew out of the water, dripping with tufts of Spanish moss. Sam recognized the moss, but the trees were unfamiliar. She pointed to them and asked, "What are those?"

"Cypress."

"I've never considered myself someone who's into plants, but the stuff around here is fascinating."

"Definitely the hallmark of Acadiana. There's a lot of Louisiana you won't find in the Crescent City."

Sam nodded. "I like to venture out of the city limits when I'm in a new place, but I don't always. I hate to admit it, but having brown skin and being masculine of center has put me in some uncomfortable situations. It helps to have a guide."

"Yeah. I went to Gulf Shores once with a group of friends and we ended up in a bar that was dicey. I don't know if I felt truly unsafe, but it was close, and definitely uncomfortable."

It was nice to know she wasn't the only one. "So tell me about where we're going today."

"Breaux Bridge. It's a little town, close enough to Lafayette to be a suburb, but with its own personality."

"Has your grandmother always lived there?"

"She grew up there, then moved to Darrow when she married my grandfather. He worked at one of the refineries on the river. When he was killed in an accident at the plant, she moved back so she could raise her kids—my dad and his five sisters—closer to the rest of her family."

"And have you always been close with her?"

"Always. I spent summers with her as a kid, then I stayed with her for a few months after Katrina. She was my biggest ally when I was going back and forth with the rest of my family about moving back."

Even more of an influence in Tess's life than Sam had realized. Definitely a big deal. "She sounds like a special woman."

"She's a force."

After exiting the highway, they drove one winding country road, then another. When they pulled into a short gravel driveway next to a white house with a screened-in porch, Sam tried to calm the sudden flurry of nerves by soaking in details. Like so many houses in Louisiana, it sat on concrete risers about three feet off the ground. A woman with white hair and who looked to be even shorter than Tess opened the screen door and waved.

They got out of the car and Tess made introductions. What Edith Arceneaux lacked in height, she more than made up for in energy. She reminded Sam of her own grandmother, minus the sternness.

The house smelled like heaven. And with the table already set, Edith wasted no time sitting them down to a dinner. The crawfish étouffée, like so much Cajun food, was at once simple and complex. It was also about ten times better than the étouffée Sam had eaten in New Orleans. Even though she didn't cook, Sam had come to embrace Tess's adage that some things were meant to be homemade.

Sam tapped into her interviewing skills to get Edith talking, being sure to avoid topics that might create awkwardness for Tess. In truth, though, Edith didn't need a lot of prompting. She was filled with stories about Tess's childhood, what it was like to grow up during the Great Depression, being an advocate for the desegregation of Louisiana schools. She was also pretty adept at asking questions of her own.

"Tell me, Sam, how you pick the places you go?" She ladled a second helping of étouffée into Sam's bowl. "How did you pick New Orleans?"

"Part of it is my own interest—places I've never been or only visited briefly."

Tess gave her a quizzical look. "I thought you worked on assignment."

"I do," Sam said quickly. That wasn't a total lie; she gave herself assignments and deadlines. "I get some leeway in location, though, places I'd find interesting."

"I'm surprised you waited so long for New Orleans, then." Edith winked at her. "And what about your mama and daddy? Where are they?"

Sam talked about her childhood in Philly. She threw in the fact that her parents had honeymooned in New Orleans. "I guess there was quite the Cuban district back then."

Edith nodded. "I don't know about now, but back in the sixties, they called New Orleans New Havana."

"I didn't know that." Tess shook her head. "I learn something new every time I visit."

Tess and Sam helped clear the table and Edith brought out a cake covered in snowy white coconut. Despite her better judgment, Sam ate two slices, much to the amusement of both Tess and Edith. They lingered for a while over coffee, talking about family histories and traditions.

During the years Edith lived in Darrow, one of her best friends was the wife of a Cuban immigrant who worked at the plant with her husband. They'd introduced Edith and her husband to the Cuban neighborhoods of New Orleans, the same ones Sam's parents had visited during their honeymoon. Sam laughed and Tess pretended to be scandalized by the amount of rum and cigars consumed in those days. Although Edith had lost touch with them after moving back to Breaux Bridge, talking about them seemed to be a pleasant trip down memory lane.

When they offered to help with the dishes, Edith waved a hand and made a noise that conveyed dismissal. Tess rolled her eyes in a way Sam found endearing. "You said on the phone there were a couple of things you wanted help with."

Edith sighed. "There's a branch in the backyard that needs trimming and I promised your mother I wouldn't get on the ladder anymore, at least not without someone on the ground to hold it steady."

Sam had no trouble imagining the tiny woman teetering on a ladder with a pair of trimmers. Tess said, "I don't agree with my mother about much, but she's right. You don't mind holding the ladder for me, do you, Sam?"

"At your service."

"It's the pecan tree. There's a limb sitting on the roof of the house that has to go."

"We'll take care of it."

Sam followed Tess out the back door and to the small shed in the corner of the yard. With surprising dexterity, Tess pulled what had to be an eight-foot ladder from inside and started carrying it across the yard.

"I can help, you know."

Tess glanced back over her shoulder. "There's a pair of loppers hanging on a nail. Would you grab them?"

By the time Sam located them and joined Tess, Tess had the ladder set up and ready to go. "I'm happy to do it if you'd like. My reach is a bit longer than yours."

"Hero complex? Really?"

"Not at all. Just trying to earn my dinner."

"Likely story. I've got it, though. Will you hold the ladder and hand these to me once I'm up far enough?"

"Of course." Sam braced one hand on the ladder and her opposite foot on the bottom bar. As Tess began to climb, Sam asked, "Do I have to promise not to look up your skirt?"

"Nope."

Sam didn't actively try to peek, but she did enjoy the shape of Tess's legs as she made her way to the fourth rung. "Please be careful."

"Always. Hand me the loppers, will you?"

Sam flipped the tool so she could hand it to Tess handle first. The ladder wiggled slightly as Tess maneuvered. Sam heard the crunch of wood giving way. "Should I be covering my head?"

"No, Mawmaw was right. It's all just sitting on the roof. I'll give you a warning before I chuck it down."

Tess worked for another few minutes and Sam ruminated on how she was spending her day. As a writer, she made a point of putting herself into new and interesting situations. Still, she couldn't ever remember standing in a backyard, trimming trees.

She thought about her own grandmother. Sam had spent huge amounts of time with her as a child, but Abuelita had been the strong and capable one. By the time those tables had turned, Sam was off at school or exploring a new book location. Her brothers were around, so it wasn't like Abuelita wanted for helpers—or grandchildren, for that matter—but Sam couldn't help but feel a pang of sadness that she wasn't around for chores like these.

"I think I'm about done up here. Look out below."

Sam snapped out of her reverie and ducked her head a little farther under the ladder. Sticks and branches started falling around her. Aside from a couple brushes on the arm, Tess managed to avoid hitting her. "You're quite good at this."

One more snip, one more branch. "You sound surprised."

"Not surprised," Sam said quickly. "Impressed. Probably because I'm completely unaccustomed to yard work."

"Oh. Well, in that case, thank you. Will you take these from me?"

Sam took the loppers, keeping her other hand securely on the ladder while Tess climbed down. "Very impressed indeed."

Back on the ground, Tess smiled. "If we bring these out to the street, the town will pick them up. Will you give me a hand?"

"Of course."

They dragged and carried the branches around the side of the house, making a pile near the mailbox. They returned to the backyard to stow the tools, then stood for a moment admiring their work. Edith emerged from the house, wiping her hands on a dish towel. Tess put her hand on Sam's arm. "Would you mind if I invited her to go out with us? She loves zydeco and I don't think she gets to hear it live as much as she'd like."

"Seriously?" Sam hadn't thought she could like Tess's grandmother any more than she already did.

"We don't have to. I understand if you'd rather it be more like a date."

Sam looked at Tess's frown and realized she'd misunderstood Sam's meaning. "No, no. I'd love her to join us. I just don't normally associate grandmothers with bars."

Tess's face relaxed. "Technically, it's a dance hall."

"Right, right. Well, I think it's a great idea." Not that they were keeping score, but based on the smile Tess flashed, Sam was fairly certain she'd just earned a lot of girlfriend points.

CHAPTER TWENTY-SIX

An hour later, Sam found herself in a large space not unlike other dance clubs she'd patronized. Sure, exposed incandescent bulbs took the place of disco lights and the walls had wood paneling to match the scarred wood floors, but the essence of the space—and its purpose—came through. They sat at one of the square tables lining the dance floor, sipping beers and watching the band set up. Between Edith and Tess, it seemed like they knew half the people in the place by name. Sam got introduced more often than not, and the warm greetings made her feel less like an outsider.

Once Edith settled in, she looked at Sam. "Did Tess tell you her cousin is in the band?"

Sam turned to Tess with a raised brow. "She did not."

"Third cousin. He's my mama's age, so more like an uncle."

"Nice." Keeping tabs on complicated extended relatives felt like something Cajuns and Cubans had in common.

Tess pointed at the stage. "The guy with the accordion, T-Frank." As if on cue, he glanced up, made eye contact with Tess, and offered a wave.

"What's with the T on the front of names? I hear it a lot."

Edith chuckled. "It's a shortening of petite, the French word for small. When little boys are named after their daddies, families throw on the T to know which one they're talking about."

"Ah. I've never heard that."

Tess added, "And when you hear people called Trey, it's usually not their name so much as they're the third in the family with the name."

"Fascinating." Sam decided she needed to work that into the book somehow.

A few minutes later, T-Frank stood at the microphone and welcomed everyone. With a quick glance back at the rest of the group, someone called out a count and the music started. The accordion reminded Sam of the six months she spent in Paris writing *The Long Shadow*. Then, however, the songs were languid and romantic. This was more buoyant. Paired with the violins—or maybe they were fiddles—the resulting tune had a definite bounce. She watched couples move onto the dance floor and fall into an easy rhythm. Most of them formed a circle around the perimeter, moving together in a way that made Sam think of a classic ballroom waltz. Others remained in the middle, keeping the beat, but throwing in more elaborate turns and circles.

"Are they singing in French?"

"Cajun French, which is pretty close," Edith said.

"I've never seen anything like this."

Tess turned to her. "Like what?"

"I mean, it's not weird or exotic or anything, but I kind of thought I'd seen all the variations of juke joints and dance halls there were. The music is unique and the dancing, it's like a cross between country and ballroom. Can you even find something like this in New Orleans?"

"There are one or two places, but you really have to look for them. Cajun is definitely not the same thing as Creole—music, food, or otherwise."

Sam mulled that over. It was a distinction she'd not given much thought to. "Are we allowed to dance?"

Tess raised a brow.

"Together, I mean." Sam hated having to ask, but she knew how small towns and conservative communities worked. Things had come a long way, but acceptance wasn't universal. Even if she didn't fear for their safety, she didn't want to put Tess in an awkward position. Even now, she'd think twice about dancing with a woman at any gathering of her family.

"Yes, we're allowed. Are you asking?"

Sam stood and extended a hand. "I most certainly am."

Tess took her hand and smiled. "Do you know how to two-step?"

"I can probably fake it well enough."

"That'll do." They made their way to an unoccupied corner of the dance floor. "Let's start with the basics and then maybe work up to something fancy."

"Yes, ma'am."

Tess took the position of follower, but her grip on Sam's hand was firm. "It's one-and-two, one-and-two. I can reverse lead. Just move in the direction I guide us."

Tess wasn't joking. Despite her position and her smaller size, she led them in a simple back-and-forth step to the music. She explained traveling and the most basic of turns. They danced one song on the perimeter, then joined in the traveling circle. Aside from an occasional misstep, dancing with Tess was easy, natural. And although it felt like a PG version compared to their night of salsa dancing, Sam relished having Tess in her arms. At once both intimate and casual, it made Sam think about being with Tess differently.

The next song was a waltz, which turned out to be almost identical to a traditional waltz. It gave Sam the opportunity to actually lead, not simply assume the position. They made their way around the room and Sam was struck by the idea that they'd essentially abandoned Edith at the table all alone.

"Do you think your grandmother would dance with me?"

Tess smiled. "I'm sure she would, but you'll have to get in line."

Tess angled her head and Sam glanced in that direction. Sure enough, Edith was on the dance floor, being spun around by a man who had to be half her age. "Why does that not even surprise me?"

"Because you're a quick learner?"

Sam chuckled. "Thanks. Really, though, she is a remarkable woman."

"She is. I love my parents, but I like to think that I take after her."

"Oh, definitely."

When the music ended, they returned to the table to sit and watch for a bit. Just as they did so, T-Frank spoke. "Some of y'all may know Tess Arceneaux, my little city mouse cousin. She's visiting today and I was hoping I might get her up here to do a couple songs with us. What do y'all say? Would y'all like that?"

There were a few claps and cheers from the crowd and glances in their direction. Sam looked over at Tess, who'd folded her arms and looked at T-Frank with feigned exasperation. Tess made eye contact with her. "Do you mind?"

"Quite the opposite."

Tess shook her head and stood, inspiring more claps and cheers. She made her way to the stage and Edith rejoined Sam at the table. "Have you seen Tess sing?" she asked.

"A couple of times. Once with her band and once doing jazz with just a piano."

Edith nodded. "She's got a gift. And she might be a city mouse, but this music is in her blood."

Sam watched as Tess climbed onto the stage. When she slipped a corrugated piece of metal over her head, Sam looked back to Edith. "Is that a washboard?"

"It certainly is."

Tess slipped something onto her fingers and gave T-Frank a nod. The music started and, sure enough, Tess joined in, tapping and scraping in time with the beat. She looked as though she'd been doing it her whole life. The song was a duet, with T-Frank and Tess singing back and forth at one another. Sam had no idea what the words were, but it felt playful, silly more than flirtatious.

The song ended and Sam asked, "What was that song about?"

Edith smiled. "A frog trying to sweet-talk a pretty girl into kissing him."

"So he can become a handsome prince?"

"Not this one. He just likes kisses from pretty girls."

"Does he get one?"

"In the end. He's quite a charmer."

Sam laughed and returned her attention to the stage. Tess removed the washboard and nodded when T-Frank whispered to her. The music began again, but slower this time. When Tess began to sing, Sam felt something shift in her chest. Although she expected Tess's sensuous contralto voice, something about her singing in French seemed deeply personal, intrinsic to who she was as a person. It wasn't that Tess refused to open up, but Sam found moments like this—unguarded and not actually intimate—were the times she caught glimpses of Tess's soul.

Edith's hand on her arm brought Sam back to her surroundings and made her realize a few tears had found their way down her cheeks. She wiped them away quickly and smiled. "Let me guess. That was a plaintive love song."

Edith shrugged. "In a way."

Sam nodded. "It was beautiful. I'm always amazed how much can be conveyed even without understanding the words. Sort of like opera, I guess."

"You're in love with her, aren't you?"

Sam considered denying it, but Edith's eyes were filled with understanding. "I'm not sure the feeling is mutual."

Edith sighed. "Tess can be a tough nut. She feels more deeply than anyone I've known, but she keeps it close."

"Did someone break her heart?"

"Not in the way you're thinking. Now, I'm sure there's been a time or two when a girl, or maybe a boy, has left her a bit bruised."

"But you're talking about something else."

"Katrina took her toll on buildings and neighborhoods, but she took her toll on people, too. And not just the ones who lost a loved one or their homes. She tore at the fabric of what people felt about New Orleans, their lives there."

For Sam, the dominant sense she got after the storm was one of resilience and determination to rebuild. Talking with Tess about her family, the decision whether or not to move back, had given Sam a glimpse into how much more complicated things were. Sam realized now, however, that she'd downplayed just how profoundly that time had impacted her.

"She learned that the things you think you can count on without fail aren't so certain after all. I wouldn't say she closed off her heart, but she definitely insulated it some."

"That makes sense." Sam understood it. She didn't know what to do with it, but she understood it.

"You shouldn't give up on her. She's not making it hard on you on purpose."

Sam had to chuckle at that assertion. Although she'd gotten over just how much of a hard time Tess had given her at first, it remained clear to her that Tess sat firmly in the driver's seat of how far things between them got.

"Do I even want to know what y'all are talking about?" Tess asked.

Sam had been so absorbed in her thoughts, she'd not even noticed Tess rejoin them. "We are waxing poetic on your rare talent."

"You're trying to distract me with flattery."

Edith wagged a finger. "Not at all. I haven't heard you sing in ages and I forget just how lovely it is."

Sam nodded her agreement. "And I've never heard you sing like this."

Tess rolled her eyes. "If y'all say so."

They stayed for another hour, talking about Tess's family—who had talent, who had kids, who had better get their act together before life passed them by. When they dropped Edith off at her house, she insisted on sending them home with the cake she'd made for their visit. Sam knew enough from her family that it would be rude to refuse. Besides, it was coconut cake.

Hugs were exchanged all around. When Edith pulled Sam close, she whispered in her ear. "Don't you let her scare you off, now. She wouldn't have brought you here if you didn't mean something to her."

Sam nodded, half thrilled and half terrified by the assertion. She turned her attention to Tess before her emotions got the best of her for the second time that evening. "Do you want to drive again?"

Tess shrugged. "I'm okay. Driving at night isn't nearly as fun."

"If you say so. Thank you again, Mrs. Arceneaux. I hope our paths cross again sometime."

"Please, call me Edith. And the feeling is mutual, my dear."

Sam and Tess climbed into the car, then made their way through town and back to I-10. Once they were on the highway and directions wouldn't be needed for a while, Tess allowed her mind to wander. Now that the day was over, she realized how much it was bringing a girlfriend home to meet the family. Even if she hadn't intended that, the end result shifted their relationship to a new level.

If she didn't think too hard about what it meant, Tess didn't mind it so much. She liked spending time with Sam. A lot. Regardless of the situation, Sam seemed at ease. She was attentive without smothering, smart but never condescending. And she couldn't forget amazing in bed. Being with Sam was the exact thing Tess had been looking for, even when she refused to actively look.

But that didn't change the fact that Sam would only be around for another month or two. She'd said nothing about sticking around longer. Other than that brief mention of being in Spain for the summer and fall, she hadn't talked about her future plans at all. Much less their future plans. All of which led Tess to believe there was no such thing as their future. As much as that had been the arrangement going in—what she signed up for and what she wanted—the uncertainty of it left Tess feeling hollow.

Tess shook her head and shifted in her seat, trying to shake off the melancholy that threatened to settle around her. She didn't obsess about the future, or the past. She refused to start now.

"You okay?" Sam asked. "Do you need to stop?"

Tess shook her head again and smiled. "I'm good. Just ready to be home, I think."

"You and me both. I hope, when you say home, you're not ruling out spending the night at my place."

Living life in the moment—that was her mantra. "I think that could be arranged."

Sam glanced over at her. "I had a really nice time today. Thank you for inviting me."

It had been a good day. That's what she needed to focus on. "I'm glad you came."

"I loved seeing a different side of Louisiana. I feel like I got to see another side of you, too."

Tess nodded, thinking about Sam charming stories out of her grandmother, helping with yard work. "I could say the same about you."

CHAPTER TWENTY-SEVEN

S am knew something was wrong the moment they pulled into the driveway. The porch light she'd left on was dark; upstairs, a light in the bedroom she never used was on. "Wait in the car."

Tess gave her a quizzical look. "What? Why?"

"Someone is in the house, or was."

Tess's eyes darted toward the house, then back to Sam. "How do you know?"

"The door is open."

Tess scowled. "Are you sure you didn't forget to close it all the way?"

"I'm sure." Sam tried to swallow the mixture of anger and panic rising in her chest.

"We should call the police. You shouldn't go in there." Tess placed a hand on her arm.

"There's a chance they're still there. I don't want to wait for the police."

"That's exactly why you shouldn't go in. They could be armed. Or high. Or both."

"Okay, you call the police. I'm going in." She didn't wait for Tess's response before climbing out and heading toward the house.

Figuring the element of surprise was the biggest thing in her favor, she crept through the front door and flipped the entire bank of switches. Light flooded the foyer and living room, as well as the front porch. The culprit was long gone, but had left one hell of a mess.

Overturned chairs and decorative pillows littered the floor, along with books and magazines. But the television remained on the wall, seemingly untouched. Sam walked toward the kitchen and found most of the cabinets had been emptied. Broken dishes mixed with emptied boxes of cereal, utensils, and cans of soup.

She walked to the office and switched on the light. More chaos, but her laptop sat undisturbed on the desk. Sam took the stairs two at a time. She stuck her head into the two guest rooms—not a thread out of place. Her room, however, was a different matter. The bed had been stripped. Sheets and pillows and the duvet sat in a tangled pile on the floor. What appeared to be every article of clothing she owned had been pulled from the closet and dresser. Again, the television sat untouched.

Sam looked over at the dresser. The small wooden box from her grandmother was gone. She'd kept the few pieces of jewelry she owned in it, along with mementos. Nothing of any real value. Something caught her eye and she walked over to investigate. A small square of white paper sat where the box had been. The message was in neat, block letters:

TAKING WHAT'S MINE.

Sam swallowed. What the fuck? She stood for a long moment, trying to decide what to do. A sound behind her made her spin around, brace for an attacker. Seeing Tess in the doorway sent a wave of relief through her. "What are you doing in here?"

"You didn't come out and I was worried something had happened to you."

"So you decided putting yourself in danger was the answer?" The idea of Tess caught up in this mess made her queasy. Sam stuffed the note in her pocket.

"You're the one who came in first. I wanted you to wait for the police."

Sam took a deep breath, tried to get a handle on the myriad of emotions that prevented her from focusing on any one thing. "Did you call them?"

"I did."

"What did you say?"

"That there had been a break-in. Then I gave them your address."

"Are they coming?"

"On their way."

"Okay." Sam ran her fingers through her hair. She needed a game plan and wished desperately she could have called Prita before the police. "Let's go downstairs and wait."

Tess gave her a puzzled look, but didn't say anything. Back in the living room, she looked at the television and cocked her head to one side. "They didn't take the TV."

"I know."

"Did they take anything?"

"Just a small jewelry box."

"Not your computer?"

"No."

"Do you keep any cash around?"

"Not much." Sam walked over to the console table where she kept a few twenties to make ordering takeout easier. They remained in the drawer, neatly folded. "The little bit I do have is still here."

"It doesn't make sense."

On the surface, Sam agreed. Her mind, however, had more of the pieces and was working to put them all together. Still not sure how everything fit, and not wanting to freak Tess out, she kept it to herself. "I know."

Tess didn't say anything else. She stood with her arms hugging her chest. Sam wanted to say something reassuring, but no words came. Instead, she paced back and forth, waiting for the police to arrive and trying to will away the angry knot in her stomach. Her mind continued to turn over the details. As desperately as she wanted it to be a random crime—someone looking for cash or things that could be easily sold—she knew it was something more sinister. Whoever had been watching her just took things to the next level.

When the police arrived, Tess kept herself in the background. It didn't take a rocket scientist to know that what had happened was no ordinary break-in. What Tess couldn't figure out, however, was the underlying motivation or who the perpetrator might be. She kept her mouth shut while Sam talked to the police, which included giving them a note she'd found. A note she hadn't shared with Tess.

They took photos, told Sam she could put things back together. They promised to keep an eye on the house. When they left, Sam said she needed to make a few phone calls. It was clear to Tess she wanted privacy. Part of her considered going home, but Sam seemed shaken and Tess didn't like the idea of leaving her alone. The one thing Tess could sense was that the intrusion had been personal, vindictive. But it hadn't seemed her place to say so, at least not to the police. She could decide later whether or not to press Sam. In the meantime, she offered to put Sam's bedroom back together.

Upstairs, she surveyed the damage. It was an even bigger mess than she remembered from the few seconds she'd seen of it earlier. Still, nothing looked damaged. Nothing seemed stolen, either. That made her more uneasy than the idea of being robbed.

Tess took her time putting Sam's clothes back in order. She didn't know Sam's preferences, but she hung and folded until everything fit somewhere and looked tidy. The bed, as far as she was concerned, was a different matter. The idea of a stranger's hands on the sheets where she and Sam slept, made love, skeeved her out.

She pulled clean sheets and a spare blanket from the linen closet, making the bed as best she could. Then she gathered up the sheets and duvet from the floor. When she did, a pair of purple lace panties fell from the pile. Tess stared at them with a combination of confusion and disgust.

They weren't hers. She was pretty sure they weren't Sam's either. While her first thought was that Sam was sleeping with someone else, it didn't make sense. Tess had stayed over more nights than not in the last few weeks. Unless they'd been left the night before, or intentionally hidden in or under the bed, she would have noticed them. After a moment of contemplation, she picked them up with two fingers and made her way downstairs. Not that Tess wanted to kick her while she was down, but Sam had some explaining to do.

Sam ended the call she'd been on and looked at her. "I really appreciate the help, but I don't want you to feel like a maid or—what are those?"

Tess dropped the pile of linens at the bottom of the stairs, then let the underwear fall on top. "I was hoping you could tell me."

"Where were they?"

"In the pile of bedding on the floor. Or under it. They fell out when I picked everything up."

"They're not yours."

From Sam's tone, Tess couldn't tell if it was a statement or a question. "They are not."

"They're not mine."

"I didn't think so."

Sam's eyes got big. "I'm not sleeping with anyone else."

"I didn't say you were."

"No, but I'm saying it anyway. We haven't talked about being exclusive, but we haven't talked about seeing other people, either. I'm not seeing, or sleeping with, anyone else."

"Okay." Hearing Sam say it out loud, and so adamantly, eased some of the tension in Tess's chest. Even if she told herself it didn't matter, of course it did. "For the record, I'm not, either. That leaves a pretty big question, then."

Sam looked at the pile and took a deep breath. "I think I know who broke into my house."

Not where she thought that was going. "What do you mean?"

"Some weird stuff has been going on. I had a feeling they might be related, but nothing concrete."

"I don't understand. What weird stuff?"

"A note on my car. A voodoo doll on my doorstep. I thought they might be pranks, or maybe not meant for me, but I'm pretty sure they're all connected."

"Who is it? Did you tell the police? I didn't hear you say anything."

"I'm not one hundred percent sure, so I didn't. Once I know, I will."

"Sam, you're not making any sense. Do you know or don't you?"

"I think it's a woman I used to date."

"What?" The word came out louder than she'd meant, more accusation than question. Tess took a deep breath and tried to calm down. If she had any hope of figuring out what was going on, she needed Sam to open up. "I'm sorry. I didn't mean to yell."

"Why don't we sit down?"

Tess couldn't decide if the request was for her benefit or Sam's, but she followed Sam over to the sofa and sat. "Okay. Tell me everything."

"Before coming to New Orleans, I was in Dallas for a few months. I dated a woman for a couple of those months. Nothing serious."

Tess raised a brow.

"At least, I thought it was nothing serious. No, more than that. We discussed it. She didn't want strings any more than I did."

"Then why would she break into your house?" Tess bit her lip. Stop talking.

"When I told her I was leaving, she started getting clingy. When I reminded her of our arrangement, she didn't take it well. She kept saying, 'We're so good together.' In her mind, she still didn't want the white picket fence and the two-point-five kids, so there was no reason we wouldn't stay together."

Tess had joked to Carly that Sam left a trail of broken hearts everywhere she went. The stark reality of it made her stomach turn. "I take it she wasn't interested in a long-distance relationship."

"I wasn't." Sam sighed. "She was beautiful, smart, ambitious. Something was missing, though. We didn't connect on any deep level."

Tess couldn't help but wonder if Sam would say the same about her. She hated herself for going there. "So you ended it. You left."

"I did. She called and texted a lot at first. Sometimes angry, sometimes sad, sometimes upbeat and hopeful. Eventually, I blocked her number. It feels callous to say that, but I didn't know what else to do. I thought engaging her would only make things worse."

Tess couldn't fault Sam. She likely would have done the same thing had she been in that situation. "What makes you think she's the one who's behind all this?"

Sam sighed again and tried to decide how much detail to share. If there'd been a shred of doubt in her mind, seeing the underwear vaporized it. Purple lace was a signature part of Francesca's wardrobe, so much so that Sam had teased her about starting her own line of purple lingerie.

She didn't want to freak Tess out, but at this point she needed Tess to understand what they were dealing with. On top of that, she didn't want to risk Francesca tracking Tess down and harassing her. Francesca seemed more than vindictive. Sam thought she might be unstable. She gave the highlights of what had occurred in the last few weeks, culminating with the missing jewelry box and the note left in its place. She couldn't bring herself to mention the photos. "She'd given me a pair of cuff links. I kept them in that box."

"Sam, this is fucked up."

"I know."

"Do you think she's the one that trashed my bike?"

The knots in Sam's stomach grew even tighter. "Shit. I didn't even think of that."

"I mean, I don't know if she has anything against me, or even if she knows who I am. The police thought it seemed like a personal kind of attack, though."

Sam's mind flashed to the envelope of photos. Photos of her with Tess. If it was Francesca, she knew who Tess was. Sam felt sick. "God, Tess. I'm so sorry. I have no idea, but if it is her, I will find a way to make it up to you."

Tess shook her head. "It's not about that."

"I'm going to get to the bottom of this."

"But you didn't tell the police about your suspicions."

"All I had was a gut feeling."

"And several threatening notes and a pair of purple lace underwear." Tess curled her lip as she finished her sentence, leaving Sam unsure of what to say to make her feel better.

"Yeah. Those are definitely hers." Sam shook her head. "I thought it was done. I haven't heard from her in a while."

"You blocked her from contacting you, Sam. That's hardly a point in her favor."

"It seemed so unlikely at first, not to mention egotistical."

Tess closed her eyes and shook her head, making Sam wish they'd been together long enough to have a better idea of what she was thinking. "What are you going to do?"

"I'm going to try to contact her."

"Then what?"

"If she takes my call, I'll talk with her. I think I'll be able to tell from that if something is off."

"Off?" Tess made a sound of disgust. "And then what? Are you going to bring the police into it then?"

"Maybe. I don't know. I don't wish her ill. I think I need to figure out if she's simply harassing me or if it's more than that."

"I think the 'more than that' line was crossed a while ago, but you do what you need to do."

"So you'll let me do this my way? You're okay with that?"

"I don't know if I'm okay with it, but that's beside the point. If you've learned anything about me, I'd hope it's that I don't tell people what to do or how to live their lives."

It wasn't the vote of confidence Sam was hoping for, but at this point, she'd take what she could get. "Thank you. I promise I'll resolve it soon. If I can't, I'll hand it over to the police."

"You know the longer you wait, the worse it's going to be."

Sam sighed. She didn't want to think about that possibility. She didn't want to think about any of it. As much as she made her living concocting elaborate crimes, she liked to keep her life tidy and uneventful, at least when it came to illegal activity. "Yeah."

Tess didn't say anything else. She looked around the room, as though searching for clues, or answers.

"I understand if you don't want to, but I hope you'll stay." Sam didn't want to admit it, but wanting Tess to stay went beyond the symbolic message that they were okay, that everything was going to be okay. She certainly didn't expect Tess to protect her, but she bought into the idea of safety in numbers. And if Francesca had it in for Tess as much as she did for Sam, Sam definitely didn't want Tess being alone.

"I'll stay." Again, Tess didn't offer much in the way of enthusiasm or reassurance. That said, Tess didn't mince words and she didn't hold back her opinion. Agreeing to stay meant something.

"Thank you. Unless…Would you rather go to your place?" Sam didn't want to come across as weak, but she felt unsettled.

Tess, who'd started up the stairs, paused. "No. I'm okay. But how about we sleep in one of the spare rooms tonight?"

Sam chuckled. "Is that dumb? Not the idea. I mean, is it dumb to be so weirded out?"

"Not at all. I know I'd rather not be in the room where someone rifled through everything." Especially if that someone was a crazy ex-girlfriend.

Even with the judgment in her voice, Tess's matter-of-fact tone did more to make Sam feel better than her agreeing to stay. She took a deep breath and felt a little of the tension ease from her shoulders. "I'm glad it's not just me."

They went into the room across the hall from Sam's bedroom. Tess slipped out of her clothes, then looked around. "Do you mind if I grab one of your T-shirts?"

"I'll get it." Sam crossed the hall and grabbed one from the dresser. She opted to keep a T-shirt and boxers on as well.

"Thanks," Tess said when Sam handed her the shirt.

They had a moment of awkward hesitation figuring out whose side of the bed was whose. Tess immediately curled up on her side. Sam slid in behind her, unsure if her touch was wanted, but craving to feel

Tess close to her. Tess didn't protest, but she didn't wiggle closer as she usually did, so Sam left her arm draped lightly around Tess's middle.

After about an hour, Tess's breathing evened out, telling Sam she'd finally fallen asleep. Knowing that sleep was unlikely to find her, Sam turned her attention to formulating a plan. Was it overly simplistic to think she could, with a single phone call, determine Francesca's state of mind? Then again, it couldn't hurt to try. Sam figured she owed her that much. She'd try to talk to her and see if there was any hope of resolution without pressing charges.

Sam continued to stare at the window, a shade brighter than the rest of the room courtesy of the outside security light shining against the curtains. Of all the calamities that had played out recently, one stuck in her mind. The very first note—the one left on her car and the one she so easily dismissed. *I know who you are.*

Sam didn't think it possible for Francesca to have figured out her alter ego. But still. The statement wouldn't carry much weight as a threat if it didn't have a secret to back it up. If Francesca had somehow figured out Sam was also Sid Packett, reasoning with her, or even having her arrested, would not solve Sam's problems.

Sam had already considered telling Tess. Whether or not they stayed together, she felt like Tess could be trusted. And if they did stay together, she should know such an important thing about the woman she was with—sooner rather than later. If she was being honest with herself, the question of whether or not they would stay together weighed on Sam's mind at least as much as dealing with a stalker. Ironically, the stakes with Tess seemed much higher.

CHAPTER TWENTY-EIGHT

Sam woke the next morning feeling, if not rested, resolved. She needed to tell Tess who she was. Part of her motivation came from the increasing unease about Francesca and what she might do. If things blew up, she did not want Tess finding out from some crazy woman with a grudge. Even more importantly, she wanted to be with Tess. And she couldn't imagine taking things to the next level with secrets hanging between them.

She encouraged Tess to roll around in bed while she made coffee. She'd just turned the pot on when Tess padded into the kitchen. She still wore the T-shirt Sam had given her the night before; even in the shapeless, faded gray material, she was gorgeous. Sam swallowed the lump that had risen in her throat.

"Tess, we need to talk." God, could she sound like any more of a cliché?

Tess furrowed her brow. "Are you breaking up with me?"

"No. God, no." Why would she think such a thing?

"Are you sleeping with someone else?"

Sam resented that question even more, but her behavior had been increasingly erratic. And given what she'd told Tess about Francesca, Sam couldn't blame her for going there. "Didn't we establish last night that neither of us is sleeping with anyone else?"

"Okay, what is it then? Wait. Can I have coffee first?"

Sam smiled at the request. She poured two cups and handed one to Tess, who took a sip then perched herself on one of the stools at the island. "Better?"

"Much. Now speak. The suspense is killing me."

Sam forced herself to make eye contact. "I haven't been entirely truthful with you."

Sam watched a shadow pass through Tess's eyes—concern becoming suspicion. "Truthful about what?"

"What I do." She swallowed. "And the weird stuff that's been going on."

"You mean they're related?"

"Yes. Sort of. At least I think so."

Tess's mind raced through possibilities. Aside from what Sam had told her the night before, along with some far-fetched ideas involving undercover cops or mafia connections, she couldn't imagine what all this could have in common. "I'm listening."

Sam seemed almost painfully uncomfortable, a fact that made Tess even more uneasy. "I told you when we first met that I'm a writer."

"You did."

"That part is true."

Was that a good thing or a bad thing? "Okay."

"What I didn't tell you was exactly what I write."

Tess wanted to scream at her to just spit it out already, but she refrained. "Okay."

"I write novels. Mystery novels, to be exact."

Tess couldn't figure out why that would be such a big deal. "And you didn't tell me this because…"

"Because I write under a pen name."

Again, not a huge deal. "I guess I'm not sure why—"

Sam cut her off. "My pen name is Sid Packett."

Tess didn't read mysteries, but she knew who Sid Packett was. You couldn't walk through Barnes & Noble or log into Amazon and not know who Sid Packett was. She'd even read a couple of his novels when Carly passed on her copy and recommended them. She'd never seen a photo, but imagined he looked like John Grisham—middle-aged, white, kind of boring, straight. Oh, and male. None of this made sense. Tess realized she hadn't said anything. "I don't understand."

"All the books that are by Sid Packett, I wrote them."

Something in Sam's tone made Tess feel like Sam was trying to explain herself to a child. She sucked in a breath. "I understand what a pen name is."

Sam plowed on. "I knew that male authors sell better than female authors, especially in the mystery genre. Male characters sell better, too. So that's what I wrote."

Although Tess's first reaction was disbelief, her mind started turning over the possibility. Sam's weird secrecy about her work. Her parents' disapproval. Allusions to being a writer. When Sam made it clear she didn't want to talk about it, Tess hadn't pushed. Of all the possible explanations, she never would have come up with this. "Why are you telling me now?"

For the first time since she'd started talking, Sam paused. She seemed to be weighing her options. "I've wanted to for a while now. It's not something I usually tell the women I date."

"But?"

"But what we have feels like something more. I didn't like keeping such a big secret from you."

"Okay." Tess hated giving such a noncommittal response, but she didn't know what else to say.

"And I think my identity has something to do with what happened last night."

"What does your pen name have to do with the person who broke into your house? Last night you said you thought your ex-girlfriend did it."

"The break-in wasn't about stealing anything. It was about sending me a message."

Tess waited for Sam to continue, but she didn't. "You're going to have to give me more to go on than that."

"I think she somehow figured out who I am and is trying to use it against me. Or get revenge. I'm not sure exactly what the motive is."

Tess tried unsuccessfully to push down the nausea that was churning in her stomach. "And she broke into your house to send that message."

Sam sighed. "I think so. I don't know if her plan is to go public or to try to blackmail me or what."

"But, again, you didn't say anything to the police."

"Because I don't know what she wants."

"I don't think it matters what she wants."

"But if I can reason with her instead of antagonizing her, she might be less inclined to go public with what she knows. And getting the police involved will definitely antagonize her. I want to avoid that if possible."

Tess scrubbed her hands over her face. "I think there's a fundamental flaw in your logic."

"What's that?"

Was Sam being naïve or willfully ignorant? "You're assuming she can be reasoned with. If she's willing to break into your house, ransack it, leave behind a pair of underwear, my guess would be that ship has sailed."

"I still want to try."

Tess took a deep breath. "Like I said before, I'm not going to tell you what to do. I don't agree with you, but that's not really the point."

Sam nodded. "I appreciate you trusting me."

Tess started to climb down from the stool, but Sam put a hand on her arm. "What?"

"Aside from the crazy ex, are you mad?"

"Mad?"

"About Sid, that I didn't tell you."

Tess's first instinct was to say yes. She didn't like secrets and she liked being lied to even less. But at the same time, she could see why Sam wouldn't share that part of herself lightly. She might not be happy about it, but she wasn't angry. "I'm not mad."

"Thanks."

Tess hopped down then and headed up to the bathroom. She took a quick shower and decided to head home for the day. She felt like she could use some alone time. She also had no desire to be around while Sam attempted to track down and negotiate with a woman who, as far as Tess was concerned, belonged in either prison or a psych ward.

She did let Sam drive her home. She kissed her good-bye and wished her luck. Inside, she stood in her living room and looked around, unsure of what to do with herself. The conversation from the night before and that morning continued to play in her mind, leaving her uneasy and restless.

It meant a lot that Sam had chosen to confide in her. The circumstances of that, however, left much to be desired. It was hard to know if Sam told her who she was because she wanted to or because she felt backed into a corner. Tess didn't like the idea of the latter. It annoyed her that she'd been so surprised. She'd been clueless at best and, at worst, stupid.

She needed to do something—anything—to take her mind off it. Working on a new song would be a losing battle. She sat on the sofa with Marlowe and flipped on the television, but the weekday morning options left much to be desired. On top of that, she couldn't sit still and Marlowe quickly abandoned her lap for his favorite windowsill. She thought maybe she could channel the energy into a good spring cleaning, but her attempts at deciding where to start devolved into pacing back and forth in her living room.

The pacing did little to calm her down. On top of everything that had happened, Tess's mind kept going back to the afternoon at her grandmother's house and the dance hall. For the first time since they'd started spending time together, Tess felt like she and Sam were a couple. And it hadn't freaked her out.

And before she could even start to process that, all hell had broken loose. A random break-in would have left her unsettled. Sam saying she knew who was behind it was surreal. The culmination—the feeling that her life teetered on the edge of chaos—made her twitchy. She'd worked hard to keep that kind of havoc out of her life since the aftermath of Katrina, and she'd been successful up to now.

She should go for a run. Tess hated everything about running, but couldn't think of another way to burn off the tension pulsing through her. She threw on a pair of shorts and the worn-out sneakers she used to mow her tiny lawn, pausing just long enough to grab her headphones on the way out.

Tess headed straight for the levee, not wanting to run into neighbors or be slowed down by stop signs and uneven sidewalks. She took the steep hill at a sprint, ignoring the burning sensation in her legs and lungs. Deep bass and wordless techno beats filled her ears, making it hard to think. She kept her eyes on the ground in front of her, willing herself into that meditative state runners always bragged about.

When she'd finished the arc of the levee path, Tess's muscles screamed for relief. She slowed her pace to a jog, winding her way home via the streets where she'd be least likely to see someone she knew. By the time she climbed the stairs to her porch, her legs felt rubbery and unstable. She continued to suck air into her lungs, wondering if she'd ever catch her breath again. She was utterly miserable, which turned out to be exactly the distraction she'd been looking for.

She bent down to snag the key she kept hidden under the mat. As she stood, Tess sensed someone behind her. She turned to see who it was, but only caught a glimpse of a light purple towel moving toward her face. As it covered her nose and mouth, an unfamiliar sweet smell filled her nostrils. Tess lifted her hand to knock it away, but her arms suddenly felt heavy, like they were weighted down and moving through water. Dizziness quickly followed. Something was terribly wrong. Her last thought before losing consciousness was whether Sam would come looking for her.

Chapter Twenty-nine

Sam knew she should give Tess some space. Between telling Tess who she was and the fact that she had a stalker, she could hardly blame Tess for feeling shell-shocked. Really, given all that, she should be happy and relieved Tess remained even remotely positive. If she hadn't wanted time to digest it, Sam would have worried.

Still. Something in Sam's gut told her she needed to seek Tess out. Her gut didn't have any useful guidance on what the hell she should say, but it remained insistent. Sam shook her head. Gut feelings worked well for the detectives in her books, but they were doing a pretty abysmal job of steering her in the right direction.

She checked her phone for the thousandth time that hour. Francesca hadn't answered the phone and had yet to respond to the voice mail or the text Sam had sent. Nor was there a text or call from Tess. The latter shouldn't make her anxious. Tess asked to be left alone for a little while to process everything. People who asked to be left alone didn't reach out to the people they were trying to avoid.

Still.

Unable to shake the feeling, Sam grabbed her keys and got in her car. She'd do a quick drive-by. Seeing Tess's house—not on fire and with her car in the driveway and new bike parked alongside—would dispel any weird premonitions that had permeated her mind. And it wasn't like she'd get anything else accomplished while she waited to hear from Francesca.

When Sam turned the corner onto Tess's street, the sight of a police car sent a wave of panic through her. It couldn't possibly be Tess. But as she got closer to Tess's house, Sam realized the car was parked right out front. She pulled her car over and got out, relieved to see the officer talking to a young woman who wasn't Tess. The relief was short-lived. As she got closer, she realized a second officer was poking around the bushes in front of Tess's porch.

"What's going on? What happened?"

Both the officer and the woman turned toward Sam. Sam recognized the woman. She'd seen her a few times when she'd left Tess's in the morning, waiting with her little girl for the bus. She lived across the street from Tess.

"What's wrong? Did something happen to Tess?"

The officer looked Sam up and down with suspicion. "Do you know the woman who lives here?"

"Tess Arceneaux. She's my girlfriend." The word "girlfriend" came out of her mouth before Sam realized she'd said it. She wasn't sure Tess would use the same term to define them at this point, but now wasn't the time for semantics. "Will you please tell me what's going on?"

Instead of answering, the cop turned back to the other woman. "Ms. Daigle, is this true? Do you know this woman?"

"Not personally, but I've seen her around the last couple of months."

Sam turned back to the police officer, hoping that was enough to get her access to information.

"And what's your name, Miss?"

"I'm Samara Torres. I've been dating Tess for the last two months. Now would you please tell me if something has happened to her?"

"When was the last time you spoke with Ms. Arceneaux?"

Sam fought the urge to grab the cop by the front of his shirt and shake him until he gave her answers. She resisted, partially because he had at least sixty pounds on her and partially because getting herself arrested wouldn't get her closer to knowing what was wrong with Tess. "This morning. I dropped her off around eight."

"I see. And were you and Ms. Arceneaux getting along all right? Was there any strife in your relationship?"

She didn't even know what had happened to Tess and now it sounded like she might be considered a suspect. She felt morbidly relieved to have brought the police into the Francesca mess, at least peripherally. And regretted that she hadn't told them everything. "Not between us. Some weird things have been happening to me, a few to Tess. My house was broken into last night."

That seemed to get the cop's attention. "And where is your house? Did you file a report?"

"It's in the Garden District, and yes. At first I didn't think they were related, but I've come to believe they all trace back to a woman with whom I had a brief relationship." She didn't mention the fact that she'd only shared some of the details, and none of her suspicions, with the police.

"I see."

Sam wanted to punch him in the face. "This could be related. I don't know. But I need to know what happened, where Tess is now."

"I saw someone dragging Tess to a car. She didn't seem conscious," the woman, Ms. Daigle, said.

The cop shook his head like this was the last thing in the world he wanted to deal with. "Clarence, get over here. We need to separate these witnesses and get statements."

The second cop emerged, empty-handed, and ambled their way.

Sam turned to the Daigle woman. "What did the person look like? Was it a woman? What kind of car was it? Did you get the license plate?"

"Ms. Torres, I can see that you're clearly upset. Why don't you come back to the station with me to make a statement. The more specific details we have, the more likely we are to find your friend."

"Find?" Somehow, Sam had convinced her brain that Tess had been attacked—hurt maybe, but somewhere Sam could get to. The veneer of calm she'd clung to vanished, her voice taking on some of the hysteria taking root in her mind. "She's missing?"

"We don't know that for sure. Ms. Arceneaux might have been ill and asked a friend to take her to the hospital."

"She's been kidnapped. You have to find her." Sam was yelling now. Could this really be Francesca's doing? Threatening notes and destruction of property were one thing. Kidnapping was a felony. And an indication Francesca had gone completely over the edge.

"We're going to do everything we can, Ms. Torres. Your cooperation will help us."

Sam had to know if it was Francesca. If it was, she'd be able to provide a lot of useful information to the police. If not, if Tess was the victim of some random kidnapping for ransom or worse... The thought of what could happen to her made Sam think she might vomit. She forced down the bile that had risen in her throat. "Of course, I'll cooperate. I just need to know if it was a woman who took her."

"It was." The neighbor had spoken again.

"Ma'am, I need you to stop talking to her." Clarence had joined the conversation, but hadn't made any effort to physically separate them.

Sam focused her attention on the neighbor. "Was she tall, curvy, with long brown hair?"

"I couldn't tell if she was tall because she was hunched over, but she was definitely bigger than Tess. And she did have long hair. A ponytail under a black baseball cap."

Sam had no doubt the woman who took Tess was Francesca. At the moment, she couldn't decide if that made her feel better or worse. Either way, that meant she was in the clear as a potential suspect. It also meant she had a boatload of information that the police needed. "I think the woman who has been stalking me—stalking both of us—is the person who did this."

The first cop finally seemed interested in what she had to say. "What's this woman's name?"

"Francesca Romero. She lives in Dallas. I don't remember her address, but she should have a Texas driver's license. If she still has the same car, it's a silver BMW."

"The car was silver," the neighbor chimed in.

"Okay, let me radio this in and then, Ms. Torres, I'm going to ask you to come to the station with me."

"Of course." Sam felt the tiniest sliver of relief that they were finally taking action. "I filed the other police report last night. You might want to tell them to pull that file, too."

The officer stepped away to call in the information, leaving Sam standing on the sidewalk with the neighbor and Clarence. "I'm so grateful you saw something, and that you called the police."

The woman nodded. "Sure. I opened the door to go get the mail and something about it just didn't seem right. I'm Jody, by the way."

"You're a good friend, Jody. I'm Sam." Sam stuck out her hand and Jody shook it. "I can't thank you enough."

"I only hope they find her soon, and that she's okay."

"Me too. They will. I'm sure of it." Sam's words did little to reassure her. She hoped they did something for Jody.

The cop stepped back over to where they were standing. "We're running Ms. Romero's records now. We've got a BOLO out for a silver BMW and will hopefully be able to add more detail to that soon. Ms. Torres, would you like to ride to the station with me or take your own car?"

The last thing Sam wanted was to spend twenty minutes in the car with a cop. She also didn't want to be stuck at the police station with no way to leave. "I'll follow you there."

"Can I give you my number?" Jody asked Sam. "So you can call me if there's news?"

"Absolutely." Sam tapped the numbers into her phone, realizing she'd never think of getting a woman's number the same way again.

She climbed into her car and pulled up behind the patrol car. It probably only took them thirty seconds to get situated and moving, but it felt to Sam like an eternity. Their lack of urgency gave her a place to direct her anger for a moment, so she took it, letting out a string of expletives that made her feel momentarily better. When she was done, some of her anger had dissipated. Instead of making her feel better, however, it simply cleared the way for panic to settle in.

❖

The first thing to permeate Tess's consciousness was the fact that she had a splitting headache. As much as she wanted to will herself back to sleep until the pain subsided, her brain told her something was wrong. She struggled to open her eyes. Taking in her surroundings confirmed her mind's assertion. She had no idea where she was or how she got there.

"Oh, good. You're waking up. I wasn't sure how long that would take."

The silhouette of a woman came into Tess's line of sight, but her vision blurred. She didn't recognize the voice. "Where am I?"

"I wanted a private place where we could talk."

The woman's voice sounded friendly. Tess wondered if she'd been hit by a car or something. Maybe this woman was trying to help her. That didn't make sense, though. Tess was sitting up, and her surroundings looked more like a hotel room than a hospital—a pair of matching double beds with ugly floral spreads, a single wide window with the drapes pulled shut, and a door with a placard of text under the peephole. "Who are you?"

"Someone who wants to help you."

Tess tried to lift her hands to rub at her eyes, but her limbs felt heavy and weak. She looked down and realized her wrists were bound together with a zip tie. Two more ties held her ankles to the legs of the chair. That did wonders to clear the fog in her brain. "What the fuck? What's going on?"

"I'm sorry I had to tie you up. I know it seems rather extreme, but I knew it was the only way I'd get you to listen to me."

The woman's tone remained pleasant and she spoke in a matter-of-fact way that made Tess question her grip on reality, given the circumstances. "Well, I'm listening now."

"I'm trying to help you."

"This is not my definition of help."

The woman sat on the corner of the bed, crossed her legs, and leaned forward. "We're the same, you and me. Strong, independent women who fell under the spell of a handsome, charming dyke who took advantage of us."

Holy shit. The panic Tess had managed to keep at bay threatened to take over. This woman was Sam's ex. The crazy one. The stalker. She hadn't wanted to believe it, but there was no denying it now. And she was clearly every bit as crazy as Tess imagined.

"I'm trying to save you from her."

Tess obviously knew who the woman was talking about, but a voice in the back of her mind told her she needed to keep the woman talking, buy time to figure out a plan. "Who do I need saving from?"

The woman shook her head with exasperation and stood up. She began pacing back and forth in front of Tess. "She'll break your heart. Even worse, she'll humiliate you. She'll disappear one day and leave you to explain to your friends what you did to drive her away."

Tess tried to stop her mind from going in too many directions at once. She'd been kidnapped by Sam's ex. The sheer insanity of that was enough to make her head spin. But on top of that, this woman seemed to think they were on the same side. Tess wondered if what she saw in movies and on TV was true—that she should attempt to connect with the woman, win her over. "Is that what she did to you?"

"She appeared one day out of nowhere, charming as fuck."

Tess couldn't argue there.

"A little flirtation, a little romance. Lavish gifts and the best sex of my life."

Tess cringed at the surge of jealousy and swallowed the pithy comment on the tip of her tongue. What the hell was wrong with her? She needed to be nice to this woman, not antagonize her.

"And then she was all, 'Sorry, Francesca, I've got other plans. It's been fun.'"

Francesca. Tess realized that in all of Sam's explanations the night before, she'd never used a name.

"And then she was gone."

Tess knew better than to let on she knew Sam's side of the story. "That sounds really hard."

"She ignored my calls, my texts. If she hadn't made reference to Tulane, I might never have tracked her down."

The meaning of Francesca's words sank in. Even though Sam had said as much last night, part of Tess hadn't entirely believed it. Not that she didn't trust Sam, but the whole thing felt more like an episode of a cheesy cop drama than real life. Now, not only did she have to believe it, she was in the middle of it. She needed to figure out an escape plan, fast.

"Did she tell you?"

The question yanked Tess out of her thoughts. Focus. She needed to stay focused. The pounding in her head didn't help. "Tell me what?"

"Who she really is?"

Tess fought to keep any frustration from her voice. "I don't know what you mean."

"What she does for a living. Why she has more money than God."

Tess's mind flashed to the conversation she'd had with Sam not twelve hours before. Was it twelve hours? Tess realized with a jolt she had no idea how much time had passed. "Um…"

The woman—Francesca—sat again. She took a deep breath. Tess couldn't be sure whether Francesca was deciding what to say or was pausing for dramatic effect. "She's Sid fucking Packett."

Tess's stomach did a flip. All of Sam's suspicions were right.

Not that it did her any good, especially since Sam hadn't wanted to involve the police. She took a deep breath. Should she feign ignorance or pretend she'd known all along? "How do you know?"

"It was all on her computer—emails, manuscripts, everything."

Tess flashed back to one of her first afternoons with Sam. They'd gone for a walk on the levee and Sam had been late. Because her computer was stolen. That had been almost two months ago. Tess's anxiety ratcheted up another notch. "So, what's the plan? What are we going to do now?"

The question seemed to make Francesca angry. She started pacing again, this time touching her temples and tipping her head back and forth in a way that made Tess think she might be talking to herself. Francesca started mumbling something that sounded like, "What now? What now?"

Tess decided to keep talking. "I mean, as far as I'm concerned, we're fine. I'm not a huge fan of your methods, but your heart's in the right place."

"Would you shut up for a minute? I need to think."

"I'm just saying, now that I know, everything is different." That wasn't untrue. Could she convince Francesca they were on the same side? "You keeping me here will make things messy."

"It doesn't change what she did to me. The world needs to know what kind of person she is. I need to tell them."

"Yeah, but if you're in jail, who's going to believe you?"

Francesca turned then, her eyes filled with a mixture of anger and alarm. Clearly, she hadn't thought her plan through. Tess waffled between wanting to goad her and knowing it would probably be safer to placate. Francesca continued to pace. Tess's gaze followed her back and forth across the room.

"Stop staring at me, too. God, I just need a minute to think." Francesca moved in the direction of the bathroom. Tess continued staring at her until the bathroom door slammed shut.

CHAPTER THIRTY

Tess stared at the bathroom door. She heard the faucet come on. Francesca continued talking to herself. This was her chance. Tess propelled herself to a standing position. The zip ties dug into her ankles. She lifted her hands over her head like she'd seen in that video her paranoid aunt posted on Facebook, then brought them down and apart with as much force as she could muster. She heard a snapping sound and her wrists were free. Son of a bitch. It actually worked.

She had to move quickly. Tess couldn't figure out a way to break the ties around her ankles so she twisted herself around and attempted to free the legs of the chair instead. To her surprise, the chair slipped out almost easily. She looked around the room. Should she try to run on foot? She had no idea where they were or how isolated. There was no sign of a purse or keys anywhere.

The water that had been running in the bathroom stopped. Even through the closed door, she could hear Francesca talking to herself. It sounded like a pep talk. Tess did not feel confident in her ability to run. She tried the door anyway, but Francesca had done something to the lock. She'd cut the phone line, too, and there was no sign of her cell phone or Francesca's. For being off her rocker, she'd been surprisingly thorough.

Tess looked around frantically. Since she wouldn't be able to take Francesca in a physical fight, her best bet was to try and knock her out somehow. There wasn't much in the room to work with—the chair she'd been tied to, a television, and the lamp on the nightstand. Tess reached for the lamp and said a quick prayer of thanks that it wasn't bolted down. She positioned herself against the wall where Francesca would walk when she came out of the bathroom.

Tess wondered if she should make a noise or wait for Francesca to emerge. Then she wondered if she should have tried harder to bolt when she had the chance. Unable to stand the questions racing through her mind, or the doubts and fear that churned with them, Tess banged a fist on the wall to mimic someone knocking at the door.

She heard the bathroom door open. Tess rounded the corner and swung with all her might. The base of the lamp made contact with the back of Francesca's head. The resulting thud, combined with the fact that Francesca crumpled to the floor, made Tess's stomach turn and it was all she could do not to throw up.

What if she'd killed her? Unable to stop herself, Tess bent down to press her fingers to Francesca's neck. Before she could, Francesca moaned and attempted to roll over. Tess stood up, momentarily relieved, but then froze. Try to find a phone again or try to get away? She decided to run.

Tess went to the door, jiggling the handle and yanking. Because she didn't know what Francesca had done to it, she couldn't figure out how to fix it. It didn't help that her hands were trembling and her head continued to pound. The window was her next option. Tess yanked open the drapes and saw a mostly empty parking lot. She was definitely at one of those cheap chain motels. She hoped that meant there were other people nearby.

Unfortunately, the window had no mechanism to open. Tess looked back. Francesca had managed to get to her hands and knees. Feeling her panic start to rise again, Tess grabbed the chair she'd been tied to and hurled it at the window. The pane gave way and the chair landed on its side in a pile of shattered glass. Tess scrambled to climb out just as Francesca regained her feet.

Fighting dizziness, Tess tried to step through the opening she'd created. A hand grabbed her arm. Tess turned and swung with all her might, her fist connecting with Francesca's face. Francesca released her grip and Tess maneuvered herself out the window. She saw a blur of flashing lights; it took her a moment to recognize and process them as a police car. It came to a stop about fifty feet away. Tess stumbled toward them and hoped they were there to help her.

"Theresa Arceneaux?"

The sound came from one of the police officers who'd gotten out of the car. She wondered if she might be hallucinating. She had no idea what Francesca had used to knock her out or if she might have lingering side effects.

"Theresa Arceneaux? NOPD. Are you okay?"

Tess nodded and, instinctively, lifted her hands. She'd never been called at by police before. One of the officers approached her.

"Ms. Arceneaux, we're here to help. Are you hurt?"

Tess shook her head. "No. I'm…there's a…I hit her. I don't know if she's okay."

She was able to bring her vision into focus enough to see the officer who'd approached her gesture to the other cop. "The other woman? Where is she?"

Tess pointed behind her. It seemed like they were here to save her, but she wondered if they'd arrest her when they saw what she'd done. Would it count as self-defense? The second officer walked toward the room, weapon drawn. He tried to open the door, but it wouldn't budge. A lump formed in Tess's throat. "She's hurt."

The officer nodded and kicked the door next to the knob. It splintered and shot open.

Tess looked at the officer standing with her. "Could you call an ambulance? I hit her really hard."

Before he could answer her, a voice came over the radio. "We have our suspect, conscious, probably with a concussion. Jensen, will you call in a bus?"

Francesca was okay. Tess hadn't killed her. Relief flooded her system, followed by flashes of the last few hours. She started to feel dizzy again and found herself led to the patrol car. She sat on the edge of the seat, and at the encouragement of Officer Jensen, dropped her head between her knees.

The ambulance arrived and Tess glanced up. The two medics rushed into the hotel room. A few minutes later, one of them emerged and pulled the wheeled stretcher to the door. Tess couldn't tear her gaze from the scene. After what felt like an eternity, the stretcher emerged again, this time with Francesca strapped into it. One of her wrists was attached to the metal railing with handcuffs. She looked woozy, but was fully conscious. Thank God.

Tess looked at the smear of blood under Francesca's nose and realized she was the one who had caused it. Seeing Francesca awake calmed the churning in Tess's stomach. She couldn't quite feel proud of what she'd done, but she no longer felt horrified. Tess watched one of the police officers say something to Francesca. One of the EMTs walked over to the police car. He looked to be about seventeen, but maybe he just had one of those baby faces.

"Ma'am, are you okay? We can get another ambulance here in a few minutes."

Tess looked up, trying to keep her vision focused. "I'm fine."

The officer scowled. "Ma'am, even if you don't go to the hospital, you should at least let them check you out."

Although she hadn't been injured, Tess realized she'd inhaled something that knocked her out. She let the medic ask her a few questions, check her vitals. After listening to her description of what happened, he said, "If I had to guess, I'd say it was ether. I'm not a doctor, though. I'd strongly suggest you have blood work done in the next twenty-four hours. If not at the ER, your primary care physician can do it."

"Okay. I will." Tess didn't disagree, but the thought of going to the emergency room was too much at the moment.

A second police car pulled up. After a brief exchange of words, the new pair of officers went into the room. Tess had no idea how much time passed, but a third car arrived. Another exchange of words and the new arrivals got back into their car and followed the ambulance as it pulled away. The first cops turned their attention back to her. Tess was vaguely aware of being helped the rest of the way into their car, of the car in motion. The next thing she knew, they were at the police station. Inside, the flurry of activity was both overwhelming and reassuring.

"Are you up to giving a statement, ma'am?"

Tess nodded, realizing it was the second time in as many months that she'd had to give a statement to police. She was trying to process that fact when she heard Sam's voice.

"Oh, my God. Tess. You're here. You're okay. Are you okay? Are you injured? Did she hurt you?"

Tess allowed herself to be pulled into Sam's embrace. The strength and the warmth of it permeated, giving her permission to crumble just a little.

"You're trembling. You should be in the hospital." Sam turned to the police who'd driven Tess to the station. "Why didn't you take her to the ER?"

Tess lifted a hand. "I'm fine."

Sam wanted desperately to believe her. Knowing Tess wasn't physically injured might relieve some of the crushing guilt that had been pressing on her lungs and other vital organs. Sam looked Tess up and down, noticing abrasions on her wrists. While the idea of Tess being tied up made her want to punch something, or someone, Sam tried to take some comfort in seeing no other visible signs of injury.

"Ma'am? It would be good if you gave your statement right now. You lose a lot of detail even in just twenty-four hours."

Sam glared at the police officer, thinking she might find some satisfaction in punching him. Tess nodded, though, so Sam swallowed the urge. "Can I sit with her? She shouldn't have to relive the whole ordeal alone."

The officer lifted his hand and Sam fought the urge to hit him. "I'm sorry, since you're a potential witness, we can't chance having your statements influence each other."

"I already gave my statement," Sam said.

Tess lifted a hand. "Sam, I'm fine. I think I'd rather do this on my own anyway."

The flatness in Tess's tone cut into Sam. As much as she wanted to insist, to grab on to Tess and not let her out of her sight, Sam knew she needed to respect Tess's wishes. "Okay. Take as long as you need. I'll be here whenever you're done."

Without making eye contact or saying anything, Tess followed the officer down a hallway. Sam swallowed the lump in her throat. She couldn't read anything into Tess's actions. If not literally in shock, Tess was at least shell-shocked. Sam needed to stay calm and be patient.

She had no idea what Francesca had said during the hours she and Tess were together. Maybe it was nothing. Maybe it was enough that Tess would never want to see her again. Sam berated herself for worrying about their relationship when Tess's physical safety had been so violated, but she couldn't stop her mind from racing from one scenario to the next. One second, she envisioned what happily ever after with Tess might look like; the next, Tess's blank stare. Even worse than anger would be if Tess shut down completely and walked away.

Enough people brushed by her that Sam realized she hadn't moved from the spot where Tess left her and was now completely in the way. She returned to the waiting area near the main entrance to the station and took a seat in one of the hard plastic chairs. In an effort to not drive herself crazy, she focused her attention on her surroundings—the sounds of hushed conversations and a child crying, the smell of stale coffee and drugstore perfume. She watched the comings and goings, filing away details. It was a skill she'd honed for writing, but it also did wonders to pass the time.

When Tess emerged almost two hours later, she looked even more exhausted than when she'd gone in. Sam stood, the anxiety and uncertainty flooding back into her. She hung back, wanting Tess to make the choice to come to her. When she did, Sam allowed herself a modicum of relief. Tess blinked at her slowly and Sam feared she might pass out.

"Are you okay?"

Tess nodded.

"I don't want you to feel like you have to come home with me, but I'd feel better if you did."

Another nod.

"Are you sure you won't go to the hospital?"

Mention of the hospital snapped Tess out of her daze. "No hospital. I'll come home with you."

"Okay, good. Let's get out of here." Sam resisted putting her arm around Tess's shoulder, but did take her hand as they exited the building and walked to Sam's car.

Tess said nothing during the drive and Sam didn't press her to talk. Sam told herself that was a perfectly natural reaction to the kind of ordeal Tess had endured, not to mention the two hours of questioning that followed. Things might not be great between them, but at least Tess had agreed to come home with her. That had to count for something. And Tess was safe. That's what mattered most of all.

CHAPTER THIRTY-ONE

When they pulled into Sam's driveway, Tess realized she'd spaced out for almost the entire ride. By the time she undid her seat belt, Sam had rounded the front of her car and was opening Tess's door. She wanted to argue about Sam coddling her—for the second time in what felt like as many days—but she didn't have the energy.

Inside, Tess looked around, thinking back to the night of the break-in. Tess corrected herself; it was the night Francesca broke into Sam's house. It had only been yesterday, but in some ways it felt like ages ago. She'd been worried, but not at all for herself. In a thousand years, she'd never have imagined the way the last twenty-four hours had played out.

"Would you like to take a shower?" Again, Sam's voice snapped her back to reality.

"That sounds like a good idea." Tess made her way upstairs slowly, feeling old and frail. Maybe that's why Sam was being so delicate with her.

"You go on in. I'll get you something to put on."

"Thanks."

In the bathroom, Tess stripped off the clothes she'd put on that morning to go for a run. She stepped into the shower and cranked the water as hot as she could stand it. It felt good to scrub off the residue of the day—sweat and police station and the places where Francesca had touched her. She flipped the showerhead to massage and let the water pelt her muscles, hoping it would ease the tension and fatigue that had settled in them.

After about twenty minutes, Tess reluctantly turned off the water.

She toweled off and pulled on the pajamas Sam had set out for her. She combed her damp hair and stood for a long moment looking at herself in the bathroom mirror. She put so much stock in being a rational, reasonable sort of woman, the kind of woman who steered clear of chaos and drama. How the hell had she gotten herself into this mess?

She should ask Sam to take her home. If she had any hope of regaining a sense of order and balance, she should put some distance between herself and everything that had happened. Distance between herself and Sam. But even as she told herself that, she couldn't bear the thought of being alone, much less alone in her house.

She hated herself for being a coward. She also couldn't remember a time when she'd felt more exhausted. Tonight, she'd try to sleep. All the shit she needed to deal with would still be waiting for her in the morning. Tess emerged from the bathroom and found Sam hovering in the hallway.

"I wanted to be close by in case you needed anything."

Under normal circumstances, the gesture would irritate her, make her feel smothered. Then again, nothing about today had been normal. "Thanks."

"Are you hungry? I've got some Indian in the fridge, one more container of your gumbo in the freezer. Or I could order something. It's not that late."

Tess found the options both overwhelming and unappealing. "Not really."

Sam frowned. "You should probably try to eat something. I'm guessing you haven't had anything all day."

Tess sighed. Sam had a point. The queasiness from whatever Francesca had used to knock her out remained, but food would likely help rather than make it worse. "Okay. Nothing big, though. Are there any biscuits left? Or toast?"

"Biscuits. Coming right up."

"And some hot tea?"

"You got it. I'll bring it to you up here if you want to crawl into bed or you can relax on the sofa."

"I'll come down." Tess didn't add that the idea of being by herself made her pulse race.

They headed downstairs and Tess curled up with a blanket. Sam appeared a few moments later with a plate of biscuits smothered with butter and jam and a cup of steaming tea. Maybe being coddled wasn't entirely a bad thing.

"I'll be right back." Sam disappeared for a moment and returned with a plate of her own. She joined Tess on the sofa.

They ate in silence for a few minutes. Sam had been right. Putting some food in her stomach helped her feel steadier, more like herself. "Thanks for this."

Sam set down her plate. "It's the least I can do. Can I get you anything else?"

Tess didn't know if it was the food or just the whole day finally catching up with her, but she found her eyes getting heavy. "I'm good."

Sam nodded, then looked at her nervously. "Do you want to talk about it?"

Tess took a deep breath. "Maybe. I don't know. But definitely not tonight."

"Of course. I'm sure you're exhausted. Let's get you to bed." They made their way back up the stairs and Tess headed to the guest room where they'd slept the night before. She turned and found Sam hovering a few feet behind her. "I didn't…Would you rather be alone?" Sam asked.

She appreciated that Sam asked, especially given the circumstances. The brave part of her wanted to say yes, to assert that she felt confused and betrayed and needed space to sort that out. That part of her didn't prevail. She refrained, at least, from admitting it and said simply, "No."

They climbed into bed and Tess allowed herself to curl up against Sam. Sam felt warm and solid. If she could keep her focus on that—and only that—she might be able to fall asleep. And if she slept, she might be able to sort out the chaotic jumble in her mind.

Sam had worried that Tess wouldn't be able to sleep. She'd conked out almost immediately, however, and didn't stir. Sam knew this because she'd spent most of the night awake. Images of Tess unconscious and tied up filled her mind and were shockingly vivid. While that played on an endless loop, Sam obsessed about how much Tess would blame her for what had happened. Clearly Francesca had lost touch with reality, and Sam had no way of knowing whether what she'd said to Tess had any basis in truth. She also had no way of knowing if it would have any weight with Tess.

When Tess woke up a little after six, Sam was stiff from not moving all night. The vicious cycle of questions and doubt remained. But as much as she wanted to talk to Tess, to understand what had transpired the day before and to—hopefully—find a way to put it behind them, she almost wished she could freeze time and keep Tess wrapped safely in her arms. She took a deep breath and steeled herself for whatever would come next.

"Hey. How're you feeling?"

Tess furrowed her brow. "Like I've been hit by a truck."

"That's not surprising, given everything you went through. Does anything in particular hurt?"

Tess maintained her serious expression and Sam imagined her taking inventory of herself. "My head is killing me. And my wrist."

Sam worked not to cringe. "I think you should let me take you to the hospital or at least your doctor."

"Can I start with ibuprofen, maybe, and some coffee?"

"Fair enough. Why don't you stay here and I'll go rustle it up?"

"I'm not an invalid." Tess sat up, but she immediately flinched and pressed her fingers to her head.

"No, but you've been through a lot. Why don't you try to take it easy, at least for a little bit."

Tess sighed. "Okay. I'll wait here."

Sam extricated herself from the bed. She grabbed the ibuprofen and a glass of water from the bathroom, handed them to Tess, then headed down to make coffee. She made scrambled eggs while the coffee brewed. Even if Tess didn't want them, it made her feel useful. Since there were still a few leftover biscuits, she warmed them up as well. She piled everything on a tray and returned to the bedroom, where she found Tess sitting up and hugging her knees. "I thought I might be able to talk you into some breakfast, too."

Tess offered her a half smile. "Thanks."

Sam didn't want to pry, but she felt like, if she didn't get some of the details about yesterday, she'd go crazy. She was trying to find a non-aggressive way of saying that when Tess set down her coffee. "I guess you want to know what happened."

Sam let out a breath. "I do. I don't need a blow by blow, but I want to hear whatever you feel comfortable talking about."

Tess shook her head and kept her gaze focused on the duvet. She wasn't sure she was comfortable talking about any of it, but Sam needed to know. And Tess needed some answers about how much Sam knew, and when. She gave Sam the medium-length version of the story. When she finished, Sam sat staring at her like she'd grown a second head.

"You knocked her unconscious with a lamp?"

Tess had to admit there was an almost comical, movie-like element to the culmination of her kidnapping. Had she not had the weight of the last few days on her, she might have been able to laugh about it. Maybe. "I didn't think about it, really. I didn't know where we were and I figured I should try to stop her from following me."

"You're an amazing woman."

"Stop."

Sam's expression softened. "No, really. You were smart and brave and managed to rescue yourself. I don't think a lot of people would have had the wherewithal to do that."

Tess hadn't felt brave. If anything, she'd been grateful she hadn't slipped into a full panic. "I don't think it was a well-thought-out plan to begin with."

"True, but the fact that she was unstable makes your composure all the more impressive." Sam took her hand. "I'm just so glad you did what you did, and that you're safe."

For some reason, Sam's tenderness made Tess cringe. It felt heavy, insincere. That might not be fair, but she couldn't help but feel like Sam's choices had a lot to do with how far out of hand the situation had gotten. "You were right about her."

Sam visibly stiffened. Tess didn't want to take satisfaction in that, but she did. "What do you mean?"

"She figured out who you were. She followed you to New Orleans. She's the one who stole your computer."

"Oh, my God. Of course. Why didn't I think of that?" Sam shook her head. She was either genuinely surprised or a really good liar.

"So you never told her?"

"I never told any of the women I dated. Like I said when I told you, it started out as a way to get published. I never thought my books would take off like they did. I mean, I fantasized about it. I think most writers do. There were a couple of times I thought about going public, but I didn't want to mess with a good thing. I'm pretty sure a lot of men would stop reading my work if they knew I was a woman, and a Latina one at that."

"I get it."

"And I was never interested in being famous. I loved the fact that I could make good money, be a successful author, but without all the trappings."

"Sure." It made sense. Tess didn't want it to, but it did.

"I get to live how and where I want. I've never had to worry about being recognized. It felt like the best of both worlds. And it certainly made dating easier."

Tess shook her head. It all sounded perfectly reasonable. Up until the last bit. "Easier, yes. You lie about who you are, though."

Sam took a deep breath. "Yes and no. For the most part, I'm vague. And for the most part, that's more than enough."

"What does that mean?"

"It means that most of the women I date aren't interested in my life story."

Tess thought about how much she'd kept Sam at bay when they'd first met. Part of it had been the fact that Sam was just passing through. Tess had sensed something about her, though, something that felt a little too smooth. Tess had ultimately written it off as her own prejudices toward Sam's flirtatious personality and wealth. Now, she was reminded that her gut was one of the most reliable things about her.

"Tess, things between us are so much more than that."

Tess raised a brow.

"You know they are. I couldn't put my finger on when exactly they changed, but when I realized it, I told you."

Again, it made sense, but Tess was not in the mood to give Sam even an inch. "You told me because you didn't have a choice. You were afraid she would blow your cover and had to beat her to it."

Sam looked pained. "I know it seems like that."

"How else is it supposed to seem?"

"At first, when weird shit started happening, it was much easier to focus my attention on figuring that out."

That was a can of worms they hadn't even opened yet. "So you knew it was her? I don't understand why you didn't tell the police sooner. Tell me sooner."

"It's not like I knew all along. And I certainly didn't realize everything was connected. I didn't want to admit that it was. I wasn't trying to keep it from you."

"Weren't you? Seems to me like that's your M.O." An M.O. Tess had easily fallen for.

"Tess."

Feeling stupid fueled her anger. "You mean to tell me that if you'd not been obsessed with keeping your identity a secret—from me, from the rest of the world—that the last couple of weeks wouldn't have played out very differently?"

"Your safety was my top priority."

Tess sniffed her disdain. "No, actually, I don't think it was. It seems like your secret was your top priority and keeping me in the dark didn't keep me safe at all."

"The moment I thought you might be in danger, I acted. You have to believe that. You have to know that I would never intentionally put you in harm's way."

"Intentionally? No. But I do think your judgment was skewed by wanting to protect your own interests."

"I thought they were our interests. How can I convince you of that?" Sam's eyes were pleading.

Tess sighed. "I'm not sure you can."

"What are you saying?"

Tess pressed her fingers to her eyes. "I don't know."

"What can I do?"

"I don't know that, either. I do know I need some space. I need to sort this out in my own head."

"I want you to trust me again. Just tell me what I have to do."

"I wish it was that simple. And at the moment, that's only part of the problem."

Sam looked confused.

"The other part is that you didn't trust me."

"Tess, it isn't that I—"

Tess lifted her hand. "Don't. You trying to explain isn't helping right now. It's only making me feel worse."

That shut Sam up. Tess took a deep breath and climbed out of bed. Grateful that she'd left some clothes at Sam's, she went to the otherwise empty dresser and pulled out shorts and a T-shirt.

"Do you want to go home for a bit? I'll drive you."

Tess would have much preferred taking the street car into the Quarter, then the ferry—both for the fresh air and the solitude. She didn't have her wallet, though, or her ferry pass. The thought of having to ask Sam for money seemed more humiliating than enduring fifteen minutes in the car with her. "That would be great. Thanks."

When they pulled up at Tess's half an hour later, Tess had a flash of the day before—coming home from her run, sensing someone behind her. The memory sent a chill through her.

"Are you okay?" Sam's hand was on her knee and her eyes were filled with concern.

"I'm fine. Thanks for the ride."

"I want to give you space, but I'm worried about you. Can I check on you later?"

"I'd rather you didn't, at least for a couple of days. I'll call Carly and fill her in. I'll be in touch when I'm ready." Tess climbed out of Sam's car without waiting for an answer.

She found the key under the mat where she'd left it the day before. She let herself in, deciding to take the key in with her instead of putting it back. Sam waited for a minute before driving off, but eventually did.

Marlowe, who'd been alone for close to twenty-four hours and denied his dinner, meowed his discontent. Tess headed to the kitchen to feed him, feeling comforted by the routine. She put on a fresh pot of coffee for herself and, deciding her clothes smelled faintly of Sam, took a quick shower. Once she was clean and caffeinated, she could start the process of figuring out what the hell she should do next.

CHAPTER THIRTY-TWO

By early afternoon, Tess was feeling more than a little stir crazy. She'd called in sick to work but couldn't seem to relax. She waited until she knew Carly would be almost done with work, then called her, asking if she could come over. It wasn't like she could casually say, "Oh, hey, by the way, I was kidnapped yesterday by my girlfriend's crazy ex" over the phone.

When Carly arrived, Tess launched into the story. She told Carly about the break-in at Sam's, Francesca, the hotel room, her daring-slash-ridiculous escape. She left out the part about Sam's identity, not because she wanted to keep it a secret from her, but because it wasn't her secret to tell. And the story was plenty crazy without it. By the time she finished, Carly gaped at her.

"Holy shit."

"I know."

"No, like, really. Holy shit."

"I. Know."

Carly went into full-on nurturing mode. She arranged with Becca to stay over, made dinner, and distracted Tess with old movies. "You need to process, but you need to recover first."

To Tess's surprise, it worked. The security of having Carly there, combined with a huge bowl of pasta and the antics of Cary Grant and Katharine Hepburn and a pet leopard, relaxed her. As they sat on the sofa, sharing a blanket and a pint of Blue Bell mint chocolate chip, Tess felt almost normal.

The next morning, she gave into Carly's badgering and went to the doctor, who confirmed she was fine. Well, fine physically. Her mind still felt like mush, but she insisted Carly get home to her family.

She spent the day cleaning her house from top to bottom. It felt good to use her muscles, helped to clear the fog. It tired her out, too. According to her doctor, ether didn't typically have lingering effects, but Tess was convinced it had sapped her stamina, much like a cold or the flu. As frustrating as she'd find that normally, she found the exhaustion reassuring.

Sam had texted her a few times, mostly to check in and offer anything Tess might need. Tess appreciated the sentiment, and was able to say as much, but she couldn't bring herself to open a bigger conversation. Nor did she invite Sam over. Fortunately, Sam didn't press.

She sat at her kitchen table with a plate of Carly's leftover spaghetti and tried to figure out what to do next. Even though her body was tired, her brain remained full steam ahead. She couldn't seem to get a handle on the torrent of questions spinning around her mind. Her thoughts jumped, without bidding or much rational organization, from the day they met, to the night her bike was torn up, to the day they spent in Breaux Bridge, to the night they first made love. Interspersed, flashes of the hotel room and the look in Francesca's eyes when she talked about Sam.

Part of her was searching for clues, anything Sam said or did that might have hinted at how she spent her time. Part of her tried to suss out lies that Sam may have told along the way. The more Tess tried to pin down, however, the slipperier everything became. Sam had been deliberately—artfully—vague in how she talked about her work.

That felt somehow worse than outright lies. Lies wouldn't have made Sam a better person, but they would have made Tess feel better. A good liar could be hard to detect. All the omissions, though, and the half answers should have triggered something. But they didn't. She hated to think she got so swept up in the romance that she stopped paying attention to details or started ignoring red flags. She hated even more to think she wasn't very smart, easily duped by the sophisticated writer.

But then she thought about Sam's track record with women, not to mention her own conviction that things with Sam would never lead to anything serious. Nothing about the early part of their relationship would have made her expect Sam to confide in her. On top of that, she could hardly begrudge Sam wanting privacy. Their first fight had been, at least in part, about Tess not wanting to live her life surrounded by public attention.

She tried to separate Sam's revelation from the kidnapping. She knew it wasn't fair to blame Sam for Francesca's actions. As easy as it was to throw around blame after the fact, she couldn't expect Sam to have known just how far over the edge Francesca had gone. Would she even be questioning Sam's integrity had the admission not been wrapped up in the fact that Sam had a stalker who was hell-bent on revenge? That said, had Sam not felt the pressure, would she have said anything? As much as she could have told Tess sooner, she could just as easily have said nothing at all.

Carly told her to give it time, that things would feel a lot clearer when the dust settled. But Tess wasn't a patient person. She needed to figure things out, and to do that, she would have to talk to Sam. But knowing it and having the wherewithal to do it were two entirely different matters.

She gave up any chance of finding answers and went to bed. Despite her exhaustion, she tossed and turned for a long time before falling asleep. When she did, strange dreams followed her. The sound of her phone ringing pulled her back to reality. The sunlight pouring in made her realize that, despite the dreams, she'd slept soundly.

Seeing Carly's name on the caller ID made her smile. She'd been keeping close tabs on her, which was sweet. "Hey."

"Sam is on WGNO."

"What?"

"She's on *Good Morning New Orleans*, giving an exclusive interview."

The meaning of Carly's words sank in. "Wait."

Tess clamored out of bed, walked into the living room, and picked up the remote. She switched on the television and flipped to channel eleven. Sam's face filled the screen; underneath, the headline read "Sid Packett: Mystery Solved."

"Shit."

"Do you know anything about this?" Carly's voice reminded Tess she was still on the phone with her.

"Yes."

"Are you going to share?"

"Yes, I just need to see what she says."

"It's okay. Dustin just spit up and I have to change him before I take him to daycare. Are you working? Do you want me to come by the restaurant after work?"

"Yes and yes. I'll see you then."

"Tess?"

"Uh-huh?"

"Are you okay?"

Tess shook her head. That was a loaded question if she'd ever heard one. "I'm fine. I'll explain everything later."

"All right. I'll see you around four."

Carly hung up and Tess turned up the volume. Sam sat on a sofa across from a perky blonde who seemed to hang on Sam's every word. Despite coming in mid-interview, Tess registered immediately what Sam was doing.

"So, why now?" The blonde leaned forward. "What made you decided to reveal yourself today, on our show?"

Sam gave the woman her signature flirtatious smile. Tess rolled her eyes. "I've always enjoyed my anonymity, but it comes at a price. When I meet people, I have to keep a huge part of myself secret. It's gotten old."

The woman nodded sympathetically. "And do you think this will have an impact on the way readers look at your work, or on your sales?"

"I sure hope not." That earned a laugh from the perky blonde. Sam was such a natural at this, Tess had a hard time believing it was her first public appearance. Sam folded her hands and her face grew serious. "I hope my readers know that the books are, and will be, the same. The person doing the writing isn't changing."

"Anything else?"

"I hope the people in my life, especially those who didn't know about my books, understand that I'm the same person I've always been."

The blonde smiled. "And from where I'm sitting, that's a brilliant writer who also happens to be utterly charming. Thank you, Sam, or should I say Sid?" She winked at Sam, then turned to the camera. "Wayne, back to you."

Tess sat on the sofa, remote still in hand. The man on the screen started talking about improvements to a wastewater treatment facility in Terrebonne Parish. She clicked through the other channels, half expecting Sam's revelation to be headline news. It wasn't. That was a relief.

She turned off the television and continued to sit, trying to make sense of it. Did Sam do this for her? The thought that Sam had upended her life, and possibly her career, sat heavy in Tess's stomach. Sure there was a small thrill in the idea Sam might make such a grand gesture for her. Yet guilt pressed into her. She never wanted to be a woman who needed grand gestures. If she'd somehow pressured Sam into this decision, she'd hate herself.

Then again, maybe this wasn't all about her. Sam had made a comment about how having secrets gave other people power. Maybe she'd decided to go public for that reason. And there was still the whole Francesca thing. Even from prison, she could likely stir up trouble if she set her mind to it.

Tess picked up her phone, then set it down. Sam would still be at the television station. Her phone was probably exploding with phone calls and texts. She might be giving other interviews. While it might not be a national headline, the news would make the rounds and Sam would be plenty busy.

Tess got ready for work in a fog, her mind playing a loop of Sam's words. It might be one giant publicity stunt, staged to garner attention and sell more books. But Tess kept coming back to the idea that the decision had something to do with her. Sam's last statement, especially, could have been made directly to Tess.

Tess climbed on her bike and rode to the ferry. On the short trip across the water, she thought about the ride she and Sam took together. Sam had a way of soaking in experiences, details. She'd not thought about it at the time, but it was clearly a writer thing. At the restaurant, she locked up her bike and went in the back.

Even though the kitchen already bustled with activity, the pace and energy in the morning were different. Terrence and Jocelyn were prepping vegetables; T-Jacques put away pots and pans that had been left to dry overnight. They exchanged good mornings while Tess gathered her tools and headed out to the oyster station.

"Was that your girlfriend on *Good Morning New Orleans*?"

Tess turned to find Chantelle standing behind her. Chantelle was one of the waitresses who Tess felt pretty certain had a crush on Sam. Given that she had just finished high school, it was more cute than threatening. "It was."

"I can't believe she's Sid Packett. I love his books. I guess I should say her books. How crazy is that? Did you know?"

The final question caused Tess's insides to clench. She'd intentionally not mentioned the whole Francesca fiasco to anyone besides Carly. She didn't want the attention and she sure as hell didn't want to have to provide the whole back story. Sam's revelation, however, was public now. Tess had been so busy trying to process her feelings, she'd hadn't even thought about the inevitable questions from everyone who knew they were together.

"I found out a while ago. We didn't talk a lot about work." Tess fought the urge to cringe. What a pathetic answer. It made their relationship seem so superficial. Or it made Tess seem superficial. Or both.

"Do you know why she decided to go public?" Chantelle's eyes got big. "Did it have something to do with you?"

Tess cringed outwardly at that. "I don't really know. It's kind of complicated."

"Oh."

Chantelle's exaggerated pronunciation grated on Tess's nerves and she fought the urge to roll her eyes. "I've got to finish setting up, okay?"

"Okay."

Chantelle didn't seem bothered by the brush-off. Tess sighed. Probably because she was in a hurry to go share the little bit of scoop she did have with the other waitresses. If Sam had given her a heads-up about what she was going to do, Tess could have figured out how she wanted to handle the questions. Tess shook her head, dismissing the thought as self-absorbed. She finished setting up her station, wondering how and when she'd talk to Sam next.

Fortunately, the lunch crowd was steady and kept her from being able to stew. There was, however, no sign of Sam. Tess told herself that was a good thing, but she wasn't very convincing. When things began to slow around two, Tess went into the kitchen to look for something to keep her busy. She emerged with a fresh sack of oysters and found Sam standing on the other side of the bar.

"Hi." Sam offered her a tentative smile.

"Hi."

"I don't know if you watch television in the—"

"I saw."

"I wanted to tell you ahead of time, but I didn't want to chance you maybe trying to talk me out of it."

Tess frowned. "I wouldn't try to talk you into or out of anything."

"I didn't mean…I just…"

Tess didn't think she'd ever seen Sam at a loss for words. "I hope you didn't do it for me."

"Let's just say you helped me realize it was time."

Tess nodded slowly, but didn't say anything. What a perfect, noncommittal answer. She didn't know if that made her feel better, or worse.

"I was hoping we could talk. Do you get off soon?"

"Five, but Carly is meeting me here when she gets out of work."

"Ah." Sam looked crestfallen.

"But she'll have to get home for dinner. I could do later, if you're free."

"Absolutely."

"Do you want to meet somewhere?"

"Would it be okay to do my house? Or yours?"

Tess raised a brow. "Afraid the paparazzi might be relentless?"

Sam chuckled. "I doubt it. But I'd rather not have to worry about being interrupted one way or the other."

"Fair enough. I'll come to you. Around seven?"

"Perfect. I'll get dinner."

Tess thought of their adventures—and misadventures—in the kitchen and smiled. "Don't go to too much trouble."

Sam smiled sheepishly. "I'll see you then."

Sam didn't say anything about staying to eat and Tess didn't ask. She watched Sam walk toward the exit. While there were no photographers or fans milling around her, three separate people stopped her to talk. Based on the nods and smiles and handshakes that followed, Tess had to assume people recognized her from the television appearance. Although Tess had sensed what a big deal doing the interview had been, it was only in that moment she realized how much of an impact it would have on Sam's daily life. She tried to shake off the nagging discomfort and went back to work.

By the time Carly arrived at four, Tess had cleaned every nook and cranny, reorganized her entire station, and rolled six dozen sets of silverware for the waitstaff station. But the moment they were done exchanging greetings, a gaggle of tourists streamed in and took up residence at her bar. She set Carly up with a dozen oysters and a glass of Sauvignon Blanc, then moved to greet her new customers and take their orders.

Fortunately, they were a group of friends—chatty and frequent visitors to New Orleans—so once Tess had put in their drink order and shucked a few dozen oysters, she was able to leave them to their own devices. She made her way back down to Carly just as Carly slurped one of her oysters, closed her eyes, and smiled.

"Why don't I come and visit you at work more often?"

"I don't know. The oysters are cheap and fresh and the company is impeccable."

"Indeed. How is my impeccable company doing?"

"Okay." Tess sighed. "Sam stopped by."

"When? What did she say?"

"About an hour ago. I told her I was meeting you."

Carly cocked her head to one side. "We could have rescheduled."

"I didn't want to do that, for a lot of reasons. I'm going over to her place later. To talk."

Carly nodded. "So what are you going to do?"

"Damned if I know."

"Well, we'll figure it out. Despite how delicious these are, that's not why I'm here."

A pair of tickets printed behind her. Tess grabbed them and started prepping new trays. "You're the best. Tell me about you while I do these and then we'll get to me."

Carly sipped her wine and made a face. "My boss is leaving, moving to Charlotte."

"The one on maternity leave?"

"Yeah. Her husband took a promotion and they're moving so she can stay home with the baby. She's talking about putting in a good word for me to take her position."

"Carly, that's awesome. You'd be so great."

"Maybe. I'm not sure."

"You're so good at your job. You have the best ideas and people love you."

"Yeah, but part of that is because I don't tell them what to do, hold them to deadlines, or fire them."

Tess could definitely empathize with that. "I think you'd be great at it, but I get maybe not wanting it."

"Plus I don't have an MBA. Not a big deal for a graphic designer, but a potential problem for an account manager."

"Do you want an MBA?"

"I didn't think so, but I'm actually considering it. Does that make me a sellout?"

Despite how different their lines of work were, they'd bonded plenty over bad bosses and stuffy corporate types. While Tess still didn't want that for herself, she could see Carly doing it well, and not becoming stuffy or overbearing. "Not at all. The world needs more cool bosses. And I bet there's a nice pay bump."

"More than nice."

"Well, if you decide to do it, I'll be happy to pick up some extra babysitting while you study."

Carly's face softened. "Thanks, Tess. That means a lot. Now, enough about me."

As if on cue, Danny came through the swinging door to the kitchen. "Afternoon, Miss Tess."

He was only a few years her junior, but she'd been unable to convince him to drop the "Miss." "Hey, D. I didn't realize you had the dinner shift tonight."

"Covering for Antoine. His girl went into labor this morning."

"Aw. Well, I'm sure he appreciates it and I do, too. I'm so not feeling a double shift today."

Danny grinned. "Well, I'm here, so you is officially off for the night."

Tess gave his arm a squeeze. "Let me hand the ladies at the end of the bar off to you and I'll be out of your hair."

Twenty minutes later, she was in her street clothes and sitting with Carly at one of the high-top tables in the bar. She took a swig from the beer Gary had pulled for her and tried to gather her thoughts. Maybe if she did that, she'd be able to get a handle on her feelings.

"You said you knew about Sam before this morning. How long have you known?"

Tess sighed. "She told me the morning after the break-in. She said she'd been wanting—planning—to for a while, but I can't shake the feeling that she did it because she felt trapped."

"Because that Francesca woman knew."

"Right. I can't see how that wouldn't have played into her decision."

"And she didn't tell you she was doing the interview ahead of time?"

"No. When she stopped by earlier, she said she didn't want to chance me trying to change her mind."

Carly shook her head. "This is even more complicated than I thought."

Tess rolled her eyes. "Tell me about it."

"So tell me what you're feeling right now."

"Um, okay. In no particular order, I feel betrayed, stupid, special, overwhelmed, hopeful, doubtful, and terrified."

"That's a lot."

"That's my problem."

Carly nodded. "It doesn't sound unreasonable, though, to feel all those things."

"Thanks?"

"I just mean it shows you're processing. If you felt nothing, or only angry, I think that would be worse."

Tess rolled her eyes. "Easier, though."

Carly shrugged. "Maybe in the moment. But if the plan is to sort things out—with or without Sam—it sounds like you've already started moving forward."

With or without Sam. Those words seemed to hang in the air. At the end of the day, that was the million-dollar question. Could she fix things with Sam? Did she want to? "So what do I do now?"

"Well, you did agree to talk to her."

Tess sighed. "Yeah."

"If you're not sure what to say, you can start with listening. I imagine Sam has at least a couple of things to get off her chest."

"I guess."

"I know Sam is at the forefront of your mind, but I'm kind of still hung up on the fact that you were kidnapped. Are you sure you're okay?"

"I am, or I will be. It sounds weird to say, but I didn't ever feel like she was going to hurt me. And the whole thing only lasted a few hours."

"Tess, I know you loathe the idea of being dramatic, but come on."

Tess smiled. "I'm not trying to downplay it, I swear. It's just… it feels over and done. Everything else is still hanging over my head."

Carly shook her head. "If you say so."

After paying the tab, Tess and Carly walked out of the restaurant. Even with the sun beginning to set, the air remained thick and hot. And it was only March. Carly hugged her and wished her luck. "Please let me know if you need anything. We're here for you."

"I know. Thanks."

CHAPTER THIRTY-THREE

Tess knocked on Sam's door and thought back to the first time she'd visited. She'd been intimidated by the luxury of it, and by the fact that Sam clearly had money. It hadn't taken long for that unease to pass. In fact, most of her hesitation about Sam had been vanquished. She'd never expected it, but they'd become friends as much as lovers. Tess couldn't put her finger on when, but she'd started to think of them as a couple. Did the events of the last few days change that? Did she want them to?

Sam opened the door with a hesitant smile. "I'm so glad you're here."

Tess stepped inside. "I knew we needed to talk, even before your appearance this morning. Thanks for giving me some space."

Sam shut the door behind them, then stuffed her hands in her pockets. It was a habit, Tess had learned, she used to prevent herself from fidgeting. "Can I get you something to drink?"

God, this felt more awkward than their first date. "That would be great."

"Beer? I have wine and soda, too. Or I could make tea."

"I'll have a beer. Thanks."

"Make yourself comfortable. I'll be right back."

Tess took a seat on one end of the sofa. Sam disappeared into the kitchen and quickly returned holding two bottles. She sat down next to Tess, close but not touching. Tess considered starting with pleasantries, but decided the Band-Aid approach would be better. "I keep coming back to this feeling that the only reason you told me who you are is because you felt backed into a corner, afraid Francesca would out you to me, to the world."

Sam shifted so that she faced Tess. She put her hand on Tess's knee, but quickly removed it. "I can see how you might think that, but it's not true."

"I mean, what did you think before that? Poor, dumb Tess. She'll never figure it out."

"I've never thought you were dumb."

Tess found that answer not even remotely satisfying. "But you did think I'd never figure it out."

Sam shook her head emphatically. "It's not like that. I mean, did you ever try to figure it out?"

Tess huffed. "I didn't think there was something to figure out."

"Exactly."

Tess was surprised that Sam didn't immediately back down. Rather than making her angry, though, it gave her confidence. It told her Sam had some convictions, even if Tess didn't agree with them. "I don't see—"

"You were never pushy about it, for which I was grateful. If you had been, in the beginning, I would have had to think about how much to share."

"Because you thought I might snoop."

"Because I wanted—want—you to trust me. Tess, I know it's really hard for you to believe me at this point, but I'd already decided to tell you. I wanted to let you in because I'd started to see a future for us and I knew secrets weren't going to cut it."

Tess looked at Sam and sighed. She hadn't come here to pick a fight. She didn't know why she was stirring all of this up again. Actually, she did know why. She was being a coward. "I do believe you."

The relief on Sam's face was palpable. "That means a lot to me."

Time for a little bit of her own honesty. "Before all this happened, I'd started to think about a future with you, too."

Sam set down her beer, untouched. Based on Tess's terse replies to her texts and her tone at the restaurant this afternoon, she'd started to fear Tess didn't share any of her feelings. For the first time in days, she allowed herself to feel some hope. "Really?"

Tess nodded. "It was a little terrifying, but I thought we might be able to make it work."

Just as quickly as it came, Sam's hope faltered. "You're talking about us as if we're in the past tense."

Tess took a sip of her beer and looked out the window. "After Katrina, everything was chaos. We evacuated, thinking we'd be gone two or three days. It was weeks before we were able to get back in and even assess the damage. No one knew what would be waiting for them. People, my family, questioned whether to come back at all. And I'm saying that as someone whose house and place of employment survived."

Sam knew how much the storm had impacted her, and her family. She tried to connect that to the conversation they were having now. "I can only imagine the toll it took."

"After, there were two things I knew for sure. One, New Orleans is my home. I sacrificed a lot to come back and I'm not leaving again."

Sam swallowed. "And the second?"

"I'm not going to let anyone tell me how to live my life."

As far as Sam could tell, neither of those things meant she and Tess couldn't be together. "I wouldn't ask you to leave. And I hope you know I would never want you to be anything that you're not."

Tess offered her a half smile. "I was starting to believe that when everything blew up."

Sam didn't want to beg, but she needed Tess to understand where she was coming from. "Nothing that happened changes that—not who I am, not my feelings for you, not how I feel when we're together."

"Doesn't it? You're a jet-setter, Sam, a famous author. You're used to a life of travel and adventure and beautiful women. Someone who writes their own ticket doesn't suddenly stop and settle down."

Sam shook her head and smiled. "They do when they've found what makes them happy."

Tess raised a brow. "You're trying to tell me I've inspired you to completely change your lifestyle."

"No. I mean, yes, but not only you." Sam hated that she fumbled over the words. "I like it here. I like the city and its history. I like the culture, the food."

Tess chuckled at Sam's mention of food.

"It feels like home. You're a huge part of that, but so are Elisa and the friends I've made. I feel like part of the community. I've never felt that before." Only when she said it out loud did Sam realize how much that feeling had driven her nomadic life. She always left places while they were still fresh and exciting, before she had a chance to feel dissatisfied or like she didn't fit in. "I like it."

"You sound like me."

Sam grinned. "I probably got some of it from you. You eat, sleep, and breathe your community."

Tess shrugged. "It's not perfect by any means, but it's mine."

"Exactly. You made me see how much I wanted that. You made me think maybe I could have it." Tess nodded and Sam thought she'd finally said something that seemed to resonate. She decided it was time to lay all her cards on the table. "Tess, I didn't do that interview to get you back."

"I…"

"I mean, I would have. I want you back and am willing to do all sorts of things to prove that to you, but I did it for me, too. I hope, instead of sounding selfish, it helps you to see that I've changed. I want a different life than the one I had." Sam feared she might be rambling, but she couldn't help herself. "I want a life with you."

Tess took a deep breath; Sam held hers. "What about your next big plot?"

If Tess was asking, things couldn't be all bad. "I don't know. I think New Orleans might have a few good stories left in her."

"And then?"

"And then I conduct research trips like most writers—a week or two at a time." Sam realized it could be as easy as that. She didn't have to pick up her life every six months. She didn't have to live out of suitcases or take up residence somewhere to be able to write about it.

"I see."

As the idea took shape in her mind, the promise of a life with Tess grew alongside. "Maybe I could convince you to come with me sometimes."

"Really?"

"Have you ever been to Barcelona?" She could see Tess sipping wine and eating tapas on the balcony of a little restaurant, in a bikini and her movie star sunglasses on the beach.

Tess rolled her eyes. "I've never been anywhere."

"You'd love it. All you need is a passport."

"I'll have to add that to my to-do list."

"Well, I have a house there for the next six months, so you definitely should." When Tess's face registered alarm, Sam quickly continued. "I arranged it almost right after I arrived in New Orleans. I'd planned to give it up, but if you'll go with me, I won't. For however long as you can get away. We can hire someone to keep an eye on your house. Oh, and Marlowe. I almost forgot about him. I'm sure we can find a kitty hotel. Or maybe you'd prefer a house sitter who can take care of him and the house. Whatever you want is fine."

"Could you…Could you slow down for a minute? You're making my head spin."

Sam laced her fingers together and smiled. "Sorry. I get ahead of myself sometimes."

Tess shook her head and looked Sam in the eyes. "You're telling me you have a house waiting for you in Spain and yet you really want to stay here?"

Had someone asked her that question three months ago, she would have laughed and dismissed it out of hand. It hit her just how drastically things had changed. And she'd meant what she said, it wasn't only about Tess. "I'm ready to have a home base. A home."

"And New Orleans is it?"

"Like I said, I love New Orleans. That is entirely true. Mostly, though, I love you. I'm in it for the package deal." Only after the words were out of her mouth did Sam realize what she'd said. *I love you.* How long had it been since she'd uttered those words to a woman? Her chest tightened and she realized she didn't know what made her more nervous—saying it or not knowing how Tess would respond.

Tess blinked a few times. "You love me?"

Sam let the reality of that sink it. Whether or not Tess reciprocated her feelings, Sam realized how much power there was in owning it. "I do."

Tess narrowed her eyes. "Love me like you love seafood gumbo or love me like in love with me?"

Sam couldn't help but laugh at the analogy. "Not to disparage my deep affection for seafood gumbo, but the latter. I love you, Tess. I'm in love with you and I want to be with you."

Tess nodded slowly. Sam couldn't tell if she was processing or formulating a response or contemplating an escape route. Eventually, she smiled. "I love you, too."

After everything they'd been through, it seemed too easy. Sam held her emotions in check. "You don't have to say it just because I did."

Tess continued to nod and her face got serious. "I'm not. I do love you. I didn't want to at first. And truthfully, when everything went down, it seemed like the perfect opportunity to cut and run. But then I realized I didn't want to run."

Sam took her hand. Despite her efforts, joy bubbled up, filling her chest. "I'm so glad you didn't."

"I could say the same thing to you."

Sam couldn't think of a time her heart felt more full. Telling Tess she loved her, having Tess say it back, made all her other accomplishments pale in comparison. Even breaking onto the *New York Times* Best Seller List for the first time couldn't hold a candle. Since saying it that way might be overwhelming, she settled for, "I'm glad that's settled."

Tess frowned suddenly. "Not to rush things, but you should know I don't want to live in some chi-chi mansion in the Garden District."

If that was the biggest of their problems, Sam wasn't about to complain. "You keep your place. I keep mine. For now. Maybe we can pick out a place for both of us, together."

Tess got a dreamy look on her face that Sam couldn't interpret. "You know, I've never done that before."

"What? Moved in with someone?"

"No, picked out a place. My house is the one I grew up in with my parents. When they decided not to come back, I worked out a plan to buy it from them."

"If you're really attached to it—"

"No, it's not that. I love my house, but if I'm being honest, it's never felt one hundred percent mine. I wonder…" Tess trailed off for a moment, as though she was considering something for the first time. "I wonder if that's part of why I've never been able to shake the feeling of being the one who stayed behind."

Sam thought about her life, moving around so that she never had the risk of being left behind, or left out. As different as their experiences had been, Sam realized some of the underlying motivations weren't that different after all. "I think there's something to be said for blazing your own path."

"Yeah, I guess I thought I'd been doing that all along."

Sam had thought the same thing, yet it hadn't shielded her from the feeling that something was missing. "I know what you mean."

Tess picked up her beer and raised it toward Sam. "Well, here's to new paths."

Sam clinked her bottle against Tess's. "And to blazing them together."

Tess leaned in and pressed her lips to Sam's. "I'll definitely drink to that."

About the Author

Aurora Rey (aurorarey.com) grew up in a small town in south Louisiana, daydreaming about New England. She keeps a special place in her heart for the South, especially the food and the ways women are raised to be strong, even if they're taught not to show it. After a brief dalliance with biochemistry, she completed both a B.A. and an M.A. in English.

When she's not writing or at her day job in higher education, she moonlights as a baker and is slightly addicted to Pinterest. She loves to cook and dreams of a big farmhouse in the country with a garden and some goats. She lives in Ithaca, New York, with her partner and two dogs.

Books Available From Bold Strokes Books

Amounting to Nothing by Karis Walsh. When mounted police officer Billie Mitchell steps in to save beautiful murder witness Merissa Karr, worlds collide on the rough city streets of Tacoma, Washington. (978-1-62639-728-6)

Becoming You by Michelle Grubb. Airlie Porter has a secret. A deep, dark, destructive secret that threatens to engulf her if she can't find the courage to face who she really is and who she really wants to be with. (978-1-62639-811-5)

Birthright by Missouri Vaun. When spies bring news that a swordswoman imprisoned in a neighboring kingdom bears the Royal mark, Princess Kathryn sets out to rescue Aiden, true heir to the Belstaff throne. (978-1-62639-485-8)

Crescent City Confidential by Aurora Rey. When romance and danger are in the air, writer Sam Torres learns the Big Easy is anything but. (978-1-62639-764-4)

Love Down Under by MJ Williamz. Wylie loves Amarina, but if Amarina isn't out, can their relationship last? (978-1-62639-726-2)

Privacy Glass by Missouri Vaun. Things heat up when Nash Wiley commandeers a limo and her best friend for a late drive out to the beach: Champagne on ice, seat belts optional, and privacy glass a must. (978-1-62639-705-7)

The Impasse by Franci McMahon. A horse-packing excursion into the Montana Wilderness becomes an adventure of terrifying proportions for Miles and ten women on an outfitter-led trip. (978-1-62639-781-1)

The Right Kind of Wrong by PJ Trebelhorn. Bartender Quinn Burke is happy with her life as a playgirl until she realizes she can't fight her feelings any longer for her best friend, bookstore owner Grace Everett. (978-1-62639-771-2)

Wishing on a Dream by Julie Cannon. Can two women change everything for the chance at love? (978-1-62639-762-0)

A Quiet Death by Cari Hunter. When the body of a young Pakistani girl is found out on the moors, the investigation leaves Detective Sanne Jensen facing an ordeal she may not survive. (978-1-62639-815-3)

Buried Heart by Laydin Michaels. When Drew Chambliss meets Cicely Jones, her buried past finds its way to the surface. Will they survive its discovery or will their chance at love turn to dust? (978-1-62639-801-6)

Escape: Exodus Book Three by Gun Brooke. Aboard the Exodus ship *Pathfinder*, President Thea Tylio still holds Caya Lindemay, a clairvoyant changer, in protective custody, which has devastating consequences endangering their relationship and the entire Exodus mission. (978-1-62639-635-7)

Genuine Gold by Ann Aptaker. New York, 1952. Outlaw Cantor Gold is thrown back into her honky-tonk Coney Island past, where crime and passion simmer in a neon glare. (978-1-62639-730-9)

Into Thin Air by Jeannie Levig. When her girlfriend disappears, Hannah Lewis discovers her world isn't as orderly as she thought it was. (978-1-62639-722-4)

Night Voice by CF Frizzell. When talk show host Sable finally acknowledges her risqué radio relationship with a mysterious caller, she welcomes a *real* relationship with local tradeswoman Riley Burke. (978-1-62639-813-9)

Raging at the Stars by Lesley Davis. When the unbelievable theories start revealing themselves as truths, can you trust in the ones who have conspired against you from the start? (978-1-62639-720-0)

She Wolf by Sheri Lewis Wohl. When the hunter becomes the hunted, more than love might be lost. (978-1-62639-741-5)